ADD ROMANCE AND MIX

ADD ROMANCE AND MIX

SHANNON M. HARRIS

SAPPHIRE BOOKS

SALINAS, CALIFORNIA

Dedication

This book is dedicated to my Grandma, whose red cake is a staple at holidays and special occasions. It doesn't make an appearance in this book but it is hands down my favorite cake.

Acknowledgments

This has not been an easy writing year for me and this book is testament to me pushing on. It went through three plot changes until I was satisfied with the finished draft. I have to give a huge shoutout to Linda North whose help was instrumental in this book being completed. Thanks to Chris and everyone at Sapphire Books for all they do to ensure a quality product is produced.

Chapter One

B riley leaned against the wall as she looked out the window with her arms crossed. With keen interest, she watched as Leah, her next-door neighbor, moved around in her front yard. The tight khaki pants Leah wore made her ass look fantastic. Briley groaned but couldn't take her eyes off Leah's slim frame.

From a distance, Leah looked larger than life, but in reality, Briley thought she was around five feet two, a good three to four inches shorter than her. All she had to go on was that one time she'd passed Leah on the sidewalk. When Leah had smiled at her, Briley became so flustered that she'd quickly walked past her without saying a word. Briley hadn't made a move to introduce herself. It was not one of her finer moments.

Today, Leah wore her ever-present oversized sunglasses and had her curly blond hair in a ponytail sticking out from the back of a ball cap. Briley would never admit it, but watching Leah was her favorite pastime. Just not in a stalker or creeper way. At least she hoped not.

Leah and her son, Evan, had moved into the house next door ten months ago. Briley knew Leah was fifty and her son was sixteen because Mrs. Hanlin had told her the day after they'd moved in; she'd also mentioned Leah had an ex-wife, another daughter, and two grandkids.

Briley pushed her black framed glasses up the

bridge of her nose as her eyes moved from Leah's tight ass, up a toned body, only to lock eyes with the woman who had taken her sunglasses off and now nibbled on the earpiece. With a squeak, Briley jumped back from her window, lost her footing, and fell backward to land on the floor. "Oh."

Kat, Briley's older sister by two years, jumped up from the couch. "You okay?" She popped the rest of her cheese Danish in her mouth, then looked out the window to see what held her sister's attention. "Does this have anything to do with that woman staring at your house and laughing?"

"What?" Briley scrambled up, leaned back against the wall, then crept toward the window, where she glanced out. Leah was turned away from her and talking to Ms. Hanlin, their busybody with a heart of gold neighbor, and gesturing to Briley's house.

"Do you have a thing for your neighbor? You sure do stare at her a lot." Kat was tall and imposing at almost six feet and all lean muscle, as opposed to Briley's five-foot-six frame. They both took after their mom with chestnut hair, but Kat had their dad's blue eyes and Briley their mom's green.

Kat had arrived the previous day after quitting her job the month before, packing up, and driving halfway across the country to move in with Briley. They'd talked about Kat needing a change for months and Briley had offered her spare room, as long as Kat paid part of the expenses, got a job, and figured out what she wanted to do with the rest of her life. The sale of Kat's condo, which netted her a tidy sum, also helped her make up her mind. Briley understood being stagnant, but she also knew Kat would go crazy if she sat around doing nothing for too long, hence the requirement of her looking for work.

Briley grimaced and flicked her hand in the air, hoping Kat would let it drop. "I don't even know her." Luck was not on her side.

Kat looked skeptical. "You don't? That doesn't sound like you at all. You know all your neighbors." Kat pointed out the window and scrunched her nose up. "She lives right next door."

"Your point?" Briley lifted her eyebrows.

"Is her house the one you and Brandon wanted to flip, but the owners wouldn't sell to you?"

Eight years ago, she and Brandon, one of Briley's best friends, had decided to pair up and try their hand at flipping houses. They'd researched for months before they felt ready to take the plunge. The first year they'd only flipped two houses, and although they'd made a good profit, they'd also made countless mistakes. Every year since, they'd improved, and last year they flipped ten houses and banked a sizable profit. Jacob Anderson, LLC was flourishing and a dream come true.

"The owner's reason was that she wanted the house to keep its integrity." Briley shrugged. "Who knows? I still don't think that was the reason, but I guess we'll never know." She peeked out the window again.

"You haven't introduced yourself yet?"

Ignoring Kat, Briley walked into the kitchen, where she topped off her glass of milk and downed half of it before setting it on the counter. She scratched her nose. "Well…" She ran her hands through her long hair and slumped against the black granite counter top.

"I see," Kat said slowly. "How long has she lived here?"

"Ten months," Briley mumbled.

"You have to speak up if you want me to hear you."

Before speaking, Briley drained her glass. "I said ten months. Okay." She threw her hands in the air. "Ten months and no, I don't know her." She avoided her sister's penetrating gaze. "I have yet to introduce myself to her, at least properly, but I have spoken to her son quite a few times."

That made Kat sit up straighter in her chair. "Seriously? You've spoken to her son, but not her?" Kat pointed to the table and Briley pulled out a chair and flopped down in it.

"I...I." Briley clamped her mouth shut and decided not to mention the sidewalk incident. "I...I attempted to, but when I was walking up to her house, with a basket of baked goods, I became flustered and came back here and never attempted to again. I doubt if she even saw me." Leah stood on her porch at the time. Of course she saw her.

Kat laughed. "You ran back home? Good grief." She quickly sobered. "But, don't you give baked goods to all of your neighbors weekly? Surely, with her having a kid, you would make sure and deliver a basket to their house?"

"Yes, I do give baskets out weekly and her son has caught on and comes out to get theirs." Briley suddenly found something interesting on the ceiling. When the stress of her flipping houses got the best of her, she would bake. Some people used drugs, alcohol, or sex to take the edge off. She used baking.

"Wait a minute." Kat snapped her fingers in front of her face to draw her attention away from the ceiling. "You talk to her son and give him their basket and yet you are able to avoid her. You live in the same neighborhood. She lives right next door. You know you're being an asshole, right?" Kat paused and wrinkled her brow. "Do you have a crush on her?"

Briley shook her head and laughed. "I do *not* have a crush on her." At Kat's, 'you're lying' face, she quickly added, "Okay. I have a crush on her."

Kat shot her right hand, palm out, to stop Briley from saying more. "She's straight, isn't she?"

"No. Mrs. Hanlin said her ex is a woman. I've never met her but I am attracted to her and everyone that mentions her, particularly Mrs. Hanlin, always says how nice she is. I see her and Evan laughing outside when they grill out every week. I like her from a distance. I haven't worked up the nerve to actually talk to her yet." She sighed, dragged herself out of the chair, walked into the living room, and fell onto the couch.

After settling in the recliner, Kat motioned for her to go on.

"It started out as me not giving her my cupcakes when they first moved in, then Halloween happened and what I'm calling the First Incident."

"Wait, let me get comfortable." Kat wiggled against the recliner cushion. "This is going to be good."

Briley rolled her eyes. "You know I always put decorations out. Well, I put mine up, then she put some out. When she saw me looking at her yard, she winked at me. She *winked.* So, I did what any reasonable person would do. I bought and put out more decorations. Then Mrs. Hanlin told me that Leah was going to give out full size candy bars." She slapped her hands on the couch cushions.

Kat laughed and pulled a knee to her chest and wrapped an arm around it. "You went out and bought full sized candy bars, didn't you?"

"Of course I did." A small smile graced her lips. "The kids loved it."

"I bet they did. Didn't you dress up as Supergirl?"

She nodded. "It was a big hit with everybody."

"What did Leah dress up as?"

"She dressed up as Captain Marvel. Her son dressed up as Spiderman. Her daughter and son-in-law were in town with their two kids. Before you ask, no, I did not talk to them either, but the kids were super cute." She had a silly smile on her face, thinking about the kids in their Superman and Harry Potter costumes.

"Actually, that's awesome. I would love to have seen Leah's costume."

Without missing a beat, Briley picked up her phone, scrolled through the pictures, then handed the phone over to her sister.

"Briley, she looks wickedly cool." Kat scrolled through a few photos. "Her grandkids are adorable." She handed the phone back. "She must have put a lot of work into her costume and you just happened to get a picture of her wearing it. It's like she's posing for you."

Briley ignored Kat's remark about Leah being a grandmother and tossed the phone to the end of the couch. "Mrs. Hanlin said she spent months working on it. Her son enjoys cosplaying, so she thought it would be a good bonding experience for them both."

"You do, too." Briley waved her off. "Okay. Is that the end of your feud?"

"You know how much I love Christmas." Briley placed her arm over her eyes.

"Briley, what happened?"

"The Third Incident. I decorated, then she decorated. Then I decorated some more, then she did. For a solid week, we would one-up each other. I ended up spending half of my Christmas money on decorations. Mr. Balkin would sit bundled up in his lawn chair across the street and watch us to see what the other one would come up with. You know how competitive I am. She just wouldn't stop." Briley sat up and lifted her legs onto the coffee table. "I won the Christmas decorating competition and was mentioned in the paper." She had the paper displayed in a frame on her bedroom wall. It had taken her years to place first.

"I know. You sent Mom and me both a copy of the paper. Framed." She paused for a moment. "It seems to me that you both have a part in this. She obviously was trying to get your attention. Maybe this was the only way since you've been ignoring her. Which doesn't sound like you at all."

"You know I bake every Christmas and I went all out this year. Spent weeks baking and making candy, then packing everything up. I made everyone a small basket of goodies and passed them out."

"You didn't give her one?" Kat picked up a throw pillow and hit Briley in the head. "What the hell is wrong with you?"

Briley glared at her, straightened her glasses, then hugged the pillow to her chest. "Evan, Leah's son, had told me they were going to his sister's for Christmas. I thought about giving them one for a hot second, but decided not to since they were leaving. Then Mrs. Hanlin, because it's always her, said that Leah saw her basket and asked her about it the day before they left. Mrs. Hanlin told her that it was from me. Leah then proceeded to tell her that she didn't get one, and Mrs. Hanlin said for a second, she and her son looked sad."

Kat shook her head. "Wow. That's…I don't know what to say. Wow."

"Stop looking at me like that."

"Like what?"

"Like you're disappointed in me. I'm disappointed enough in myself for the both of us. I should have given her a huge basket to take with her for everyone to share." Briley waved her hands in the air. "She makes me nervous. Kat, you don't even know."

Kat's gaze bored into Briley. "It doesn't bother you that she's a grandma?"

"She may be a grandma but she's only fifty. You know age doesn't matter to me. She's gorgeous, right?" Briley had thought about the age difference, but the sixteen years between the two of them didn't matter to her. There had been a twenty-year difference between their parents and they were married almost forty years before their dad had died in a motorcycle accident a few years back.

"She is and I just wanted to make sure about the age difference." Kat stood, walked around the coffee table, sat down on the couch, and drew Briley against her side. "I don't care how big of a crush you have on her; you need to do something to make up for your shitty ways. Maybe bake her some cupcakes." She frowned when Briley stiffened in her arms. "Is there more?"

"Incident Four." Briley glanced away sheepishly. "Look. You know I don't have a green thumb, but did you get a look at her flowers? They are amazing. So, when I saw her planting them, I went out, bought a few pallets of flowers for myself, and planted them. I thought that if I impressed her with my mad gardening skills it would be easier to strike up a conversation.

One day while I was watering said flowers, I caught her staring at me. She shook her head, winked at me, then walked into her house."

"Briley, what flowers? I didn't see any when I got here yesterday."

"They died."

"Say what?"

"They all died." Briley buried her head in Kat's neck. "I couldn't even keep some stupid flowers alive. What kind of loser am I?"

Kat laughed and kissed her on the head. "Don't be dramatic. So your mad gardening skills are nonexistent. Just the fact that you tried tells me that you like her." Kat laughed and squeezed her once more, before standing up. "I think it's time we settled this."

"Wait." It took a moment for Kat's words to register but when they did, Briley jumped up from the couch, misjudged her momentum, and tripped over the coffee table. Kat barely caught her in time to stop a minor catastrophe.

"Easy."

Briley threw her arm off, heart pounding in her chest. "Where are you going?" She ran in front of Kat and plastered herself against the front door. "You are not going over there." She didn't know why she told Kat anything.

The glare Kat threw her way should have stopped Briley in her tracks, but she wasn't thinking straight.

"Don't tell me what I'm not going to do." Kat crossed her arms. "It never worked when we were growing up and it's not going to work now. I am going to do what you haven't worked up the nerve to do yet. I am going to introduce myself to Leah." She grasped Briley by the shoulders and shoved her aside. "You should find a way to make this right. Besides, I could have gone through the backdoor. Oh, and," she said, "don't think I didn't catch that you skipped over the second incident."

Briley slid to the floor when the door shut behind Kat, then quickly scrambled to the window, peeked out it, and couldn't believe her eyes when Kat marched next door and joined Leah, who was walking away from her mailbox.

They shook hands, exchanged words, then Leah pointed to her house. Kat nodded, followed her down the walkway, up the steps, and disappeared behind Leah's bright red front door. Briley flung the curtain back and dropped down on the floor, staring up at the ceiling.

She had really stepped in it this time. Whatever *it* was. How would she climb out of a hole she was still digging? She didn't know how, but she had a feeling she was about to find out. Briley knew Kat wouldn't let this go, and in a way, she didn't want her to. Maybe a push was exactly what she needed.

Chapter Two

After flinging the curtain back in place, Briley ran to the couch, flopped down on it, and had just opened the book she swiped from the coffee table when the front door opened and Kat walked in. There was no way she would ever admit to Kat that she had divided her time for the last hour between pacing the living room floor and looking out the window. Briley peeked at her from over the top of the book.

The blank look stayed plastered to Kat's face, even as she shut the front door, walked to the couch, picked up Briley's feet, sat down, then laid them in her lap. She grabbed the remote from where it lay beside Briley and turned the television on before resting her arm on the back of the couch.

Briley pretended to read, but the words blurred together. Her eyes widened in surprise when she realized the book was upside down. If she flipped it, would Kat notice? Probably. She noticed everything. Since Kat seemed content to stay quiet, Briley decided to bite the bullet. "Did you have a good time?" Briley lowered the book to gauge Kat's reaction.

Kat kept her eyes on the TV. "I did. Have you enjoyed reading your book?" After a beat. "Upside down."

Briley flung the offending book on the floor. "She invited you in?"

"Since you were watching us, you would know

this."

Busted. "I hope she served you refreshments."

"She was a perfect hostess."

As Briley knew she would be. When nothing else was forthcoming, Briley sat up, swung her feet to the floor, and snatched the remote from Kat's hands. "That's it?"

"Yes." Kat turned slowly toward her.

Briley moved closer to her and sweetly smiled. "Oh, come on. What did you talk about? Did she mention me?"

"She did mention you."

"Well, what did she say?" Briley wiggled to get comfortable on the couch.

"Look." Kat took Briley's hand and sighed. "I wasn't sure if your crush was for real or not and I hope you don't get mad at me, but..."

Briley jerked her hand back and covered her mouth. "You told her I had a crush on her? How could you, Kat. Really?" Why didn't the earth open and swallow her whole?

"No." Kat ran her hand through her hair. "I didn't tell her you had a crush on her. Please understand. She was charming."

Oh, God. What did she do? "Go on."

"I asked her out," she said, in a rush.

Briley smacked her on the arm. "You what?"

"I asked her out. You were right. She is attractive, and I can see why you are gone on her. Besides that, she's funny, and sweet. I like her and I wasn't going to pass this opportunity up. You snooze, you lose." She stood, tapped Briley on the tip of her nose, and skipped out of the living room and down the hall to her room.

Briley dropped her head in her hands. She

couldn't believe this. How could Kat ask her out after finding out Briley liked her? She knew she had no reason to be jealous, but this sucked. On the other hand, what did she think would happen? Shit. Kat asking her out wouldn't be at the top of her list and the list wasn't even that long.

Why was she getting worked up? Briley, jumped up, shook her hands out, and bounced on her feet. It was only a crush. She'd had plenty of those in her thirty-four years. She walked to the window and looked out it, watching Leah getting in her Escalade and back out of her driveway. This called for drastic measures.

Three hours later and out of the corner of her eye, she saw Kat walk into the kitchen, stop, then lean back against the wall. "Briley, what are you doing?" Kat eyed the table and the counter that was covered in cookies, turnovers, and several different types of pastries.

"It's obvious, isn't it?" Briley smiled and turned from the stove. "I had the urge to bake." She spread her arms wide. When she noticed the extent of her impromptu baking marathon, her smile faltered. "I guess I got a bit carried away."

"Are you all right?" Kat picked up a chocolate chip cookie and took a bite of it.

"Of course. You know I love to bake. This way I'll have lots of treats to hand out." With the side of her hand, she wiped the hair out of her eyes, leaving a smidge of flour in its wake.

"Bri, you're not mad at me, are you?"

Briley forced a laugh and quickly turned her back to her sister. "Of course not. What would I have to be jealous about?"

"I didn't say jealous. I said mad."

"Same difference."

"No, it's not."

"Whatever." She picked the dough up and flung it back on the counter. "I'm not mad."

"You seem a bit…"

Briley whirled around. "I'm not mad. Do what you want. Have dinner with Leah. I don't care. Get married. Have babies," she muttered. She knew she was being a bitch, but she and Kat had never been interested in the same woman before. Even when they both came out in their teens, the type of woman that drew each of them had always been opposites. All this was a new experience and she didn't like it. Not one iota. The dread swirling in the pit of her stomach only added to her overall turmoil to dampen her mood.

"Okay." Kat lifted her hands up in defeat.

Briley ignored her, wrapped the dough up, and put it in the fridge to rest. She walked past her sister and picked up the caramel sauce.

"Apple turnovers with caramel sauce. That will be good for us to take to Leah's for dinner tonight."

Once she poured the caramel over the top of the pastries, set the pot in the sink, and wiped her hands, she turned to Kat. "Say what?"

"Leah. Dinner. We'll have something to take for dessert now." Kat pointed to the pastries.

Briley narrowed her eyes and gripped the edge of the counter top. "I think I missed something. You mean you'll have something to take to dinner?"

Kat grinned like the Cheshire Cat, which gave Briley a really bad feeling. "No. Leah invited both of us over for dinner tonight." She picked up a glazed donut hole and popped it in her mouth.

"You said you asked her out!" Briley accused.

"I lied." She shrugged. "I wanted to see how

worked up you would get and by the number of baked goods, I would say you were worked up thinking about us dating." She chuckled and poured a glass of milk.

Damn Kat and her meddling ways. "What the… Kat, and you called me an asshole."

"This will give you a chance to turn around your asshole standing. Dinner is in an hour. You need to shower and change." Kat pointed to her head and face. "You have flour on your face and in your hair."

Briley planted her hands on her hips but the insult died on her lips. Kat was right; she did need to change. After everything that had happened between her and Leah, could all it really take was her sister to narrow the divide? It seemed too good to be true. Briley gnawed at her bottom lip. "Why did she invite me?"

Kat hesitated with the donut hole halfway to her mouth. "Contrary to what you might think, she doesn't hate you. In fact, she said she's been enjoying your competitions. She did add she doesn't know why you dislike her." Kat eyed her over her glass of milk. "I didn't tell her that you had a ginormous crush on her or who she reminds you of." Briley looked appalled. "Come on, you didn't think I wouldn't notice."

"Whatever. She really said all of that?" Maybe the time had arrived to try and work this out. She was an adult. She could do this.

"Yes, Briley. If only you would give her a chance. I know you've had some bad luck in the relationship department, but maybe it's time to put your heart on the line."

"That's hard to do." Her last relationship ended two years ago, and she hadn't had the heart to start something serious again. Not after the way that one ended. Briley didn't know if she could do it again.

Kat eyed the clock. "You need to get ready."

"Yes." After her shower, she searched through her closet for fifteen minutes, then had to talk herself down from a panic attack. This wasn't a date. It was dinner with her neighbor and her sister, but she still wanted to make a good impression.

She settled on a pair of plaid Bermuda shorts, and a cream colored, V-neck sleeveless top, with a yellow cardigan. Simple, but practical. She couldn't believe she was doing this. She'd been such an asshole to her neighbor, but since her sister was involved, she knew there was no getting out of this. She arranged her hair up with a clip, then slipped on a pair of sandals. She walked down the hall to the kitchen, pulled a basket from her stash in the pantry, and loaded it with treats.

"Ready?" Kat asked when she stepped into the kitchen. She looked Briley up and down. "You look nice."

"Thanks. Are you sure this is a good idea?" The basket in her arms felt like it was filled with lead.

Kat patted her arm. "What are you afraid of? If the evening falls apart, just come home and continue ignoring her like you have been, and if all goes well, maybe you've made a new friend or something more."

"It's the something more that scares me." She pushed her glasses up the bridge of her nose.

"Let's go."

Like a prisoner being dragged to the gallows, Briley followed behind Kat. The walk to Leah's house felt like the longest of her life. She paused at the steps and admired the flowers that lined the path and surrounded the porch. Leah really did have a knack for growing them. She should ask her for pointers.

When the door opened, Briley turned slowly and

watched as Leah stepped out dressed in a pair of black tailored trousers, a short sleeve pink polo, and a pair of black Wonder Woman socks. Briley's heart skipped a beat. Could this woman be any more perfect?

"It's a beautiful evening." Leah leaned against the railing and looked from one to the other.

All Briley could do was gape, as all words had fled. Leah looked tiny up close. Why did Leah have to look effortlessly amazing? Even if Briley could regain the use of speech, she knew what ever came out of her mouth would be utter gibberish. How, after only a few words from Leah, could she get tongue-tied? "I…" Panic seized her chest and Kat rescued her.

"It is." Kat climbed the steps.

Briley didn't know where the bout of courage had come from, but she shot up the steps, and thrust the basket into Leah's arms. "Look." She reached up and fiddled with her glasses. Kat nodded at her encouragingly. "I am sorry, I've been such an asshole to you. I think, maybe, I've let my competitive nature get the best of me and I have never given you a chance. It's not like me at all." She then pinched at her cardigan. "Please accept this basket with my apologies."

"Apology accepted." Leah looked down at the contents of the basket before raising her head and arching her brow, a small teasing smile appearing. "Everything looks and smells wonderful."

"Ladies, I hate to do this, but I'm not going to be able to stay for dinner. I hope you both enjoy your evening," Kat said.

Briley jerked her head around and grabbed onto Kat's arm. Kat pried off the death grip, and scampered down the stairs, Briley right behind her. Kat whirled around and stopped Briley with a hand to her chest.

"You didn't mention that at my house." Briley swiped the hand away and leaned in close to whisper in Kat's ear. "Don't do this to me. She made dinner for both of us." She stiffened when she caught the mischief in her sister's eyes. Then it dawned on her. Kat had set her up.

"Have a good time. Both of you." Kat patted Briley on the hand then lowered her voice. "You can thank me later." She winked.

As Kat walked down the pathway, Briley's eyes stayed glued to her until she entered through the back door of her house. Briley took a deep breath. *I can do this. I want to do this.* After a count of ten, she turned around, walked back up the steps, and plastered a smile on her face. "So?"

"Dinner should be ready now." Leah walked to the door and held it open for her. Her smile should have helped to put Briley at ease, but it had the complete opposite effect on her.

Leah didn't seem fazed by Kat's declaration at all. Briley's steps faltered when it dawned on her that Leah was also in on it. They had both played her. Surely, that was a good sign. "Dinner?"

"Yes, dinner."

With a quick look from Leah's house to her house, Briley finally made up her mind. This was her chance and she wasn't going to throw it away. "After you."

Chapter Three

As she stepped into the living room, Briley couldn't help but admire the rustic chic layout. It was warm and welcoming, with photos of Leah and her family scattered throughout, and not at all what she expected. A large couch sat in front of the fireplace and two chairs were adjacent to the couch with a large area rug between them. She nodded in approval and followed Leah toward the kitchen.

Briley's heart almost stopped when her eyes greedily took in the straight out of a magazine space. The cream-colored shaker style cabinets, combined with the gray granite countertops, and warm wood accents had a calming effect on her. As she stepped onto the dark gray slate flooring and her eyes latched onto the range, her heart started racing and she had to keep herself from swooning on the spot. The kitchen was nicer than any of the houses her company had flipped.

She held back a whimper and pointed at the counter. "Is that a forty-eight-inch dual fuel Wolf range with four burners, infrared char broiler, and infrared griddle?" She had to stop herself from salivating all over the kitchen. On some nights, she dreamed about this stove. She was almost afraid to approach it since she knew how much one of them cost.

With each word out of Briley's mouth, Leah's eyes widened. "Yes, it is. I take it you like it." She chuckled when Briley nodded. "Well." She wiped her hands on a dishtowel. "I've always wanted someone to look at me the way you're looking at my stove."

A gasp fell from Briley's lips when she took a step forward. "This isn't just a stove. It's a work of art."

"It is. Evan enjoys using it as much as I do."

"It is beautiful." She reached toward it, but pulled her hand back at the last second.

Leah laughed and pointed to the small table tucked into the corner of the kitchen. "Have a seat; I'll dish up our dinner before you start drooling over my fridge."

Briley eyed the Sub-Zero 48 fridge with glass door and nodded her approval. The cost of the appliances was extreme and only a serious home chef would shell out the cash for them. Leah must be quite the cook and Briley couldn't wait to try her food. She shifted her eyes from the fridge to Leah as she worked at the counter. Briley didn't want to be a sleaze, but she'd never been this close to her before and she tried but lost the battle not to stare at Leah's perfect ass.

A delicate cough had her jerking her head up and she met the amused green eyes of Leah, who stared over her left shoulder with arched brows. Briley flushed, and held her gaze. "Wine?"

"Sure." Briley wasn't much of a drinker, but having a nip of liquid courage couldn't hurt. Good grief, the evening was just starting and she already felt like she'd run a marathon. "Thank you," she said when Leah handed her the glass of wine. "Are you sure you don't need any help?"

"I've got it, but thank you."

Once seated, Briley sniffed the air and her stomach grumbled when Leah placed a large bowl on the table, then went back to the counter for another one. It didn't take a genius to figure out they were having chicken and dumplings and mashed potatoes. Comfort food. The chicken and dumplings were the best she'd ever had and she moaned with the first bite.

"I'll take that as a compliment," Leah said.

"They're amazing. Best I've ever had."

They were halfway through their meal when Leah asked her first question. "So, Briley, how's the flipping business?"

Briley swallowed the mouthful of dumplings she'd taken, then sipped her wine. It didn't surprise her that Leah knew what she did for a living. Mrs. Hanlin and Kat would have told her. Her nerves had settled over the course of the meal, and she took a few seconds to gather her thoughts. "Good. We just finished a house a couple of weeks ago. It sold quickly. Brandon has an eye out for another one."

Leah nodded. "Is flipping houses like what you watch on TV?"

"Yes and no. It's somewhat more in-depth, and a lot harder, but the profit is there if you do it right, but if you do it wrong, the loss can be extravagant." She and Brandon had learned that the hard way on their second flip. The loss taught them a valuable lesson and one they would never forget.

"As with any job." With a twist of her hand, Leah swirled the wine in her glass. "Do you enjoy your job?"

Briley felt glad Leah decided to start with small talk. This she could handle. Being this close to Leah wasn't as scary as she expected it to be. "I love it. It gives me the freedom to do other things I enjoy and the opportunity to save for the future." She tapped her finger on the tabletop. Turnabout was fair game. "I heard you're a writer. What do you write?"

"I'm freelance." Leah leaned back in her chair.

"Really? What have you written?" She'd always wanted to write a book, but knew she didn't have the patience for it.

Leah relaxed back into her chair. "It was always my dream to write for all the big magazines and newspapers and for the most part all of them have come true. The New Yorker, Time, Vogue, and National Geographic, plus countless others. It's hard work, but fulfilling. I wouldn't trade my time spent traveling and writing for anything. I'm working on a book right now about my experiences. I wasn't sold on the idea, but my agent convinced me to give it a shot. Of course, the traveling slowed down when Evan was born."

"He's a good kid."

Leah quirked her lips. "I think so. He does tend to get into things he shouldn't, though, but I miss him when he's with his other mother."

"You also have a daughter."

"Madison is twenty-four and married with two kids. Evelyn is three and Henry just turned two."

Her face lit up as she talked about them and Briley couldn't help but be affected by the smile on Leah's face. "I remember seeing them at Halloween."

"I wasn't always there when Madison was growing up. I promised myself if I ever had any more kids or if I was ever blessed with grandkids, I would make the time to spend with them. I don't get to see them as much as I would like because Evan is still in school, but we FaceTime quite a bit."

"That's great. Kat and I don't see our mother that much, but we talk, maybe once a month. We drifted apart after my dad died. She told us we both reminded her too much of him. It's been three years, and she's grieved, but how do you fill the hole left by your husband of forty years dying? Honestly, Kat and I both love our mother, but we were always closer to our dad. I think she resented us a bit growing up because of that, and the gulf just grew wider after his death. Don't get me wrong, if she called and needed anything, I would be there, but I like our distance right now." She took a sip of her wine. "Jesus. That makes me sound like an asshole."

Briley almost jumped out of her skin when Leah placed her hand over hers. "Everyone has a different relationship with their parents. Don't beat yourself up and no, you don't sound like an asshole." She pulled her hand away and Briley missed the contact instantly. "You sound honest."

Things had taken a turn she hadn't expected and she needed to get them back to safer ground. Talking about her mother should never be mentioned before the fifth date, if that. She swallowed and willed the butterflies in her stomach to settle. "Do you have a favorite article you've written?"

Leah settled back in her chair with a wistful smile on her face. "My first one will always be special, but I don't have a favorite. At the time, each one is my favorite. Each article represents a period in my life, and I wouldn't change any of them. Freelancing has provided the opportunity for me to travel all over. The world is a beautiful place, Briley. Even with all the turmoil, there is always something to be thankful for or something that will put a smile on your face. You just have to know where to look." She picked up her glass and saluted her before taking a drink.

The contented look Leah directed at her didn't

help to ease her nerves. "So, you enjoy it?"

"Yes, and I've done well enough to provide for my family. I can't complain."

Briley laid her spoon in her bowl. "I've always believed you should go after your dreams. Living stagnate will only end in heartache. Life is too short to work a job you hate or to be with someone that doesn't make you happy."

"No regrets?" Leah tilted her head.

"No regrets, but there are a few things, looking back, I would have done differently. Everything that happens in our lives or the people we meet shapes us. Makes us who we are. What about you. Any regrets?"

"A few, but the past is the past for a reason."

Leah picked up her wine glass and Briley watched her bring it to her lips and take a sip. When Leah's tongue peeked out and licked the rim of her glass, Briley's eyes shot up and latched onto Leah's amused ones. Briley coughed. "Dinner was delicious."

Leah beamed. "Thank you. It happens to be Evan's favorite and he told me I should make it when I informed him we would be having dinner together."

"That's good." So, Leah had told her son. Did that mean this was a date or just dinner? Briley nervously twiddled the stem of her wine glass. Leah reached out and stopped Briley's fingers. Briley's breath caught in her chest as she gazed into the most startling pair of green eyes she had ever seen.

"Why don't we go in the living room," Leah said. "You head in and I'll get our dessert."

"Okay." On shaky legs, Briley got up, and walked into the living room. As soon as she sat on the plush tan leather sofa, she knew she could live there for the rest of her life. It was the most comfortable thing she'd ever sat on. So far, so good. All she had to do was make it through dessert, then she could go home. This was going better than she expected. Maybe she would bake a cake for Kat for setting this up.

"Here you go." Leah handed a bowl over. "One of your turnovers and some vanilla ice cream. Enjoy." Their hands brushed and Briley shivered, but accepted the bowl without dropping it. Leah settled on the couch, far closer than Briley expected, but she wasn't about to complain.

After a couple of bites, Leah broke the silence. "I'm not sure if you are aware, but some of our neighbors have a bet on how long it will take for us to talk to each other." She grinned, a sparkle of mischief in her eyes, then took another spoonful of her ice cream.

"Yes, I'm aware." Briley licked her spoon. "You have to watch these people; they'll bet on anyone or anything. Last year Mr. Dekers, three houses down from mine, bet on whether Ted, Mrs. Conway's dog, would get Brown, the Macaroys' dog, pregnant."

"That must have been before I moved in. Go on. Don't leave me in suspense."

Briley chuckled. "By the time the Macaroys fenced in their backyard, Mr. Dekers had thirty-one people down for different bets. Brown gave birth to four puppies two months later. Puppies that looked just like Ted." After a second's pause, Briley added, "That was the quickest two hundred dollars I've ever won." Briley refused to look in Leah's direction.

"There's something you're not telling me." Leah was so close their legs were touching.

"I might have. Might have seen Ted and Brown in a private moment in my backyard. But, that's pure speculation at this point. I'm sure it could have been any two dogs running around." Briley was surprised how comfortable she felt with Leah. All pistons were firing. Knock on wood.

Leah laughed. "What did you do with the money?"

"I bought baking supplies. So," Briley pointed her spoon at her. "The money went to a good place and in a way, everyone got a bit of their bet money back."

Leah shifted on the couch and placed her hand on Briley's knee. "Speaking of baking."

After her mind cleared from the sensations rushing through her body at Leah's touch, it finally dawned on her what Leah had said. Briley wiped her mouth, then set her empty bowl on the coffee table and sighed. She knew this would come up at some point, but she hoped it wouldn't. She turned and faced Leah, lifting her hand off her knee and settling it on the couch between them and adjusting her body so she faced Leah. Thinking was hard enough without Leah touching her. "I really am sorry about everything. I should have given you a Christmas basket to take with you. I know I was an ass and I'm sorry it's taken this long to talk to you."

Leah frowned, then placed her bowl on the coffee table beside Briley's before speaking. "You think this is about Christmas? I think we need to rewind a few months before that."

With a nervous motion, Briley ran her hands down her shorts. If it wasn't Christmas or Thanksgiving, Incident Two, which she had purposely not told Kat about, what was she talking about? She thought back, but couldn't come up with anything that was even remotely on par with Christmas. "I don't understand."

Leah placed her elbow on the back of the couch and rested her head in her hand. "Do you not remember our first meeting?" Briley blushed. "From the look on your face, I would say you do. I have had a lovely evening, but the air does need to be cleared between us. Don't you think so?"

"Yes." Briley groaned. She really didn't want to talk about this, not with Leah sitting close, looking kissable, and smelling like sunshine, happiness, and laughter. She made a move to get up when Leah stopped her with a hand on her arm.

"Please stay and talk to me. I don't understand why you ran from me and never came back. I searched my mind and haven't come up with anything. I don't want you to be uncomfortable, but I would like to know, if we're going to have any type of friendship, that is."

Friendship. The word sunk deep into the pit of Briley's stomach. Friendship. How would she get out of this without looking like an idiot? Could she get out of this? She shook her head to focus and knew from the look on Leah's face she wouldn't be getting out of this one without the truth. Not if they were to be friends. Friendship first, then, maybe, something else. "Do you want the truth?"

"Yes. I would really like that." Leah squeezed her arm.

"Fine." Sucking in a deep breath, Briley tried to steady her nerves, but plowed ahead. Consequences be damned. Go big or go home. "The first time I saw you…just looking at you got me so flustered that I couldn't think straight. So instead of staying and talking, I ran back home and felt embarrassed with the way I behaved. I couldn't work up the nerve to come back. As for the other things, well, it wasn't my fault your inflatable turkey ended up on top of the Jenkins' garage." Briley got to her feet and started pacing. Her worry started to spike with each second of silence.

Leah jumped up. "Wait a minute." She stood in front of Briley and stopped her pacing. "You're attracted to me? That's the reason you ran and never came back?"

After a hard swallow, Briley nodded. She eyed Leah from the opposite side of the coffee table. When Leah started laughing, Briley's stomach dropped and her heart started racing. Well, she hadn't expected that reaction. She wasn't an anxious person by nature, but she also didn't like being laughed at. "What the hell?" she blurted out.

The laughing suddenly stopped, and the smile fell from Leah's face. She took a step in Briley's direction, and reached for her, but Briley took a step back. Leah held both of her hands out. "It's not what you think. I wasn't laughing at you or your confession."

Briley couldn't remember the last time she was this embarrassed and just wanted to go home and drown her sorrows in some donut holes. That is, if Kat hadn't eaten them all already. The best thing to do would be to bow out gracefully. "Thank you for dinner, but it's late and I should be getting home." She made a move past Leah when Leah stopped her with a hand on her arm.

"No, you don't understand. Please. I wasn't laughing at you. I promise. This entire situation is messed up. I thought I had done something horrible to have, by our neighbor's standards, the nicest woman on the block shun me. I truly wasn't laughing at you."

The look on Leah's face held sincerity. Briley nodded once. "Okay." She rocked back on her heels. The tension in the air became almost stifling. "So."

"So." Leah squeezed her arm. "Let's sit back down." Briley agreed, but this time there was a couple of feet between them. Leah wrung her hands together. "I've lived here for ten months and you ran away from me that first week we moved in."

"Yes." Briley wasn't sure where she was headed with this.

"So, I know the first reason you ran, but why in all these months haven't you ever said anything? You talk to Evan and give him weekly treats, but you never speak to me."

Now it was Briley's turn to frown. What was she playing at? "I told you the reason I haven't talked to you."

"You told me why you didn't the first time you approached me. What are your reasons for staying away?"

The butterflies were back in full force now. Leah thought Briley was only attracted to her the first time she saw her. Oh, boy. This did not seem like the appropriate time to tell her ninety percent of the time Leah occupied her thoughts. She took a few calming breaths then looked up and into Leah's eyes. Leah's face was open and fully invested in this conversation. "I'm attracted to you," Briley said quietly.

Leah's eyes widened. "Oh." She ran her hand along the back of the couch. "I thought that was only the first time."

"No, not just the first time. It doesn't have to mean anything. Well, it doesn't mean anything. Of course not. We don't even know each other. We haven't spent any time together. I could do friends." She fingered her glasses. "Be friends. Friendship works for me." She clasped her hands in her lap.

Leah took a deep breath. "Briley, it would have to be friendship. If you haven't noticed, there is quite a bit of an age difference between us. I'm old enough to be your mother."

"A teenage mother. Do you know how old I am?"

"No, but you look to be in your mid-twenties."

Briley puffed up. "I'm actually thirty-four."

"That's not what I expected, but the same applies. I'm sixteen years older than you are. I'm flattered, but I'm not sure a relationship between us would work. Briley, I'm sorry."

Briley hadn't expected any less from her. "I know." She rubbed her palms down her thighs. "I know."

Leah placed her fingers on Briley's chin and tilted her face up and toward her. She ran her finger along Briley's jaw then took her hand back. "Briley, I have two kids, and two grandkids. I'm fifty."

"You don't have to explain yourself to me. You don't owe me anything." She picked up Leah's hand and kissed it before standing. "It's getting late. I've had a lovely time and I promise the next time I see you out I won't ignore you and maybe I can get some gardening tips." This wasn't how she pictured the night ending and it sucked, but at least they had cleared the air and there was a chance at friendship.

"Okay." Leah walked her to the door. "I would really like to be your friend, Briley."

"I would like that, too."

"Good." Leah kissed her on the cheek.

Briley stepped onto the porch, down the steps and toward her house, ignoring her tingling cheek. Kat opened the kitchen door, ushered Briley into a kitchen chair, and placed a steaming cup of tea in front of her.

"Why do you look like someone kicked your puppy? What happened? Tell me."

"It's stupid." She shook her head. "She just wants to be friends. Not sure a relationship would work."

"You have to start somewhere. Friendship is a good first step."

"I know you're right. I know." She closed her eyes as the hot tea warmed her belly. "On another note, I believe I've managed to fill that hole I dug for myself. I know I didn't lose anything, but it feels that way. You know?"

"I do." Kat scooted her chair by Briley's and drew her into a hug. "You've semi-stalked her for a long time. It will take time but I've got to tell you I think she's interested in you."

Briley pulled back. "What? Why?"

"Briley, she asked tons of questions about you and showed interest. We can work with that. Just give her time and don't give up. Not yet. We're only in the first inning."

"I don't even think we've made it to the first inning. I'm sure we're still in the locker room before the game."

"Still game day."

"I love you." She punched Kat in the arm.

Kat mocked glared and grabbed her arm. "What was that for?"

"You didn't tell me how awesome her kitchen was."

Kat smiled. "If you play your cards right, you could be making her breakfast from that kitchen one morning." She winked at her.

"Friends make breakfast for each other."

"Not naked friends after a wild night of sex with

each other. At least not my friends."

Briley laughed. "Maybe you should get different friends."

"Maybe I should." She picked both their empty cups up and put them in the sink. "Tomorrow is another day."

Briley took a step back from her. "What's that look on your face for?"

"What look?" Kat held her hands up.

"Your up to something look. Please, don't do anything else. You've already got the teams to the field."

"And as your coach it's my job to make sure you have the right playbook. Don't worry, Briley. We've got this. Leah won't know what hit her. Trust me."

"I think we've used too many sports analogies for one night."

As Briley lay in bed that night, staring at the ceiling, she replayed the entire non-date in her head. There was something there. Leah wouldn't be able to deny that. Whether she changed her mind on them dating remained another matter. She'd make her cupcakes tomorrow. No one could say no to her cupcakes. She rolled over and closed her eyes.

Chapter Four

I don't know why we have to go to the grocery store this early," Kat grumbled, and fastened her seat belt.

Briley ignored Kat's bitching and pulled out of the driveway. Besides her house, the black Silverado 2500HD WT Double Cab was her only major purchase. She'd bought it last year and hadn't regretted the purchase once.

She'd woken at a quarter to six and decided today would be a good day to do her weekly shopping. If it kept her mind off a certain someone, all the better.

"Quit being such a baby. It's not that early." Sleep had eluded her the night before because she couldn't stop thinking about the dinner at Leah's. Briley wasn't going to push Leah into anything she didn't want or wasn't ready for, and after she avoided her for a week or two, she would start initiating conversation with her. Maybe that would allow her the time she needed not to combust in Leah's presence.

"What are you making for dinner?" Kat asked as she focused on her phone.

"What do you want?" She eyed her sister as she flipped the turn signal.

"Beef tips, broccoli, and rice."

"Fine." It did sound good and the beef wouldn't take that long to cook in the pressure cooker.

"Have you decided what you're going to do?"

Briley drummed her hands on the steering wheel and bobbed her head to the radio. "About what?"

"Leah. What else?"

"I'm going to give it time, then and only then, if I can manage, I'm going to try a friendship with her. But, before I start avoiding her, I've decided to make cupcakes for her because of the way I've acted. No one can resist them." Briley hummed along with the radio, lost in her own world until Kat snickered beside her, then she flipped the radio off. "Why'd you do that?" Briley reached to turn the radio back on, but Kat swatted her hand away.

"So, you want her to taste your cream filling, huh?"

"What?" Briley spluttered. "Grow up, Kat." She flipped her off, never taking her eyes off the road.

"Oh, God. You should see the look on your face." At the stoplight, Briley turned to glare at a laughing Kat, who took the opportunity to lift her phone and snap a picture.

"You are such a shit."

"Oh, Bri, I think it's admirable you want her to taste your cupcake considering who she looks like."

"Keep your mouth shut about that. Besides," Briley said, pulling into the parking lot of the grocery store, and parking the truck. "She doesn't look exactly like her."

"Whatever you say, sis."

Briley fought the urge to pull away from her when Kat slipped her arm around her waist but decided it wasn't worth the effort. She scanned the parking lot, then came to a complete stop when she spotted a familiar SUV parked close to the store. Plenty of people owned Escalades in Garriety, but Leah was the only one that owned a burgundy one in their neighborhood. Her heart pounded when she took in the familiar license plate to confirm her suspicions. Really? What were the odds she'd be here today? At this hour?

"Bri?"

"I…" Of course Leah would be here before Briley started phase one of avoiding the woman. Why didn't the universe just take her now?

Kat saw where she looked, grinned, and slapped her back. "Perfect. You know she has to eat too, and if you're lucky, she'll find something else just as tasty." She steered Briley toward the grocery store, ignoring the pout on her face.

"I can't go in there." She stepped away from Kat. "There's another grocery store across town."

"We are here now." She grasped Briley's shoulders. "Take a deep breath. Now another one. Good." She dropped her hands from Briley's shoulders and pointed to the store. "Don't be a baby. Isn't that what you told me? Let's go."

"Boy, Kat. I always look forward to your pep talks. So inspiring."

"Damn straight. I can record you a bunch, if you like. That way you'll never forget."

Briley rolled her eyes and avoided Kat's arm, bypassing her and entering the store. Kat grabbed a cart and followed behind her. It only took twenty minutes for Briley to find the items on her list, and she hadn't seen Leah once. Considering the store wasn't that big, she would chalk this up to a miracle. Briley: One. Fate: Zero.

When she turned around after grabbing two cans of pumpkin to place them in her cart, Kat had disappeared with it. "She was just here." Her grumbling came to a halt when she turned the corner toward the produce section. She backpedaled and plastered herself against the closest shelf, heart pounding in her chest. Leah and Mrs. Hanlin were talking by the produce section.

The first step to avoiding your prey is to know where they're located. Step one, check. Now she had to find Kat before Kat found Leah and Mrs. Hanlin. All she had to do was make sure they were still there, then she would head in the opposite direction, looking for Kat.

A few deep breaths later, Briley peeked her head around the shelf and gulped, dread filling the pit of her stomach. Kat had stopped beside Leah and Mrs. Hanlin at the apples. Okay. She was a grown woman. She could do this. Maybe. Before she could escape, Kat caught her eye and Briley shook her head, mouthing 'no' to her. When Kat smiled, and lifted her phone, both Leah and Mrs. Hanlin turned in her direction, but she quickly moved out of sight.

"Hey, Briley. Come say hello."

Kat's voice carried further than it should have in the small store. Crap. Why hadn't she thought just to call Kat? She would have to say hello now. *I can do this.* All she had to do was pretend she hadn't seen them or wasn't avoiding them so as not to look like a complete idiot. Piece of cake.

Briley glared at the old woman giving her dirty looks by the canned peaches, took a deep breath, then rounded the shelf. With more confidence than she felt, she walked toward the three women that watched her approach. Mrs. Hanlin looked genuinely happy to see her. Leah smiled at her and Kat had an evil grin on her face.

"Hello. I didn't see you all over here." She set her two cans in the cart then gripped the handle. "It's such a pleasant day to grocery shop." As soon as the words left her mouth, a huge clap of thunder shook the building. "I just love a good thunderstorm."

Disbelievingly, Leah eyed her. "We saw you peeking around the corner over there." She pointed to the aisle Briley had hid in.

"I don't know what you're talking about." She pushed her glasses up higher on the bridge of her nose even as Kat shook her head at her. Briley had always been a terrible liar.

"Oh, Bri, here you go." Kat lifted her phone and showed her a picture of her peeking around the shelf with a strained look on her face, then proceeded to show it to the other two women. Briley kept her cool and ignored the pointed stare Leah aimed her way.

"Thanks, Kat."

"You're welcome. What are sisters for?"

"Briley." Mrs. Hanlin touched her arm. "We were just talking about how Leah resembles some of the actors you're fans of."

Briley gulped and avoided Leah's gaze; she instead focused her death glare on Kat. "Really?"

Kat shrugged. "Mrs. Hanlin brought it up. She has been in your house, you know?"

"That's good," Briley said.

"So, Briley, who is it I resemble?" Leah asked. It took all of Briley's self-control not to fidget at the look in Leah's eyes. How could just a glance from the woman throw her in a tailspin?

"Oh." Mrs. Hanlin tapped her fingers on her cart. "What's her name? Cal...Calista Flockhart and Kyra Sedgwick. I was always a fan of *The Closer*."

"Who isn't? She's amazing." Briley wanted to crawl under a rock and die. She decided to downplay it and turned to Leah. She looked at her without really looking at her. "I don't see it."

"I've been told I favor them before," Leah added, but continued to stare at Briley as if she was trying to figure her out.

"No." Briley shook her head and wiped her brow. Jesus. Did they have the heat on in this store? "I still don't see it." Of course she saw it. How could she not? Leah was a dead ringer for Flockhart. The woman whose face, along with Sedgwick's, plastered her entertainment room. Her most prized possession was an eleven by seventeen-inch poster of *Cat Grant* autographed by Calista. It had taken her forever to get it signed and that was only from sheer dumb luck.

"Hmm." Kat fingered her phone's number pad then walked around Mrs. Hanlin and stood beside Leah. She raised her phone that showed a picture of Calista and placed it by Leah's face. "Do you see the resemblance now?"

Briley was going to kill her when they got home, slowly, and with a blunt knife. She leaned forward and squinted. "I guess there's some likeness."

Kat nodded, then slipped her phone back in her pocket. "Are you ladies making anything special or just doing a bit of shopping?"

"I always do my weekly shopping on Friday morning," Mrs. Hanlin said.

"I just needed to pick up a few things," Leah said.

Briley glanced in Leah's cart. Chicken, fresh fruits, vegetables, a pack of Oreos, and several other items.

"What about you, Briley?" Leah asked. "Doing a

bit of light shopping?"

"Actually, she's…"

"Yes," Briley blurted, before Kat could finish. "Just picking up a few things."

Leah eyed Briley's cart then her face. "Are you going to bake something?"

"Oh, I hope so." Mrs. Hanlin clapped her hands.

"She's going to bake a batch of cupcakes," Kat rushed out before Briley could cut her off.

"Cupcakes." Briley nodded. Oh God. Did Leah just take a step closer to her? Stupid crush and stupid Kat. "That's what I'm going to make." She couldn't help the blush that raced up her neck. Now every time she thought of cupcakes she would think about what Kat said.

"Are you all right?" Leah asked, placing a hand on Briley's forearm.

Briley fought the urge not to pull away from her. For one, it would be rude and the last thing she wanted was to hurt Leah's feelings. Leah hadn't done anything wrong.

"You do seem a mite flushed, Briley, dear," Mrs. Hanlin said.

Briley waved her free hand in the air as if she was swatting flies. "I'm fine." She laughed. "F…fine."

Kat snickered and the other two turned to her. Briley warned her with her eyes not to say anything, but she knew it was a losing battle. She would poison her dinner tonight. "She's just nervous about what her cupcake tastes like," Kat said.

"You sure you're all right, Briley? You're even redder now." Leah looked between them and squeezed Briley's arm.

Kat leaned close to Leah. "I think she's just

worried about whether someone will like the filling of her cupcake." Kat winked at her.

"Oh, my God." Briley hung her head.

Leah's eyes were on Briley and she patted Briley's arm before pulling her hand back, placing them on her own cart. "What kind of cupcakes?"

"Turtle," Briley muttered, thankful Leah had changed the subject.

Mrs. Hanlin placed a hand over Briley's that clutched the cart. "If I'm not mistaken, the last time you made them was a few years ago, and you were trying to woo Beth without really wooing her. Weren't you?"

Briley opened her mouth then clamped it shut. She hadn't remembered that. Come to think of it, the only time she did make them was to impress someone. Mrs. Hanlin was as old as dirt. How could she remember so much? "Yes, it was. But this time," she turned to Leah, "it is a gesture to forge the divide between us." Oh, for fuck's sake. Did those words really just come out of her mouth? One look at Kat's face confirmed that, yes, they had. The faster she got this over, the quicker she could get her first murder out of the way. "I am really sorry for the way I've treated you."

"Apology accepted, just like last night. Let's put all that behind us," Leah said and Briley nodded in agreement. "I've never had turtle cupcakes before. So, since you apologized twice, I hope I'm still getting some?"

"Oh, Leah," Kat said. "I don't think that's anything you have to worry about. You will definitely be eating her cupcake."

"And with that," Briley said, her stomach doing some weird flip flop movement she'd never felt before when Leah tilted her head and smiled at her, "I think it's time to go. Kat, you can either come with me, or stay here and walk home." The faster they got away from Mrs. Hanlin and Leah, the better.

Kat's eyes widened. "That's fifteen miles away and it could start raining at any minute."

"It would be good exercise and you could get a free shower. I'm trying to save money since the city jacked up our water bill."

"It is a shame. Seems every month they up it," Mrs. Hanlin threw in.

"I'll see you ladies later," Kat said.

"Briley," Mrs. Hanlin called out. "Why don't you and your sister join me for brunch next Sunday?"

"We would love to," Briley said, pushing her cart away and toward the register. After she paid for her things, loaded them in the truck, then strapped herself in, she turned to Kat. "What did you think you were doing in there?"

Kat flinched. "You're not really mad, are you? Bri, I love you. She likes you. While I think you need to take your time getting to know her, I do believe she really likes you, but is probably scared. You just need to talk to her. Spend time with her."

"That's easier said than done." Briley thumped her forehead on the steering wheel. "When every time I look at her I want to kiss her."

"She is a looker. Besides, you can think of brunch as your second date if you don't manage to spend any time with her between now and then," Kat happily threw in.

"What?" Briley whipped her head around. "Second date. What are you talking about? What did you do?" She poked Kat on the shoulder.

"Me?" Kat pointed to her chest. "I didn't do

anything. You're the one who agreed to brunch."

"Well, hell. You played me again."

"Not just me. Mrs. Hanlin also believes you two would make a good pair. We only want what's best for you."

With a sigh, Briley rested her forehead on the steering wheel. "I understand you both wanting to help, but Kat, please don't interfere. For now, she just wants to be friends. We should respect that. If I push, I could lose the right to even be her friend."

"I promise," Kat said.

Briley lifted her head and started the truck. "Pinky promise." She held her pinky out.

"We're not kids anymore, Bri." Briley wiggled her pinky and Kat grabbed a hold of it. "I promise."

"At least I won't have to poison your dinner tonight."

Kat did a double take. "Wait…what?"

Chapter Five

After ten minutes of driving around, Briley finally found a parking space that was only a few blocks away from the art festival. Briley hadn't made up her mind whether she wanted to come, but once she mentioned it to Kat, Kat made up her mind for her.

The cool night air, along with the sounds and smells of the festival, gave her a second wind. This was the second year for the festival and, by the looks of it, they were well on their way to outpace the attendance of last year. Briley tapped her foot to the drumbeat, as Kat used her phone. A few local bands were performing.

"Ready?" Briley stretched her arms above her head and waited for Kat's reply.

Kat slipped her phone into her pocket. "I'm glad we decided not to have dessert at the house. Whatever that delicious smell is, I want some."

"Me, too." The sidewalks weren't too crowded and Briley waved at a few people she knew as they made their way to the first tent. Local artists of all ages were sectioned off along the downtown streets, selling their wares. The food vendors were allocated to a street over, and the band had erected a small stage at the town square.

They browsed the first few stalls until something caught Kat's eye down the road. "What is it?" Briley asked.

Kat whipped back around. "Oh, nothing." She rocked back on her heels and Briley knew something was up.

"Nothing?"

Kat crossed her arms and if Briley didn't know her, she would be intimidated, but Briley knew she was a big mush ball.

"That's what I said." Kat grabbed Briley's arm and steered her toward another stall. This artist made tiny creatures out of scrap metal. Briley picked up a grasshopper, turning it this way and that way when she sensed she was being watched. Kat stood to her left, so she knew it wasn't her. She paid for her three creatures, tucked the small bag into her purse, then turned around.

It only took a second for her eyes to latch onto Leah, who, by this time, was turned away from her at another stall.

"Go talk to her," Kat said, quietly.

"Should I?" Briley gnawed on her bottom lip.

Kat gave her a slight push in Leah's direction. "Yes."

She pushed Kat's hand away. "I'm going." After brushing the non-existent lint off her shirt, Briley walked toward Leah, then stepped up beside her, glancing at the small paintings on the table.

"I like this one." Leah said, pointing at one painting while not looking up. "What do you think, Briley? Do you think it would go with the decor in my living room?" Leah turned her head and directed her attention to Briley.

Why did this woman have to be so pretty? Briley's breath caught in her chest. Get a grip. "Which one?" Leah pointed it out. Briley tilted her head, thinking back to Leah's living room. "It will."

Leah picked it up and handed it to the artist, who quickly wrapped it and rang up the sale.

"Thank you. You two enjoy your evening," the artist said.

"We will." Leah touched Briley's arm and they stepped onto the sidewalk. "Are you here with your sister?"

"Yes. She's around her somewhere." Briley looked to the stall they'd left, but Kat had vanished. Figured. She turned back to Leah. "Having fun?"

"I am. I read where this is only its second year."

"They have double the vendors this year than last year." Why was this awkward? That would never do. "Want to explore?" Briley caught Leah's eye.

"I would like that." They set off and Briley stuffed her hands in her pockets to fight the urge to hold Leah's hand. As they walked, Briley commented on several vendors she knew.

The closer they got to the music, the louder the bass was, and the faster her heart pounded. Leah slipped her arm through Briley's, who almost stumbled at the contact.

"Let's sit and listen to the band," Leah said. Once seated, Briley bounced her knee up and down and kept her hands to herself, afraid of touching the other woman. Leah moved an inch closer and their legs were touching. "Do you know the band?"

The poster was located to the right of the stage, The Longhorns. "Can't say that I do." She'd never heard them before. "They're not bad." She'd check to see if they were selling any CDs when they left. Supporting the local talent was important to Briley.

"Is it only country music that will perform

tonight?" Leah touched her arm.

Briley narrowed her eyes at Leah, but fought the urge to go on the defensive. "Do you not like country music?" Briley had no problem with differing views on music, but she'd argued with quite a few people over the years who constantly had a negative attitude toward the genre.

A smile played on her lips. "It's not my go to genre, but I have nothing against it. Almost looked like you were ready to fight me."

"Sorry." Briley fiddled with her glasses. "I just hate stereotypes and people always assuming only rednecks listen to it. I'm not a redneck, but there is nothing wrong with being one. There are many facets of country music and I have never understood why someone would tear down something someone else enjoys. A few years ago, I visited my mom. She told me to put some music on, so I did. When we were on the third song, she looked at me and said, 'she can't sing, can she?' She didn't have to like the music; I would have gladly changed it, but what got me was that she knew I liked the artist, yet she still made the comment."

"I look at it like this, Briley. I may not like a certain type of music, art, cooking, the list goes on. But, I know what it takes to put oneself out there. To show the world what you've got and it's hard. I was terrified when my first article came out. People are always going to judge you, no matter what, but I make it a point not to make fun of or tear down a dream someone has worked hard to get to." She pointed at the stage. "That may not be my type of music, but they are clearly enjoying themselves, as is the crowd." Leah shrugged and crossed her legs.

Briley's stomach flipped in that weird sort of way

it had been doing lately. "I try and support the local talent," was all she could say. What was wrong with her? Get it together, Briley. She pulled her phone out of her pocket when it vibrated. A text from Kat.

Don't do anything I wouldn't do. With a winky face.

"Everything okay?" Leah asked. "Do you need to go?"

The disappointment in Leah's voice made up Briley's mind for her. "Nope." Briley turned to Leah. "I'm all yours."

"Well, then." Leah stood. "Let's continue."

"I want to see if they're selling CDs." Briley gently pushed her way through the crowd, with Leah holding onto the back of her shirt. After she'd bought a CD, they made their way to the food vendors. "What do you want? My treat."

"I won't turn down an offer like that. What do you recommend?"

Briley leaned in closer to hear her over the noise of the crowd. "It depends on what you're in the mood for. Food or dessert?"

"Dessert," Leah said, without hesitation.

Briley pointed to a vendor off to the right. "He sells deep fried cheesecake." Then pointed to a vendor off to the left. "His closest competition is Sharon, who sells deep fried Snickers. In the middle, we have funnel cakes, brownies on a stick covered in caramel and toppings. Back behind those vendors are our traditionalists. Claire sells her 'famous' waffle cones with vanilla ice cream and toppings. Doug offers mini apple pies, and Mr. Williams, way in the back, sells slushies in a dozen flavors." Briley took in Leah's wide eyes. "I know it's a lot."

"I like variety. How about we each pick one and share?" Leah gave her an expectant look.

Briley swept one hand out in front of her. "After you."

It didn't take long for their orders to be filled. With their prizes in hand, Briley led Leah to a quiet corner, where they sat down on the curb. Briley shivered when Leah moaned at the first taste of deep fried cheesecake. "Told you." They were quiet as they shared the cheesecake and the ice cream filled waffle bowl, topped with fudge sauce and peanuts Briley had picked. It became hard to keep her cool when she breathed in Leah's pleasant scent. She had just popped the last piece of waffle in her mouth when Leah spoke.

"I know you like country music. What other music do you enjoy?"

"Pretty much anything. I'm eclectic. You?"

"I'm a fan of eighties music, but I listen to classical when I'm stressed. It keeps me calm."

"So, like Beethoven or Taylor Davis?"

"Both. Last year Evan and I saw Lindsey Stirling in concert. Which was excellent."

"Love her. I've seen everybody I wanted to, except one. Celine is at the top of my bucket list."

"She's amazing in concert."

"Lucky dog."

Leah laughed. "Madison and I saw her a few years back in Vegas."

"Wild weekend?"

"Wouldn't you like to know?" Leah smiled coyly.

"Oh, now I'm intrigued. Did you wake up naked in a fountain or something?"

Leah arched her brow and Briley had the good grace to blush. "It's really telling that's where your mind went to. I'm afraid it's nothing quite that wild. Just took in a lot of shows and spent time together."

"Sounds like you had a good time." Relief flooded her that Kat wasn't there to tell Leah about their trip to Vegas five years ago. That trip became one for the record books and was not to be repeated. It was the first and only time she'd had to bail Kat out of jail.

Leah ran her hands along her thighs. "Are you okay with us interacting like this, Briley?"

Her plan to stay away from Leah was crashing and burning and she didn't have the heart to stop it. "Thanks for considering that, but I am. I like you and we are friends." Briley kicked her legs out in front of her and cleared her throat to speak when Kat walked up to them.

Kat crossed her arms. "Leah, it's good to see you again."

"You, too."

Briley stood, holding out a hand to assist Leah up. She couldn't ignore the tremors that ran through her when Leah took her hand.

Kat must have seen the look on her face because she quickly intervened. "Are you both done looking, or…?"

"I am," Leah said.

"Briley, you?"

At that moment, Briley realized she still held Leah's hand. She pulled her hand loose from Leah's and slipped it into her pocket. "I am, too."

"Good. Good." Kat patted her on the back. "Where are you parked, Leah? We'll walk you."

"Couple of blocks up."

"Perfect."

Kat kept up the chatter until Leah motioned to

the left at her SUV. Kat veered off toward their truck while Briley followed Leah to hers.

"Let me." Briley reached around Leah to open her door when Leah unlocked it and gripped the door handle. "Even as impromptu as this was, I enjoyed myself."

"I did as well. I think we're going to be all right, Briley." Leah reached a hand out toward Briley, but drew it back at the last second. "I should get home."

Briley nodded and stepped back. "Us to."

"Don't be a stranger."

Briley let go of the door, so Leah could shut it. Her thoughts were a jumbled mess, as she stood on the curb waiting for Leah to back out. A good mess, but still a mess. Kat was lounging against her truck when Briley joined her.

Kat eyed her. "So?"

"So?" Briley rocked back on her heels.

When nothing else was forthcoming, Kat laughed. "Let's get home. I'm tired."

"I could sleep." Briley leaned her head against the window, lost in thought, as Kat drove.

Chapter Six

The week flew by much too quickly for Briley's liking. She'd been busy helping Brandon search house listings, but she also managed to have breakfast with Leah three times, and dinner once. Living next door to each other was a life saver and allowed them easy access to each other.

They were both busy with work, but managed to talk for a few minutes on the mornings they didn't have breakfast together, and text occasionally. It was wonderful and she relished getting to spend time with her, whether in person or through text. So far, she'd learned some about Leah's childhood and how she broke into the freelance field. Mostly, though, she just enjoyed being with her. It was comfortable and she hadn't felt that with another woman for a long time.

"Bri, are you ready?" Kat called from the living room early Saturday, breaking Briley from her thoughts.

Briley shrugged off thoughts about Leah even though they hadn't seen each other for the past two days. Today was about her and Kat, who still hadn't decided what type of work she wanted to do. She didn't anticipate a Leah sighting considering they were going out of town and she hadn't mentioned the toy convention to her the last time they'd talked, but she should have. With a final look in the mirror, she nodded at her reflection.

Along with hundreds of vendors at the toy convention, there would also be a feature cosplay competition and a few celebrities would be signing autographs. This year there weren't any autographs that interested her, but she couldn't wait to spend lots of money on new toys. She was an avid collector of superhero figurines and memorabilia and had been collecting since her teens. She and Kat had shared that passion with their dad. When he died, they split his collection between them.

Today Briley had opted for an easy cosplay as the Eleventh Doctor. After making sure there weren't any creases in her white, striped button down shirt, she smoothed her red suspenders, and straightened her red bowtie. She settled on navy trousers and a pair of Converse to finish off her look. She'd opted not to wear the brown suit jacket, but on her way out of her room, she made sure to grab the red Fez that set on her dresser.

Kat struck a casual pose by the front door dressed as Indiana Jones. Briley lifted her phone and took a picture just as Kat turned in her direction. "I do believe if we wanted to, we could go on quite the adventure, Doctor."

"You've got that right," Briley said. Kat gave her a sly smile and rubbed her hands together. It wasn't the first time Briley was glad that Kat shared her love of all things geeky. Snagging the clear bag she'd packed the night before, she joined Kat at the door. "Onward ho."

The drive took a little over an hour and surprisingly finding a parking spot wasn't difficult. Since they weren't going to the main lobby, they showed their passes, went through the security line, then entered the first of four large meeting rooms that was littered with dozens of vendors. Her heart picked up when she spied her favorite vendor who sold vintage superhero figurines a few tables down.

They high-fived. "Let's do this."

A few hours later, they had scoured three of the rooms, which had nabbed them both three bags each filled with dozens of figurines, t-shirts, and various other collectables. Briley added three rare Funko Pop figures to her collection, including a rare Regina from the SDCC in 2015 that limited the pieces to 1008, along with a Batwoman figurine she had been looking for the last few years. Although a common figurine, none of the local shops carried it in its original packaging and she was happy to have found it. Kat was a fan of Harley Quinn and picked up a couple of pieces.

Comic books held no interest for Briley, so when Kat stopped at a vendor that sold them, she took the opportunity to look around, and sucked in a breath when she spotted a particular someone browsing at the table across from theirs.

Briley whipped around toward Kat and tugged nervously on her suspenders. Despite spending time together, she still wasn't prepared to see Leah today and not in her Captain Marvel outfit.

"You all right?" Kat asked, after she paid for her comic books. "Bri?" she waved her had in front of her face.

"She's here," Briley whispered.

Kat frowned and leaned in close to her. "Who?"

"Me."

Briley jumped when Leah spoke from behind them, but Kat turned around and smiled at her.

"Leah, good to see you here. If I knew you would be coming, you could have ridden with us." Leah gave her a one-arm hug. "Are you having fun? You look great."

Leah held up her two bags. Briley found that she had suddenly become mute, staring at Leah's outfit. Of course, she'd seen her from a distance dressed like this, but up close was an entirely different story. The tight costume outlined every curve and every muscle. She was so sexy and Briley had to stop herself from fanning her face.

Leah ran her eyes along Briley's body, then reached toward her, and straightened her bowtie, before patting her shoulder and pulling her hand back. "I am having fun. It's my first time here. When I talked to Evan last night, he was jealous but insisted I come and enjoy myself. Next year I have a feeling he won't be spending the entire summer with Kathy. It wasn't until after I talked to him that I decided to attend today."

"Is this your first room?" Kat asked.

"No, my third." Leah pointed behind her. "I've got one more."

Kat pulled a speechless Briley into her side. "That's the last one we have to explore also. Why don't you join us? Then we can get something to eat."

"I'd love to."

Briley's heart thumped to a rhythm in her chest that started playing every time she was around Leah. If it hadn't been for Kat's arm around her, she would have swooned on the spot at the blinding smile Leah gave her. *Friends, Briley. You're just friends.*

Kat pointed around them. "Are you done in here or did you want to see more?"

"Lead the way."

"Wait." Kat stopped them, then asked a passerby dressed as Batman to take their picture. Kat sandwiched

Briley between her and Leah, and when Leah wrapped her arm around her waist, Briley felt like all the air had been sucked out of the room. Briley was sure she managed to smile and when Kat checked the photo, she seemed satisfied at the outcome.

When Kat motioned them forward, Briley took a step away from Leah and accepted the bags Kat handed her. They quickly split up when they entered the room, but at various points, Briley would feel eyes on her and when she would look up, Leah would be watching her. After another hour of searching, Kat called a time-out to get something to eat. It was all Briley could do not to vibrate from the idea of food.

They debated the different food trucks set up in the side parking lot, and decided on The O'Neil. In reality, it was Bangin' Burgers and Fries, but during the toy convention, almost all of the food trucks would come up with a flashy name for the truck and for the food. This year they had decided to cover Stargate SG1. She and Kat always had fun walking through the parking lot and taking pictures of the different food trucks and their menus. They'd made scrapbooks over the years and this year wouldn't be any different.

Still undecided, Briley pursed her lips and scanned the menu for the third time. There were so many choices and everything sounded so good. She hummed and ignored Leah and Kat, who were tapping their feet, as she scanned the list of items again. It was between the Teal'c, a double burger with three different kinds of cheese, bacon, onions, and a special sauce, or the Jackson, a deep-fried chicken patty, with lettuce, tomato, bacon, mushrooms, and a special sauce. Decisions. Decisions.

"Briley?" Kat all but shouted at her.

Briley turned and acknowledged them both. The scowls on their faces did nothing to dampen her mood. "I want the Teal'c." She scanned the menu once more. "And I think we should get a plate of the Ori." A huge platter of French fries, covered with cheese, sour cream, chili, onion, and peppers.

"Leah?" Kat asked.

"I want the Vala."

Briley squinted at the menu, not remembering seeing the Vala. There it was at the bottom of the page. Thin sliced roast beef on a sweet roll smothered in cheese and a special sauce. Briley blinked. "That sounds good too."

Kat rolled her eyes. "You've already decided, Briley. No going back now."

"Fine." Briley shoved her bags at Kat. "Find us a place to sit and I'll order. What do you want?"

"The Teal'c," Kat said, taking Leah's bags from her. "Leah, stay with Bri. She won't be able to carry all of our order."

"I could manage," Briley muttered, shoving her glasses up the bridge of her nose.

Leah gave her a look Briley recognized as her don't be silly look. "I don't mind waiting with you."

"So?" Briley rocked back on her heels and Leah mimicked her movements.

"So?"

After spending the past week getting to know each other, why was this awkward? Briley shook off her lingering doubts. She and Leah were fast becoming friends. "Having a good time?"

"I am. It got even better when I ran into you and your sister." She looked her up and down. "The bowtie is a new choice, although I prefer Twelve."

"That's nonsense." She was too nervous to debate the merits of Eleven over Twelve so she changed the subject. "Kat likes you," she blurted out and averted her gaze back down to the menu in her hand. She jerked her head up when Leah ripped it out of her hands, carried it back to the table where the condiments were, then retook her spot beside her. "That was rude."

"The only reason you were looking at it was to get out of talking to me."

"No…maybe. Okay. Yes, it was. I'm sorry."

"Excuse me."

They both turned their heads when a tall older woman dressed as Captain America walked up to them. Briley had to hand it to the woman; she had the look down pat, even down to the cropped blond hair. She smiled even when she saw the woman's fingers twitching on her phone and Briley knew what she wanted even before she asked. She couldn't fault the woman, though; Briley had already had her picture taken with countless other attendees in costume.

The stranger turned to Leah. "I was wondering if you would take a picture with me?"

Leah took the phone out of her hands and held it out. "Briley, can you take our picture?"

"Sure." Briley's heart sank when the woman, a woman closer to Leah's age, slipped her arm around Leah's small waist and pulled her flush against her side. They looked good together and if the smile on Leah's face was any indication, she enjoyed the woman's attention. She hurried up and snapped a couple of pictures before handing the phone back. She fought the urge to grab Leah and pull her back toward her. Leah wasn't hers. They were friends. "There you go." She decided not to acknowledge the smile Leah was throwing the woman's way.

The woman pulled out a business card and handed it to Leah. "Maybe we can get a coffee sometime?"

It hurt more than she expected seeing and hearing Leah's interest in the other woman. Briley averted her gaze and tried to tune out what they were saying.

Leah placed her hand on Briley's wrist. "I'm sorry."

She frowned. "You don't have anything to be sorry about."

"Yes, I do. Even though I told you there couldn't be anything between us but friendship doesn't mean I should discount your feelings, because they are valid." She sighed. "I've been where you are. If it's too hard to be around me, I understand."

Briley knew she wasn't a good liar, but she couldn't tell the truth either. "I'm a big girl. I can handle my feelings."

"That didn't answer my question."

"Next," the food truck driver hollered.

"That's us." Briley avoided the question, pasted the biggest smile on her face that she could, and turned to give the man their orders. When she turned back, Kat stood beside her. "Where'd you come from?"

Kat shook her head. "What happened this time?"

"I honestly don't know. I was jealous she talked to that woman, but I think I conducted myself well."

"You did, honey," the woman in line behind them said and winked.

"Thank you," Briley said, even as Kat pulled her toward the pickup window.

"I really don't know what I said wrong," Briley said.

"Okay. You have to understand, she's dealing

with her feelings as well."

"I know." When their numbers were called, they grabbed both their trays, drink caddy, then walked back to the table. Captain America had made her way back to Leah and was talking to her. Briley thought she was done with her when she handed the business card to Leah.

"I'll keep that in mind," Leah said to the woman, as Briley and Kat sat their trays on the table.

"You do that." Captain America leaned forward and pecked Leah on the cheek. "For what's it worth, I enjoyed meeting you."

"You as well," Leah said.

Briley thought it was a bit brazen for the stranger to kiss Leah, but kept her mouth shut. If Leah wanted to date the woman, Briley would deal with it. Probably with a lot of binge baking and late night movie marathons with Kat, but she would deal. She shook off the thoughts, picked up her burger, and took a bite as the conversation flowed easily between Kat and Leah, but Briley kept her mouth shut for the most part. One, because her burger tasted damn good, and two, because she didn't want to say the wrong thing to Leah. She didn't know what she'd said wrong in the first place.

After take out, throwing away their trash, they finished searching the last vendor room. Briley was pulled from her thoughts when Leah touched her arm. "Yes."

"Take a picture with me?"

"Sure." They stopped a passerby, who was more than happy to take their picture. It gave Briley an excuse to put her arm around Leah's waist and draw her close.

Chapter Seven

Once seated in the auditorium for the cosplay contest, Briley's nerves were out in full force when Leah sat down beside her. The seats were arranged so close together, she couldn't help their legs touching.

"I'm always amazed at some of the designs everyone comes up with," Leah said.

"I know. Their talent astounds me. You did a good job on your costume, also," Briley said.

Leah placed her hand on Briley's thigh, and Briley stiffened automatically. Leah made as to move it, but Briley stopped her. "It's fine. These seats are close together. They're probably breaking a law or something with so many people here."

Leah smiled. "Or something."

Since Leah was already touching her, Briley lifted her arm and placed it behind Leah to rest on the seat. Kat winked at her over the top of Leah's head, and Briley flipped her off. All thought fled from her mind and her throat went dry when Leah leaned into her side a bit to adjust.

"Is this all right?" Leah asked, eyes on the stage.

"It's fine." Two hours later, and countless close calls with Briley fighting not to touch Leah's shoulder, the competition ended. Briley moved her arm and stretched, a yawn breaking through. "That was fun."

Leah took a drink of her water then put the empty

bottle in her bag. "It was. Although, I didn't realize there would be so many people here."

"This is the fifth year, and it's been growing ever since." Briley helped her with her bags. "It can't compete with the big cons, but for what it is, they put on a good show."

"I've been to the big cons," Leah said. "Way too many people for me."

"Briley and I have been to a few, but I prefer something like this." Kat motioned for them to follow her as she led the way into the lobby. "Did anybody want to do anything else here?" She eyed first Briley then Leah. "Because if we're done, I'm hungry."

"Oh, Kat." Briley groaned. "Really?"

"What am I missing?" Leah asked.

"Every time we come here, Kat wants to go to Dave and Busters."

Leah shrugged. "Sounds good to me." A small smile tugged at the corners of her mouth. "Unless you're afraid of losing."

Briley crossed her arms and Kat took a step back. "Losing?" She pointed to her own chest. "Do you see who you're talking to? I am the queen of winning, lady. You name it, I'm good at it."

"Air hockey?" Leah tilted her head.

Briley licked her lips, trying not to show any weakness. "I am like the champion of air hockey. I...I always win." She reached up and adjusted her glasses. "And, I have you know, they call me puck."

"Who are they?" Kat threw in, but continued smiling at the look of death from Briley.

"Everyone, Kat. You should know this."

Kat snickered. "What I know is..."

Briley cut her off and held out her hand to Leah,

who readily took it. Even the softness of Leah's hand couldn't derail Briley's train of thought. "You're on."

"I can't wait for this." Kat slapped them both on the shoulder. "I do believe I saw in the paper where anyone coming from the convention in costume gets twenty percent off their food order." She pulled them into her sides. "Ladies, it's game time."

Briley felt relieved no one had suggested that she ride with Leah; she didn't think her heart could take it.

"Bri, she's still back there. You don't have to keep looking in the mirror."

"I'm only checking."

"What are you going to do about air hockey?" Kat asked.

"What can I do? I'll play and lose, badly, probably, but will try and keep my cool. I'm sure I can beat her at ninety percent of the other games."

"Ninety percent, huh?" Kat turned into the parking lot.

"Too high?"

"I mean, yes. We really don't know anything about her abilities. She'll probably end up kicking our asses in a lot of the games."

Briley unclipped her seatbelt. "What makes you say that?"

"Just a vibe she gives off. Let's go. She's waiting for us, or I should say you."

The place was full, but not jam-packed, and Briley felt relieved that they could snag their own table. She hated sitting at the bar. After their drinks and food were ordered, she turned to Leah. "Are you ready?"

Leah leaned forward on the table. "I've been ready. Can't you see I'm quivering from the anticipation of beating you? First is air hockey, then who knows."

She shrugged. "Maybe the kids will choose my house at Halloween over yours, or maybe." Leah tapped her finger on the table. "Maybe I'll beat you at Christmas. I'm photogenic, Briley. I can see it now, my smiling face in the front page of the paper and in the background will be my house all lit up for Christmas."

All through her speech, Briley had picked up a napkin and torn it into shreds. "You talk a good game, but frankly you're so tiny I'm not even worried about you."

Leah cocked her head. "Tiny?"

The narrowing of Leah's eyes did nothing to deter Briley. "Tiny. So, tiny. How's the weather down there? I bet you have to shop in the kid's department. I'm surprised the waitress even saw you sitting there." Briley could tell Leah tried hard not to laugh and she gave her an A for effort. Once Leah started laughing, Kat did as well. Briley huffed. "I see how it is." Briley grabbed both of their wrists and got their attention. The smiles died on their lips. "I'm coming for you both. I have eyes on you."

"Like the eyes you usually have on my ass when I'm in my yard," Leah said, with a straight face.

"What? Who?" Briley lifted her hand to Leah's forehead. "Do you have a fever? What crazy talk is this?" She gave a grateful sigh when the waitress placed their drinks on the table. She grabbed her cup and took a giant sip. "I believe we were talking about air hockey."

Leah opened and shut her mouth and Kat shook her head.

"No, Briley, I do believe we were talking about my ass," Leah threw back at her.

"Whose?" Briley hoped the floor would open and swallow her whole. "I think I missed that conversation.

I remember air hockey."

Leah sipped her drink. "I'll give you this one, but we'll come back to it eventually."

Briley let out the breath she was holding. "Fair enough. Enjoying your burger?"

"Not as good as the roast beef earlier, but it's tasty."

"My burger's good, too, Briley," Kat threw in.

"I was getting ready to ask you."

"Sure." Kat sipped her drink.

"Kat, are you dating anyone?" Leah asked.

Briley chomped into her burger, and chewed, fully invested in this conversation. Kat had been mum on this topic since she'd arrived.

Kat took a sip of her drink before answering. "I was dating someone before I decided to quit and move halfway across the country."

That was news. Briley dabbed at her lips, then took a drink of her beer, but kept quiet.

"Not serious then?" Leah asked.

"She was fun to be with, but I didn't really see it going anywhere."

When Kat started talking about her freelance accounting gig, Briley zoned out, and zeroed in on the air hockey tables. Leah wouldn't know what hit her. She was a fierce wind. She was a hurricane.

"Briley…Briley."

Briley flinched when Leah waved her hand in front of her face. "We weren't sure where you went there for a second."

Briley leaned into Leah's personal space, and gave her kudos for not backing away. "I have one question for you." She made sure to check that they were done eating before she posed her question.

"I'm listening."

They were so close, all Briley would have to do is lean in a few more inches to kiss her. "Ready to rumble?"

Leah somehow managed to keep a straight face. "I've been ready since the parking lot at the convention. Are you ready to lose?"

"You will be the only loser tonight."

"I might have forgotten to mention that when I would allow Evan to pick a place for us to spend time together, his go to place was the arcade." Leah buffed her fingers on her shirt, leaned forward, almost touching Briley's lips, then slid off her stool.

As her heart pounded in her chest, Briley wiped her palms on her pants. Good grief, Leah was sexy.

"Are you waiting for an invitation, Briley?" Leah called out, as she walked away.

Briley was still in a daze when Kat dragged her off the stool in Leah's direction. Thirty minutes and four games into air hockey, Briley knew she didn't stand a chance. Leah was a beast.

After going down in a blaze of glory, Kat led them to the basketball hoops and challenged Leah, who readily agreed. Briley stood back and cheered for Leah. After three games, Kat had thrown in the towel, bowing at Leah's talent.

"So, what's next?" Kat rubbed her hands together.

Briley scanned the area until her eyes locked onto something she knew she couldn't lose at. "How about a bet?"

"A bet?" Leah regarded Briley with a look of pity. "Do you really think you can win against me?"

This wouldn't be the first time Briley had made a bet she wasn't sure she could win. "I'm confident in my abilities, tiny human.”

"Before I bet, I need to know the game,” Kat said.

“Racing.” Briley braced herself for the refusal, but none came. “Loser buys dessert.”

Kat bounced on her toes. “You’re on. Leah, she’s good, but I’ve beat her a few times.”

Leah shook Kat, then Briley’s hand. “Deal.”

As soon as three games became available, they hopped in. They’d decided to play individuals games instead of race against each other. Once finished, they would screenshot their score and that would determine the winner. Clearly, she would come out the victor. This was her game. Kat had only beaten her a few times, and each time Briley had been drunk. She had this in the bag. She was the first to admit she lived to win. Second place belonged to the first loser. As her car sailed across the finish line in first place, she took a picture and felt quite confident in her abilities.

She climbed out and waited for the others to join her when she’d finished. But, the looks on Kat and Leah’s faces didn’t show the expected disappointment. They were smiling and holding their phones to their chest. Suddenly, her confidence started to falter. She didn’t know Leah well enough to know, but she knew when Kat was being devious. This was not one of those times.

"So, beat that, losers.” Briley turned her phone around and grinned as Kat and Leah looked at Briley’s phone then each other. At the same time, they both turned their phones around.

Chapter Eight

Early the next morning, Briley danced along to the radio while the cinnamon rolls baked that she planned to take to Mrs. Hanlin's brunch. It was always a tossup as to what Mrs. Hanlin would make and she hoped for her sausage casserole, which she should have requested.

Even the ending to their night couldn't dampen her mood. Sure, she'd lost the racing game, but she found a bit of comfort in the fact that Leah had come in second. The pleased look on Leah's face when she took her first taste of the lava cake she ordered didn't hurt either.

She knew she should reign in her emotions, but she wasn't sure if she could. Leah wasn't like anyone she'd ever known before and just the thought of her drove her crazy. Being infatuated from afar was one thing, but after getting to know Leah, she knew there was no turning back.

At a quarter to nine, Kat walked into the kitchen, dressed in a pair of black Capris and a red and white striped tank top. Briley wished she could have arms like hers, but she knew what Kat put into her workouts and didn't want to devote the time it required. Most mornings, Briley had to force herself to go for a run.

"Good morning," Kat said, after taking a sip of the coffee Briley handed her. "Looking forward to today?"

"Yes." Today was going to be a good day.

"That's the spirit." Kat joined her at the kitchen table.

While Kat nursed her coffee, Briley stood up and took the cinnamon rolls out of the oven, placed them in a container and iced them before putting the lid on and sitting down beside Kat.

"Don't take this the wrong way, Bri, but it doesn't bother you that she has a teenage son, a daughter, and two grandkids?"

"We've talked about this. Our ages are the least of my worries and Evan is great. I haven't officially met Madison or her family, but I'm sure they're also great. I think with brunch today we may be heading onto the field, Coach."

"Game on." Kat rinsed out her cup, then placed it in the dishwasher.

The jeans Briley wore were well-worn, but comfortable and didn't have any holes. The vintage M&M long sleeve t-shirt was one of her favorites. "Is this too casual?"

"If Leah is going to fall for you, she'll have to accept your sense of style."

Briley rolled her eyes, grabbed the container with the cinnamon rolls, and gestured for Kat to go ahead of her. Once they were outside, Briley waved at Mr. Balkin, then slipped her hand through Kat's arm.

"I love you, Bri, and just want you to be happy."

"I want the same for you." They walked the rest of the way to Mrs. Hanlin's house in silence. The house was smaller than both Briley and Leah's, but well maintained, and the yellow painted siding gave off a friendly vibe. Without knocking, Briley opened the front door and walked in, then directed Kat to the kitchen.

Leah was bent over to take a dish out of the oven, and Briley felt no shame that her eyes zeroed in on her backside. Her eyes jerked up when Leah cleared her throat and gave her a knowing smile. Briley returned a sheepish smile then spun around and accepted the hug Mrs. Hanlin gave her.

"I'm so glad both of you could make it," Mrs. Hanlin said. Like they really had a choice. Turning down an invitation from Mrs. Hanlin was considered sacrilege. She dropped Briley's hands and took the dish from Kat. "And you brought cinnamon rolls. Leah, if you haven't had these, you're in for a treat."

"I look forward to it." Leah pulled out a chair and sat down at the table while Briley helped Mrs. Hanlin with the dishes. Since Mrs. Hanlin always sat in the chair beside the living room, that left Briley to sit across from Leah with Kat beside her. Her stomach grumbled at the smell wafting from the platters that littered the table; hash brown casserole, turkey bacon, scrambled eggs, homemade biscuits and gravy, and her cinnamon rolls. A lot of food for just four people, but she knew Mrs. Hanlin would take the leftovers to her neighbors.

The first ten minutes, they ate in silence until Mrs. Hanlin asked them a question. "I know this is last minute, but I wondered if you girls could help me bring a few boxes down from the attic."

"Kat has to make a few calls, but I'll help you," Briley said.

"I'll help as well," Leah said.

"That's lovely. Thank you both."

"Leah, are you new to Garriety, or did you use to live here? I was going to ask last night but didn't get around to it," Kat asked.

Leah dabbed her lips. "I'm new, but so far I love the atmosphere and the people have been so welcoming."

Kat scooped up another forkful of the casserole. "So, that means you've never been to the Encampment?"

"The what?"

"Oh," Briley chimed in, mentally slapping herself for not bringing it up before now. "It's a reenactment of a war. Don't ask anyone what the war is because no one knows."

"Most people in the town believe the war is made up, and I should know because I've lived here my whole life." Mrs. Hanlin placed another cinnamon roll on her plate.

"People dress in period costumes," Briley said, only for Kat to interrupt her.

"Doesn't matter what period. Any period will do."

"That may be the case, but everyone is accepted, no matter what the costume looks like. There are vendors selling food and goods related to several different periods. There are also people dressed as soldiers that reenact the war. It's all in good fun and we go every year," Briley said.

Leah grinned. "To a made-up war. How do they know what uniforms to wear?"

"Dear," Mrs. Hanlin said. "It's an all-inclusive event." She took a sip of her water. "Because at the time, no one could decide which war to reenact. There was a lot of fighting. From reading the papers, twenty people were arrested and four were sent to the hospital. Ugly business. So, everyone decided to not pinpoint one war in particular and include any war before 1950."

"It's all quite fascinating." Briley tapped her

finger on the table. "Last year, over a hundred thousand people came. They're expecting twice that many this year. It brings in tons of revenue, and everyone has a good time. You should come with us." The invitation rushed out of her mouth before she could think it over, but it felt natural to invite Leah along. Mrs. Hanlin beamed and Kat winked at her. "If you wanted?" Briley fiddled with her napkin.

"I would love to."

"Good. You can explore with me." Kat took another spoonful of the casserole and a biscuit. "Briley always helps Mrs. King and her sisters. She bakes apple hand pies for their booth."

"What else do they sell?" Leah asked.

Briley tried not to fidget under her gaze. "My booth sells buffalo chili. It's so good."

"I'll have to try it. I guess that's what all the fliers I've been seeing around town are from. I guess I should pay more attention. I'm surprised Evan didn't say something. It would have been right up his alley."

After refilling her cup with orange juice, Kat spoke. "The Encampment is a little over a month away. It starts on a Friday and runs through Sunday. The week before the Encampment, on a Thursday, there is a dance at the convention center to kick off the month of events. They try to space the events out over the summer."

"How fun. I love to dance," Leah said. "I'll have to check it out. Do you have to wear period clothing?" She looked from Briley to Kat.

"For the dance, no, it's more of a formal event, but quite a few wear costumes to the Encampment. I don't, but Mrs. King does." Briley finished off her food and pushed her plate away. Leah picked up her and

Briley's plates and carried them to the sink, then sat back down. "Thank you."

"You're welcome."

Briley had to admit, everything was going splendid. She had just picked up her cup to take a sip when Mrs. Hanlin's words registered in her head and she set her cup back down without taking a sip. "I'm sorry; I missed that."

Mrs. Hanlin touched her arm. "Mr. Balkin is getting older and he gave Leah his Christmas decorations."

Well, hell. She'd been asking him for years for those decorations, as had countless others. It seemed he was just as charmed by Leah as she was. She couldn't blame him. That meant the Christmas competition would be fierce this year. A lot of his pieces were homemade. "That's wonderful," Briley forced out. "You didn't mention that last night, tiny." She glared at Kat when she kicked her under the table.

"No need to reveal all my secrets at once." Leah rested her elbows on the table and smiled at her. "I was surprised, but excited to get them. Briley, when I win, I'll sign a copy of the paper for you." She pointed her finger at her and grinned.

Playful Leah was starting to become her favorite. Briley sat back in her chair and crossed her arms. "I hope you know it's going to take more than a few decorations to beat me. Out of the last five years, I've placed second four times and won last year." She blew on her fingers. "I've got the touch and don't intend to be a one hit wonder."

"Is that right?" Leah had a sly grin on her face. "I do believe I have an ace on my side. Not counting the extra decorations." Leah slowly ran her finger along the top of her glass.

Briley swallowed. "Really?" She loved having Leah's undivided attention, and never wanted to lose that feeling.

"Yes. Evan has a notebook filled with ideas and is excited to get started. I do believe his exact words were, 'We are going to blow her out of the water.'"

"Well," Briley leaned forward and placed her arms on the table. "I say, bring it on. I'm not scared of you and especially not of him."

"You should be."

"Why's that?" They were so close if Briley leaned forward just a smidge, their lips would touch. The ringing of a cell phone broke the tension and Briley jerked back, blinking. What had just happened? Her sight stopped on Kat, who gave her a thumbs up and a cheeky grin. Leah moved away from the table and answered her phone. From the conversation, she was talking to Evan. She rubbed her neck and forced her racing heart to settle down. Now wasn't the time to flake out.

"Sorry about that. Evan had a question," Leah said, sitting back down.

"Don't be silly," Mrs. Hanlin said. "What mother doesn't answer when their child calls?"

Briley coughed and took a sip of water. "So, I believe we covered the Encampment and the dance."

"We did," Leah said and Briley knew their moment had passed. "And the toy convention. Evan has already told me he isn't missing next year."

"That'll be great," Briley said.

"It's a lot of fun," Kat threw in.

When Mrs. Hanlin started to clear the table, Briley jumped up and helped her finish the task. If she brushed against Leah's shoulder a few times, well, no one could fault her. After everyone had a fresh cup of coffee, and Briley a cup of tea, they headed into the living room. Kat and Mrs. Hanlin settled in the two chairs across from the couch. Briley and Leah sat at opposite ends of the couch.

"I am really glad you girls are getting along now," Mrs. Hanlin said. "It does an old woman's heart good." She lifted her hand to still Briley's words. "Briley, I know what you are going to say, but I am old. In my case, age is *not* just a number."

"You are only as old as you feel, Mrs. Hanlin. Trust me on this," Briley muttered, and lifted her cup in a toast.

"I do, dear. I do."

Briley could feel Leah's eyes on her. Leah was tucked into the corner of the couch with her legs underneath her, sipping her coffee. Her gaze remained on Briley.

"Does your age affect how you feel?" Briley asked Leah.

"Some days. Others, I've never felt better or younger."

"We all have those days. It has nothing to do with our ages," Briley said.

Leah bit her lip. "You really believe that, don't you?"

"I do."

Kat chimed in. "We learned that from our parents."

"Really?" Leah asked, looking from one to the other.

Briley relaxed. "There was a twenty-year age difference between our parents and they were married forty years. So, you see, to us," she pointed between her and Kat, "age really is just a number. Our dad was amazing and never made us feel like he couldn't keep up with us."

"He always attended our games, or competitions we participated in. We camped every summer."

"And," Briley interrupted. "We wrote down different places we wanted to visit on pieces of paper and threw them into this Mason jar." Briley held her hands up to indicate the size of the jar.

Kat scooted forward on her chair, motioning with her hands. "No matter where in the world it was, if it interested us, we wrote it down and threw it in. Twice a year, Mom and Dad would pick out a piece of paper and we would travel there." Briley and Kat both grew quiet, both lost in their thoughts.

"We stopped when Dad died," Briley said, looking up at Kat. "We shouldn't have. He wouldn't have wanted that."

"No, he wouldn't have. A few weeks after his death, I walked into the living room and found Mom holding the jar. I stopped her from breaking it. It's in my room."

"We should start that back up," Briley said.

Kat lifted her cup. "Next year."

"Next year."

"I think I'll start that with my kids. Even though Madison is married, I'm sure she would love it. I didn't have many opportunities to take them with me when I traveled for work."

"Who doesn't like to travel?" Briley nodded. "Even if your piece of paper wasn't chosen, it was still an amazing trip. Well, except for that one trip to Colorado, but we don't talk about that."

Kat chuckled. "You probably cursed us just

bringing it up." Kat and Briley both made the sign of the cross on their chest.

"I wished I would have done that with my kids," Mrs. Hanlin said. "But, I think it's a good thing you two got to experience that."

"Me too," Briley said.

"Me three," Kat threw in.

Briley finished her tea and set her cup on the coffee table, then laid her head back on the couch cushion, content just to listen to the conversation around her. She closed her eyes when she felt the lightest touch ghosting over her hand that lay between her and Leah. Every happily ever after had to start somewhere.

Chapter Nine

Briley must have fallen asleep at some point because Kat had rudely woken her up when she had to leave. Now here she stood with Leah and Mrs. Hanlin, looking up into what Briley had aptly named the dark pit of doom when Mrs. Hanlin had pointed it out to them. The switch Mrs. Hanlin had flicked to light up the attic barely put any light out at all. The last thing she wanted was to venture up, but the hopeful look on Mrs. Hanlin's face made her mind up for her.

She eyed the 'past its prime' ladder, then Leah. "You ready, soldier?"

Leah arched her brow, a smile playing on her lips. "It's what we all train for."

Briley nodded seriously, then turned to Mrs. Hanlin and took the flashlight out of her hands. "Don't worry, ma'am. We've got your back."

"I knew I called in the right people." Mrs. Hanlin shook her head, playing along. "They should be in the far corner of the room. There are three or four boxes, clearly labeled. I want the two labeled courting and children."

"We won't let you down." Briley took a deep breath. "After you, private." She pointed at the ladder.

"Oh, no. I think the leader should go in first. After you."

Briley was not looking forward to what was up

there. After a deep breath, she placed her hands on the ladder and took a step up. The wood seemed solid, which spurred on her confidence and she quickly climbed up. She held out her hand for Leah, who grabbed on, and scampered up.

One side of the attic was beams and insulation, and the other side had flooring put in and the walls were sheet rocked. Though, it didn't make it any less eerie. The only window was blocked, and several shadows played in the open space. Dust covered all available surfaces and cobwebs hung artistically around the semi-large space.

"We won't get anywhere standing here all day."

"Right." Briley turned on the flashlight, which seemed to be on its last leg. Beating it against her leg didn't improve its brightness. She cursed herself for leaving her phone downstairs. "Did you bring your phone?"

"No. We could have used the flashlight. It *is* dark in here."

"You think? I hope I don't fall on my face." Briley moved forward slowly then came to a stop when they reached a wall of boxes. "Didn't she say it was in the far right corner?"

"Yep, but we haven't reached the far wall yet."

Leah stood close enough that Briley could smell her shampoo. *Get it together.* "Hold this." She gave Leah the flashlight, then tested the weight of a few boxes and set them on the ground. Leah came over and shined her flashlight in the hole Briley made. A face stared back at them, eyes black as night. Briley screamed. Leah dropped the flashlight and they both crouched and crawled against the wall of boxes. "That wasn't…?" Briley's heart pounded in her chest.

"No." Leah shook her head, latching onto Briley's arm.

Sweat popped out on Briley's brow, as her heart continued to race. She remained too freaked out to take the time to enjoy Leah so close. That was clearly a face. A human face. She took off her glasses and rubbed her hands down her face. "Shit."

"If you weren't awake before, you are now." Leah slipped her arm through Briley's. "What the heck was that? I know what my rational mind says, but…"

Briley chuckled. "My best guess was a mannequin. Maybe. I don't hear any weird noises." This was one reason she didn't watch horror movies. They freaked her out.

"You girls okay?" Mrs. Hanlin hollered.

"Fine." Briley cursed herself when her voice cracked.

"You could have told us you had mannequins up here," Leah called back.

"I don't have any mannequins up there."

The hold Leah had on her arm tightened. "What?" Briley licked her lips.

Leah stared at Briley as she spoke to Mrs. Hanlin. "Are you sure?"

"Yes, dear. I don't know what you saw, but I don't have any mannequins." Her voice faltered. "Maybe you both should come down. Just to be safe."

What fresh hell was this? "Tell me something, Mrs. Hanlin. Was there a wall of boxes separating the room the last time you were up here?"

The longer the silence went on, the more Briley dreaded her answer. What had they got themselves into?

Mrs. Hanlin's voice carried up to them. "No,

dear." A beat later. "I'm just messing with you girls. My daughter had two mannequins when she lived at home that she used to dress up. The last time I went up there, I put the wall of boxes up."

The relief on Leah's face mirrored her own and Briley leaned back into the boxes, only for her body to fall through them. "Fuck." She shielded her face as the boxes landed on top of her.

"What was that?" Mrs. Hanlin asked.

"We're okay, Mrs. Hanlin. We've got this," Leah called down. Briley felt her move two boxes off her.

She grunted when the last box was removed, then moved her arms. Leah knelt on the floor next to her. "Are you all right? That last box I moved was heavy." She lifted Briley's t-shirt and ran her fingers all over Briley's stomach. "Any pain?" She pressed on several places and Briley hissed.

She swallowed back a moan as Leah's hands roamed across her stomach. Leah's touch was like magic. A magic she couldn't have. "Some, but I'm fine. The only thing bruised more than my side is my ego." Once Briley had broken through the boxes, a sliver of light shown through the window. Briley dusted herself off as Leah leaned down to grab the flashlight. She turned around, and shuddered, but took a deep breath when she eyed the mannequin. Her heart still pounded. She'd have a hell of a bruise tomorrow on her chest. Stupid mannequin.

"Ready?" Leah touched her arm, and eyed the mannequin. "She must have one sick sense of humor to place that there. I hope she at least got a good laugh out of this. I almost peed myself."

"Tell me about it. She's old; I guess she has to get her kicks from somewhere."

Leah patted her arm. "Over here." Sure enough, the two boxes they were looking for were stacked neatly on the shelf. Briley picked up the one labeled children and handed it to Leah. As soon as she picked up the one labeled courting, she knew she'd made a mistake. She couldn't do anything as the bottom of the box gave way and the contents spilled out onto the floor.

"You okay?" Leah asked.

"Yes. Stay here." Briley took the flashlight. "I'm going to check these other boxes and empty one. Is your box sturdy?"

"Yes."

On her fourth box, she found a collection of Ball Mason jars and one by one, she placed them on the floor. When she turned around, Leah knelt on the floor and had just gathered the contents into a pile. She held a piece of paper in her hand. "What've you got there?" Leah wordlessly handed oven an envelope neatly labeled with a woman's address on it. In the upper right hand corner Carter Hanlin was neatly printed. Briley picked up another one labeled the same. Hundreds of letters in all.

Leah crawled over next to her and leaned against her with a letter in her hand. "The label courting was quite fitting."

The memories these letters held gave her chills. That Mrs. Hanlin kept these all these years was amazing. They weren't the best preserved, but she'd still kept them.

"I have to run a couple of errands tomorrow," Leah said. "I'll pick up some acid free photo albums so she can slip these inside."

"That's a good idea." Briley knew she shouldn't have but she opened one of the envelopes and slipped the letter out.

"Briley?"

She ignored Leah and carefully unfolded the letter.

My Dearest Rachel.

Briley stopped and refolded the letter and put it back. This was someone's life...and private. "I want that, you know?" Briley said, after a moment of silence.

"What?"

"A love to transcend time. I'm not looking for perfect, just someone who gets me."

Leah rested her head on Briley's shoulder. "I think that's what everyone is looking for."

"Even you?"

"Even me."

"They were together almost sixty years."

"Do you know what happened to him?" Leah stretched her legs out.

"Sudden heart attack. She told me about it over a bowl of ice cream one evening when I first moved here. She said no matter how long he was gone, she could lay in bed and if she concentrated really hard, she could feel him in the bed next to her." After their dad died she and Kat would try and get their mom to open up, but she always kept everything bottled up.

"Jesus, that's sad." Leah squeezed Briley's arm.

"I know. I barely held my tears in until I made it home."

"I've never had that kind of love before."

"Me either. She said she wouldn't change a thing about their life together. I don't think she knows she even does it, but sometimes when we talk, she'll play with the necklace around her neck."

"Do you know what significance it holds?"

Briley sighed. "It holds their wedding rings. When her hands started to swell badly a few years back, I bought it for her. She's worn it ever since."

Leah bumped her shoulder. "You're a good egg, Briley."

"My mom used to tell me I was too soft. I needed to toughen up. Dad told me that strength wasn't determined by how much we could lift, but by how often we cried."

"He sounds like a good man."

"He was." Briley sat still, enjoying the feel of Leah against her.

"I spent three weeks in the Amazon doing a piece on one of the tribes. These people had hardly any material possessions. Their huts were well-made but simple. Their clothes were well-made, but again, simple. I learned something valuable from them. Life shouldn't be measured by how much you own or the money you make. Life is a gift that should be lived for the people we love. Memories are the souvenirs we should be taking with us. I guess that's why I like taking pictures so much. I try to enjoy the moment for what it is, but I have this overwhelming urge to capture it." She pulled her legs up to her chest. "Those people smiled and laughed more than anyone I've ever known."

"I don't want to go through the loss that Mrs. Hanlin has, but I don't think I can live without it."

"That's life, Briley. We live. We die. It's the in-between we make our own. What we have to cherish."

They stayed sitting until Briley's butt started to fall asleep. She didn't want to ruin their time together, but Mrs. Hanlin would be waiting for them. They carefully put the letters in the box and got to their feet. Briley lifted the box and followed Leah. A few feet from the stairs Briley stopped.

"What is it?"

"These have been up here for a long time." She saw Leah nod. She wouldn't ask but she would always wonder why Mrs. Hanlin decided to read them now.

"Sometimes it just takes time, Briley."

"Time," she said softly.

At the bottom of the stairs, Briley set her box down, turned off the light, and lifted the ladder back up. She picked up the box and they followed the smell of freshly baked cookies into the kitchen.

Mrs. Hanlin turned around and covered her mouth to keep from laughing.

"What?" Briley turned to Leah and held in her snicker. Patches of dirt smeared her face and she had strands of cobwebs in her hair. "Here." She swiped her thumb down Leah's cheek and showed her the dirt.

Leah grimaced. "I bet I fared better than you."

"No doubt."

They deposited the boxes on the table per Mrs. Hanlin's instructions, accepted the cookies she gave them, then headed home for the shower she ordered them to take. They stopped at the sidewalk outside Leah's house.

"Not how I expected to spend my Sunday afternoon," Briley said.

"Are you kidding? That's the most excitement I've had in weeks." Leah reached toward her and ran fingers through Briley's hair only for them to come back covered in cobwebs. "Shower, then cookies."

"Yep."

Leah squeezed Briley's arm. "I'll see you later."

"Leah." She turned back around with her foot on

the first step. "I enjoyed spending the day with you."

"I did as well." A smile fluttered on Leah's lips.

"Good. Good."

"Bye."

"Bye."

Chapter Ten

A lot had happened in the few weeks since the Sunday brunch spent with Leah at Mrs. Hanlin's. Briley's company had sold one house and started another and Kat had settled into her freelance accounting gig. Although Kat hated it, for the moment, she was sticking with it. Briley gave her credit for that, but the whole reason she moved was a change in scenery, plus a new career. If Kat didn't consider something else in the next month, Briley would sit her down for a long over-due talk.

She and Leah had eaten breakfast together a handful of times on the weekends, and dinner twice with Kat. Even though Leah still made her nervous, Briley was never overwhelmed while with her. Often, if Briley got home early from work, she would whip something up and take it to Leah and they would talk while enjoying the treat. She felt they were on the right track.

Today they were having lunch together. With a wave to Brandon, Briley made her way across town. After parking in her driveway, Briley hopped out, walked up Leah's porch, and knocked on the door.

Leah greeted her with a warm smile that instantly put Briley's nerves to rest. After ushering her into a kitchen seat, she placed the food on the table. Today's fare was chicken salad sandwiches, fruit salad, and sweet tea.

"This looks delicious. Thank you."

"You're welcome."

Halfway through the meal it dawned on Briley that, although they'd talked about a lot of things, they'd never talked about their past relationships. She didn't enjoy rehashing the subject, but she was curious about Leah's story. Briley bit her bottom lip and wanted to ask the question, but wasn't sure it was her place to.

"Briley, I can see the wheels in your head turning. Ask your question."

She went with an easy way to lead the conversation where she wanted it to go. "I was just wondering if Evan's other parent participated when you and he would cosplay?"

Leah set her empty bowl on her plate. "No. By that time, we had already gone our separate ways. We both wanted Evan and she loves him, and that's all I could ever ask of her. She's remarried now, to Lilith, a woman ten years younger than her, and they have an almost two-year-old daughter they named Griffin. Everything worked out the way it was supposed to. Sometimes marriage doesn't mean forever. Sometimes it's just a stepping stone to the rest of your life and that's what I got with Evan and with Madison and my first marriage."

"Well, I, for one, am glad things worked out like they have."

"Why's that?"

"It brought us here." Briley spread her arms out wide.

Leah smiled. "Yes, it did."

"So." Briley pushed her empty plate away. "You've been married twice."

"I have. I met Jeff when I was fifteen. We were

married at eighteen and Madison was born when I was twenty-five. We divorced a year after that and remained friends, but it's never the same. He was an amazing father, but I figured out early on that we would never really be anything other than friends. It was for the best that we divorced. I actually stayed in the marriage longer than I should have, but if I'd left earlier, I wouldn't have Madison, and I will never be sorry for that."

"Was?"

"He died five years ago. Heart attack. Then I met Kathy when I was thirty-two and two years into our relationship, we had Evan. Things went south for us quickly. We both knew it wasn't the best match and thank goodness we figured that out sooner rather than later."

Briley braced her elbows on the table. "My longest relationship was five years. I thought Beth was the one. We were talking kids and marriage. One night we had a huge fight. She stormed out, and when she came back home the next morning, I knew and she knew that I knew." Briley paused to smooth a strand of hair from her face. "She said it was a mistake and would never happen again, but the damage, at least for me, had already been done. When the woman you're planning on spending the rest of your life with tells you the woman she cheated on you with meant nothing, well, I knew I would never be able to trust her again. It wouldn't have been fair to either one of us to try and make it work. She would always be atoning for cheating and I would always be reading too much into her every move. That was two years ago."

"Jeff nor Kathy ever cheated on me, but in between those two relationships, I dated a woman for almost six months when I realized only one of us was being monogamous."

"Thankfully, my only bout with cheating was with Beth. It was hard enough dealing with that from one person. I don't know how people cope when multiple partners cheat on them."

"I don't either. I value trust above all else and when it's broken in a romantic relationship, for me, it can never be regained." Leah picked her glass up and took a sip of her tea.

"I feel the same way. It's not easy to give my heart to someone because I know what it's like to have it shattered, and sometimes I wonder if the risk is worth the reward. Then I look at people like my parents and Mrs. Hanlin and want what they had."

"I agree. I don't think I'm too old to want that forever kind of love. I'm sure she's out there somewhere."

"She?"

Leah frowned. "Yes."

Briley held her hand up. "You were married to a man. I was just wondering. I didn't mean any harm."

"None taken. Jeff and I were young. Too young. I thought I knew what I wanted, but I was wrong. When I first told him I was gay, he was furious. Threatened to fight for full custody of Madison. After a few weeks, we both sat down and had a long talk, and decided to make our friendship the best we could and to raise Madison with the full love and support of two parents. It worked out well."

"And Kathy?"

"I wouldn't say we were friends after we were divorced but we had a mutual understanding and trust between us. We, also, only wanted the best for Evan and I believe we've achieved that. She's a great mother. No love before Beth?"

"I dated, but nothing worth mentioning. No one had ever meant to me what Beth did."

"Do you still love her?"

"No. I haven't for a long time. I'm ready to move on. Settle down. Make a life together."

"Be a housewife?"

"Hey." Briley picked up her napkin and tossed it in Leah's direction. "I would make an awesome housewife. Except dishes. I hate doing dishes. At least by myself."

For the next thirty minutes, they debated the many household chores they had to do. Briley was grateful for the change in subject. She could only handle spending small doses of time on serious conversation. A glance at her watch told her she needed to be getting back to work.

"I need to be getting back. I've enjoyed lunch," Briley said.

"I did as well. How about lunch again tomorrow?"

"I would love to." At the door, Briley turned back around. "The church bazaar is in a few days. Do you want to go?"

"I would."

"Good." Briley swallowed. "I can pick you up."

"It's Thursday, right?" Briley nodded. "I have an appointment. I'll meet you there."

"Okay."

"Okay."

On her way back to work, Briley hummed along with the radio, satisfied at the success of lunch.

Chapter Eleven

The bazaar was always held twice a month. The Holy Temple of God's People and Believers Church was an all-inclusive establishment. Briley and dozens of other church members had tried to tell them an abbreviated name would suffice, but the Pastor had quickly vetoed their ideas. Briley had been quite taken with The Church, but Pastor Marks said to draw people in, they needed a catchy name. Briley didn't believe in organized religion, but she did enjoy the choir and the churchgoers had always accepted her with welcome arms.

Somehow, the volunteers had squished almost forty tables into the moderately sized church basement. Food wasn't allowed in the basement for fear of mold growing in one of the rooms. They didn't want to deal with another food related illness like the one from three years back. So the ladies who cooked made do with the small kitchen in the church. When lunch was ready, you picked it up in the kitchen and took it to one of the dozens of picnic tables set up in the back parking lot.

For ten dollars, The Church offered lunch at twelve thirty on the dot. Today's bazaar offered fried chicken and catfish, along with mac and cheese, mashed potatoes and gravy, green bean casserole, and rolls. Chocolate cake and cherry pie were offered for dessert and even though she didn't bake them, she would still eat them since Brew and Bake, a popular bakery/coffee shop in Garriety, donated them.

There were only so many tickets for lunch, so Briley had snagged her and Leah's ticket before she even made it down stairs to the vendors. This was no time to be taking chances. She'd invited Kat, but she had begged off, wanting to spend a quiet day at home, relaxing. Briley knew she couldn't fight the urge and bought a couple of brownies and rice crispy treats from the kids on the church's t-ball team, who were set up in the back-parking lot next to the building.

They raised money every year for their uniforms and supplies. Before she left the table, she slipped a fifty to the kid's coach to help them reach their goal. From the way everyone bought the treats and gave extra donations, she had a feeling they would have enough money for not only the uniforms but also whatever else they would need.

At the bottom of the stairs, Briley took in the chaos in front of her. Hundreds of people filled the small space already. Briley scrunched her nose at the smell that seemed a mixture of mold, sweat, some unknown scent, and the apple cinnamon candles Dorothy, the pastor's wife, always bought for these events to try and mask the other odors. It was a good idea in principle, but ended up making the combined smells twice as worse. Everyone dealt with it because no one had the heart to tell Dorothy otherwise.

After a quick scan, Briley stepped down and moved into the crowd. Even though Garriety's population was nearing a hundred and fifty thousand, most people tended to run in the same circles and she'd known these folks since she moved into this neighborhood ten years ago. They'd accepted her whole-heartedly and if asked, she would do whatever she could for them, as she knew they would do for her.

She was halfway down the first row, between two tables that were filled with kitchen utensils and papier-mâché angels when she caught sight of Leah haggling over the price of what looked to be another piece of art. She hadn't expected her until later, so this was a treat.

Today Leah's curls were put up off her neck and she had on a pair of dark washed jeans and a short sleeve white, blue, and yellow striped polo. Briley followed the line of Leah's leg all the way down to red colored toenails encased in strappy sandals. It took her a moment to realize those sandals were headed toward her.

Briley straightened and turned to the closest table, scanning the contents to give her a moment to compose herself before facing Leah. Even though she had felt a shift in their relationship over the last several weeks, being near Leah still made her nervous. She groaned when she realized whose table she was at. Kate Michaels was the nosiest person she had ever met. Before Briley could make her get-away, Kate grabbed her wrist.

"Briley, good to see you today." When she had Briley's attention, she let go of her wrist. "What can I interest you in?" The glint in her eyes put Briley on edge and she knew she would not be able to get out of buying something.

The table contained dozens of different trinkets. "Not sure," she mumbled. Without much thought, she picked up a small polka-dot ceramic cat and handed it over. At least she would be able to hide it behind something in her curio cabinet.

"Nice choice," Kate said, accepting the five-dollar bill Briley gave her and handing over her bag. "Have a good day."

"You too." Briley turned and ran straight into Leah. She grabbed Leah's arms to keep them both upright. "Sorry, didn't expect you so close and almost didn't see you. You're so tiny." Leah smelled like a combination of apples, vanilla, and something sweet she couldn't identify. The fragrance intoxicated and it was driving her mad.

Leah held back a smile and rested her hands over Briley's. "It was partially my fault. I was waiting until you completed your purchase when my mind wandered."

Briley let go of Leah, took a step back, and rocked back on her heels. "So?"

"So." A smile played at the corner of Leah's lips.

"Have you been here long?"

"Have you bought a lunch ticket yet?" They both spoke at the same time. Leah chuckled and slipped her arm through Briley's. "Since this is my first time here, show me around."

Instead of talking, she nodded and started walking. Quite a few times, she'd catch an envious look thrown their way and stand up straighter. She knew how lucky she was to have Leah on her arm.

They spent a few minutes at each table and Briley introduced Leah to everyone she knew that they came across. Leah bought candles and another small painting to put up in her hallway, and Briley picked up some homemade oat and honey soap for Kat for Christmas, plus a new gray and blue checkered scarf for herself. It took them over two hours but they made it around the room.

"So," Briley said. "I bought us both lunch tickets."

Leah squeezed her arm. "So, you're asking me to have lunch with you?"

"I am. Let's head out and get in line. There is always plenty of food but we don't need to take any chances. Even with a ticket, these people can be vultures. Don't mess with church people and their food." Briley patted Leah's hand then motioned for her to go ahead of her on the stairs. They walked down a hallway to the kitchen, and got in line. "You're in for a treat. Mr. Hinkley's fried chicken is awesome. He's a legend around these parts."

"You don't say." A teasing smile danced on her lips.

"I do say. I do." The other woman was so easy to be around. Briley stuffed her bag under one arm, picked up a tray, and followed beside Leah as they made the way down the line. For a small woman, Leah didn't skimp on the portions. Thank goodness. After their plates were laden with food, they headed outside and Briley shielded her eyes from the sun. She searched the area for a spot to eat, ignoring Ms. Bonds, who waved frantically at her. She smiled sweetly when Leah threw her a look.

Leah arched her brow. "Should we not sit with them?"

Briley groaned but decided to take the good with the bad. "Let's go." They were good people. Just talkative. There wasn't much room at the picnic table and Briley realized her and Leah would be separated. Nothing she could do about that now. She had to squeeze in next to Mrs. Bonds, who patted her shoulder. Her son Travis was seated across from her and Leah sat on the other end of the table beside Mr. Brink. Mrs. Dundley rounded out Briley's side of the picnic table.

As everyone introduced themselves to Leah, Briley took the opportunity to shove a forkful of food in her mouth. She moaned when the mac and cheese crossed her lips. The right ratio of cheese to pasta. "Oh my goodness. I hope you got some mac and cheese, Leah, because it's what I picture Jesus serving in Heaven along with sweet tea."

"Amen," everyone at the table said.

Leah laughed and held up a spoonful to show Briley, then put it in her mouth and closed her eyes. "Wow."

"Told you." Briley shoved another spoonful into her mouth to keep from saying anything inappropriate at the look of pleasure on Leah's face.

"So, Leah," Mrs. Bonds said. "How do you know Briley?"

"We live next to each other," Leah answered.

"Isn't that convenient?" Travis sneered and Briley narrowed her eyes at him even as he smeared his roll with butter and took a giant mouthful. Travis wasn't a bad guy. A tad on the creepy side, but harmless.

"Quite," Briley said, smearing her own roll with butter and dipping it in her gravy before taking a bite. Her focus was drawn away from him when Mr. Brink asked Leah a question.

"How are you enjoying our town? I know you haven't lived here long."

"I love it and so does Evan, my son. Although, he's disappointed he is missing all the fun. I told him I would be sure and take plenty of photos."

"Do you have any other kids?" Mrs. Bonds asked.

Briley kept one ear on the conversation as she ate. She knew she was asking for trouble, but couldn't help the pull she now felt with Leah. One could only hope she wouldn't screw this up or fall too far into the abyss that she couldn't climb out of. Who was she kidding? Falling was the only option at this point. She knew Leah liked her, or they wouldn't be spending time together. It was the kind of like she felt for her that was the issue.

What she needed was some more time with her. They needed to make breakfast a daily occurrence. She'd gladly get up earlier to make that happen. As she chewed, she stared off into space, contemplating how to go about that. How could she ask her out without it being a date? Would she find daily breakfast weird? Maybe she should ask Kat, because she knew any invitation that came out of her mouth would stray to the dating side of things. She jerked her head up when someone touched her hand. Leah sat in front of her and Briley's eyes widened when she realized everyone else had left and her plate was empty. How long had she been lost in thought?

"They only just left." Leah ran her finger along Briley's hand. "What's got you so preoccupied?"

She pushed her empty plate away. "I think we should make breakfast a daily thing." Briley blurted out then cringed. That's...not how she wanted to do that.

"Really?" Leah kept her eyes glued to Briley's, but never stopped playing with her hand.

"I...mean." She licked her lips. "Yes." She waved her free hand in the air. "I enjoy spending time with you. The time we've spent together." She frowned. "Also, maybe increase our dinners and maybe a movie sometime." That sounded too much date-like. "Or, Kat and I have movie and game nights. Evan would be welcome, of course, when he gets home from spending the summer with his mom. There is always some festival going on, as you know, and I've always wanted to join a bird watching group." What were the words coming out of her mouth?

"Briley, take a breath." Leah worried her bottom lip and seemed to be having an internal struggle. "I would love to increase our breakfasts with you. I'm not sure every morning is viable, but we can up our weekly count. Dinner and a movie also sounds good."

"That's workable," Briley hurried to say.

"Glad you think so." Leah squeezed Briley's hand.

"Okay." That wasn't as hard or as awkward as she thought it would be. She could do this and Leah didn't seem bothered in the least about her invitations.

Leah frowned. "Briley, don't be afraid to ask me something. The only way you'll know the answer is if you ask the question." She drew her hand back. "Now, I do believe you said something about dessert." Her eyes held a touch of glee.

"I did. No one can ever accuse me of leaving a woman wanting." She cringed as soon as the words left her mouth.

"My, my, Briley." Leah tried to hold back a laugh.

Briley coughed and pulled her shirt away from her neck. "That's not what I meant." Leah laughed. "Tell me what you want and I'll throw our plates away and go get it."

"Split a piece of chocolate cake with me?"

"Sounds like a plan. Be right back." Briley picked up their trash and threw it away. She made the mistake of looking back and almost tripped when Leah winked at her. *Get it together.* She nodded at the people she passed on the way to the dessert table that was situated by the back doors of the church.

"Briley, what will it be?" Haley asked when she made it to the front of the line.

"Choices. Choices." Briley looked down at the dessert table and the only two choices available. "Everything looks so good. I'll have one of each."

Haley rolled her eyes. "You know as well as I do ever since Mrs. Dallas donated her fruitcake and things went south, the only dessert we can serve has to be donated from a reputable source." She waved her hand over the table. "I hope she appreciates what she has," Haley said, looking in Briley's eyes.

Briley's eyes widened. "What?"

"Leah. I hope she appreciates you. Do I need to give her the shovel talk?" She held up the knife she used to cut the cake.

"No." Briley waved her hands in front of her. "No, it's not like that. We're friends. Please, Haley. No shovel talk." Haley, the daughter of the pastor, was friendly, but she was also quite protective of the members of their church.

"Hmm." She eyed Briley then Leah. "If you say so. Which one is yours?"

"Oh." Briley rearranged her glasses. "I'm taking the cherry pie home to Kat and Leah and I will split the piece of cake."

"Hmm." Haley gave her a knowing look when she handed her a larger than normal slice of cake, two forks, and a wrapped piece of cherry pie. Briley dropped a twenty in the church jar that sat on the dessert table and accepted the two plates.

"Have a good day, Haley."

"Looks like you're already having one."

Briley chuckled and shook her head, but couldn't disagree with her. After dodging two teenagers and stopping to share a word with an older gentleman, she made it back to their table. "Best chocolate cake around," she said, setting the plates down and handed over a fork.

"Better than yours?"

"Yes." They ate in silence until only a forkful of cake lay on the plate. Briley pushed it in Leah's direction.

"Why, thank you."

"I do what I can." Briley licked her fork clean and placed it on the table.

Leah dropped her fork on the empty plate. "Evan would love the cake. Who donated it?"

"Brew and Bake. They're up on Tenth Street."

"I'll have to go sometime."

"We could go sometime." Briley forced herself not to look away from Leah's penetrating gaze.

Leah eyed her over the rim of her cup. "I don't see why not."

"Fantastic." Briley cringed as the word left her mouth and chastised herself. Fantastic was the best word she could come up with.

Leah cleared her throat and placed her hand over Briley's on the table. "I'm not sure what I've gotten myself into."

"Maybe not, but it sure will be fun to find out."

"I do believe it will."

Briley shifted on the seat. "I'm heading to the riverfront next and was wondering if you wanted to go?"

"I have to run to the bank. They close at two, but I can join you after that."

"I would like that."

Chapter Twelve

Briley drove straight to the riverfront, parked, and headed toward the chaos. She may or may not have eaten both rice crispy treats on the way over and didn't feel one ounce of guilt. Tomorrow she would run a few extra miles to offset all the food she was eating. A glance at the clock confirmed the dragon boat races would be starting soon. Before she left the church, she called Kat, but she had begged off. There was something up with her and she would get to the bottom of it.

She eyed the crowd, trying to determine the best course of action when the smell of fried dough wafted her way. Before she knew it, she stood in front of the funnel cake truck and everyone knew turning away from a funnel cake was blasphemy.

With her plate filled with a small funnel cake, strawberries, whip cream, and powdered sugar, she slowly made her way to the riverfront. Years ago, they used to have free summer concerts on the small stage that hung out over the water. Concrete stairs that were twice as long as the stage ran up the side of a large hill that overlooked the river. She found an empty space and sat down. She'd just torn off a corner of her cake and popped it in her mouth when she spotted a familiar face headed her way.

She smiled and took a drink of her water as a body landed beside her and a hand picked up a strawberry off her plate and plopped it in her mouth. She and Nina had known each other ever since she moved to Garriety. They'd met at a bar one night and had been friends ever since. Lately, they hadn't been spending as much time together as Briley would have liked, because of their jobs, and she missed getting together with her.

"By all means, have a bite."

Nina laughed and kissed her on the cheek. "Oh, I'm sorry, was I supposed to ask first?"

"Shut up, dork." Briley tore off another chunk of the funnel cake and handed it to her. By the time they'd finished eating, the races had just begun.

"We need to get together more often. It's been almost a week. That's too long." Briley knew it was her fault and she felt like a terrible friend for spending all her down time with Leah. She'd do better in the future balancing everyone in her life.

"I agree. We should get dinner tonight. Me, you, Kat, and Ashley, at Midway."

"Sounds like a plan. How is Kat?" They spent the next twenty minutes catching up, when Nina slipped her arm through Briley's and whispered in her ear. "There's a really hot woman coming this way."

Briley's heart raced and she sucked in a breath. Leah.

"What? Who is she?" Nina squeezed her arm.

"My neighbor." Briley couldn't take her eyes off Leah.

"The one you've been telling me about? The one you like?"

"Yes. It's scary, though. I-I don't...where do I go from here? We're going the friends route and I hope we take a detour along the way. It feels like it's more than that and I hope I'm not creating something that isn't there." She wrung her hands together. "But, I am not going to push her. Whatever this is between us will have to work itself out. In the meantime, I'll just show her how awesome I am and try not to make a complete idiot of myself."

"Nobody can resist you once they spend enough time with you."

Briley groaned. "Thanks for the vote of confidence."

"You have it bad, my friend, and she's almost here."

You've got this. You just saw her not forty minutes ago and you invited her here. She jumped up and pulled Leah into a quick hug. Where the hell had that come from? She quickly let go and adjusted her glasses. "Leah, I'm glad you could make it." How did Leah look even better than from when she left her at the church? The sun played off the highlights in her hair and her eyes sparkled.

Leah for her part didn't give anything away in her facial expression. "It didn't take as long at the bank as I had expected."

Briley motioned toward Nina. "This is just Nina. She found me and here we are."

"Yes. I'm just Nina."

"I didn't mean it like that." Briley groaned.

"I know." Nina turned back to Leah. "And you are?" She held out her hand.

Leah took Nina's hand. "Leah, Briley's next door neighbor. Briley has told me a lot about you."

"Sadly, I can't say the same."

Briley patted the spot beside her. Leah settled on the empty space.

The silence wasn't uncomfortable, but Briley

started to get anxious with Leah so close. "Have you ever been to a dragon boat race before?" Leah turned her head, their lips only inches apart. Briley jerked her head back.

Leah glanced at Briley's lips, then her eyes. "No, I haven't. They seem to be having fun though. Have you ever competed?"

Before Briley could answer, Nina chimed in. "Has she ever." Then she proceeded to tell Leah an embarrassing story about her and Kat's first and last dragon boat race.

"I would have loved to have seen that," Leah said.

Briley groaned. "Trust me, the story was more dramatic than the event."

"Oh, I don't know. I have a feeling there's never a dull moment with you." Leah tucked a loose strand of hair behind Briley's ear, her finger lingering for a moment on her cheek and Briley felt the breath leave her chest.

"Well, there is a time for everything," Briley mumbled.

"Oh, I know, Briley," Leah said, softly. "A woman of many talents. There's nothing wrong with having a bit of fun. You know Evan and I cosplay. Although, he's getting to that age where he doesn't want to be seen with me like that. I might be hanging up my cape sooner than I would have expected."

"Don't be silly, I would go with you. We could play off each other." The moment fled with a cell phone ringing. Briley broke away from Leah when Nina stepped away from them and answered the call.

"That was Ashley. I need to go. Leah, it was a pleasure meeting you." Nina leaned down and kissed Briley on the cheek. "I'll see you and Kat tonight. Love you."

"I love you, too."

"Oh, Leah." Nina turned around. "If you don't have plans, you're welcome to join us tonight."

Leah looked from Briley to Nina. "Tonight?"

"We're having dinner at Midway. Seven, Briley."

"Seven," she squeaked.

Leah touched her hand and Briley's heart flipped when Nina walked away. "Should I join you, Briley?"

"Of course you can join us. You would meet my other friends eventually." Briley ran her fingers through her hair and took a deep breath.

Leah smiled and moved the hair out of her eyes. "We can ride together, if you like?"

It was the best idea Briley had ever heard. "Sounds sensible."

"You and Nina seem close," Leah said, after a moment of silence.

"We are. She and Ashley own an interior decorating business and we hire them quite a bit for our houses. It all works out and I wouldn't trade our friendship for anything. She was the first person that I met when I moved here."

"Did you two ever date?"

"No. Nina's straight." Briley closed her eyes and enjoyed the cool breeze, but was startled when Leah laid her hand over her knee. She opened her eyes, watching the fingers as they played with the material of her jeans. "It's a beautiful day."

"It is." Leah agreed.

"You mentioned you started cosplaying with Evan when he was six, but you never explained what it was like early on."

"Overwhelming, is what it was. I had no idea

what I was doing, but I knew I couldn't just go out and buy him the costumes. He's always been a fan of comics and superheroes in general. For our first comic-con, he wanted to be Spiderman, and it took me seven months to make the costume." She shook her head. "It wasn't awful, but I've learned a lot since then. How about you?"

"It feels good to be someone else occasionally. It's not only fun, but freeing. You're putting on a personality that is already well established and you know what to expect from people. Shit," she groaned. "That sounded deep even to me."

Leah laughed and bumped her shoulder. "I understand. It is freeing and fun."

"Captain Marvel, huh?"

"She's not my favorite character, but I loved the outfit."

"It was a fantastic outfit." A smile broke out on Briley's face as she remembered the way the material hugged Leah's curves. She flinched when an elbow poked her in the ribs.

"Earth to Briley." Leah chuckled.

"Sorry, tiny." God, could she embarrass herself anymore? *Get it together, Briley.*

"Don't be. That's exactly the reaction I hoped for. The Doctor was a good pick, but I was partial to Supergirl."

"I'll remember that."

"Please do."

They spent the next hour mostly in silence, with Leah throwing a question in here and there about the races they were watching.

Briley opened her mouth to say something else when Leah looked at her watch. "I hate to be the one to break this up, but if I'm having dinner with you and your friends, I have more errands I need to run before then. I also need to pick up Mrs. Hanlin's photo albums."

"Of course." Briley schooled her features not to show her disappointment and stood up, shoving her hands into her pockets. She rocked back on her heels. "Me, too. I mean…I should go, too."

"Briley." Leah touched her hand, and Briley managed not to swoon. "What time are we leaving?"

"Six-thirty."

"I'm enjoying getting to know you. We can always pick up this conversation later."

Briley licked her lips. "We can. Yes."

When Leah kissed her on the cheek, she tried not to faint, but she couldn't help the blush that heated her face.

Leah ran her thumb over Briley's cheek. "I'll see you in a few hours."

"I'm looking forward to it." Briley had the good grace not to watch Leah walk away from her and instead turned and focused on the water. Okay. Things were moving along nicely. Indeed. She would have to ask Kat what the next play was.

Chapter Thirteen

Who knew it would be so hard to pick out an outfit? It was only dinner with her friends. She balled up the shirt in her hands and threw it at the bed. It wasn't as if this was the first dinner she'd spent with Leah.

"Hey," Kat shouted from where she sprawled out on the bed.

Briley rolled her eyes, but lost her footing and fell backward into the wall with a thud when Kat threw a pillow at her and hit her in the face. "Rude. Also, I have your stupid sports analogies stuck in my head."

"Where are we at?" Kat raised her head.

"Fourth inning. One on base with one batting."

"At least we're moving along. I wish I could say the same right now. Just pick something to wear. Anything." She huffed and closed her eyes.

Currently, she was on her fifth outfit. She pulled at the top, but it didn't feel right. She pulled it off and threw it in the direction of the bed. "It's not that easy."

"Oh my God. You're changing again. This is unacceptable, Briley."

Briley ignored her as she eyed the other pieces on the bed. "I'm not sure." They both jerked their head around when the back door opened and Leah called her name. "Shit, she's here."

"Fret not." Kat jumped off the bed and placed her hands on Briley's shoulders. "I've got this. You get dressed." Kat kissed her on the cheek and walked out, shutting the door behind her.

What had she got herself into? It was just dinner. She could do this. Without overthinking things, she grabbed a shirt and pulled it on, deciding to leave the black Bermuda shorts on. After putting up her hair in a bun, she grabbed her glasses, took a deep breath, and opened the bedroom door.

As she rounded the doorway into the kitchen, she stopped in her tracks as her eyes landed on Leah leaning against the counter, talking with Kat. The white blouse and blue skirt set Briley's heart racing.

"We ready?" Briley clapped her hands together.

"I am if you both are," Leah said.

Once outside, Leah touched her arm. "You look nice."

"You as well."

Briley led the way to the truck then climbed into the backseat, giving up the front seat to Leah, and allowing Kat to drive. It was only a fifteen-minute drive and she kept quiet, content, as Leah and Kat made small talk. She took a deep breath as Kat pulled into the semi-full parking lot that was a block away from the pub.

On instinct, as soon as Leah's door opened, Briley held out her hand. Leah smiled and accepted.

"Such manners," Leah teased.

"It's what I do," Briley said.

The cool night and the dozens of restaurants in the area filled the air with a heavenly aroma. Leah walked to her right, and Kat walked a step behind them. Placing her hand on the small of Leah's back, Briley guided her in and headed in the direction Kat pointed out. Nina and Ashley looked so similar with their long blond hair and green eyes they were often mistaken for sisters.

"Hey, darling," Ashley said. She hopped up from her seat and pulled Briley into a hug. "Goodness, Kat, you get better looking every time I see you." She kissed her on the cheek and turned to Leah with her hand held out in introduction. "Ashley."

Leah shook her hand. "Leah."

"Let's sit." Briley pulled out a chair for Leah, then proceeded to sit in the seat between Ashley and Leah.

"So, Briley, what do you recommend, since I've never been here? Your choices haven't steered me wrong yet," Leah asked as she settled in her seat.

"Hmm, well, their burgers are always a safe bet, but if you prefer seafood, the crab cakes are good and you have to get their sweet potato curly fries." Briley leaned toward her and pointed at an item on the menu

"Yay." Ashley high-fived her. "I'm getting the loaded bacon burger."

"I'm getting the crab cakes tonight," Nina said.

"Surprise. Surprise." Briley grinned. "That's what you get ninety percent of the time."

"Good evening," their waitress said. "What can I get you ladies to drink?" She scribbled their drink order down. "Are you ready to order?" Everyone nodded.

"Leah," Nina said, after the waitress delivered their drinks. "What brought you to our city?" Briley already knew the answer and was hoping Leah would answer in the same way she had with her. She wasn't disappointed.

Leah tapped her finger on the tabletop. "I closed my eyes and pointed to a map."

Nina perked up. "Really?"

The twinkle in Leah's eye gave her away. "In the

last few years, Evan and I have visited a few times and we both decided this would be the perfect place to settle down."

"Evan?" Ashley said.

"My son."

"Oh, how old is he?" Ashley leaned forward to get a better look at Leah.

Briley sat back and listened as they discussed the difficulties of parenting. Ashley had an eight-year-old daughter. Kat caught her eye across the table and smiled.

As the waitress set their plates on the table, Briley's stomach rumbled as the smell of the grilled onions wafted her way. She dipped a curly fry in the special sauce they give with every order and moaned at the first bite. "So good." Ashley nodded and took a giant bite of her burger. After dabbing her lips with the napkin, she turned to Leah. "How are your crab cakes?"

"The best I've ever had. I can't believe this is the first time I've been here. I will definitely be bringing Evan."

"Leah," Kat cut in. "If you want to know the best places to eat, you should go out with Briley more often. She loves to eat out and knows all the best places."

Leah turned to Briley and grinned. "Is that right, Briley? Should we go out more?"

"I think it's a real possibility you won't be able to keep up with me, Leah." Briley wasn't sure she'd ever get enough of Leah.

"Brazen. I like it."

Briley rested her elbows on the table and clasped her hands together. "Only for you."

"Only me," Leah repeated. "I can live with that."

The emotion in Leah's gaze pulled her in. As she leaned forward, a cough broke her out of the haze she was in and she jerked up and touched her glasses. "We should make a list." What was she doing and why was Leah letting her? At a touch on her hand, she turned back to Leah, who held up her fork with a chunk of crab cake on it, offering it to Briley.

With a blush, Briley gingerly opened her mouth for the sample. She ignored the looks the others were throwing her way. "Do you want to taste mine?" she asked, after swallowing.

Leah ran her thumb over her bottom lip before answering. "Sure."

The knowing looks around the table did nothing to dampen Briley's mood. "What?" Briley cut off a piece and set it on Leah's plate. There was no way she would survive feeding Leah.

They all held their hands up. "Leah, are you going to the dance?" Ashley asked, placing her arm on the back of Briley's chair and running her fingers along her shoulder.

"Yes, I am. You?"

"Wouldn't miss it. Briley always saves a dance for me."

Briley nodded.

"Briley dances with all of us," Nina chimed in.

Briley threw her napkin on the plate and pushed it toward the middle of the table. She squeaked when Leah placed her hand on her knee and squeezed. Briley looked down at the hand, then up at Leah, who had turned to talk with Kat. If someone would hold a gun to her head, she wouldn't be able to tell them what Leah and Kat were discussing. The warm hand on her knee screwed with her head.

Ashley nudged Briley's elbow. "Do you want dessert?"

"Do you know me at all?" Briley half whispered.

"We'll have two large slices of apple pie," Ashley told the waitress, after asking everyone their preferences.

When Leah's hand on her knee became too much of a distraction, Briley reached down to move it, but to her surprise Leah intertwined their fingers. Okay. This was new. Awesome and new.

Once they'd finished eating dessert, Kat paid for dinner and Briley pulled her hand away from Leah, dug a twenty out of her purse, and laid it on the table for a tip.

Ashley insisted on darts, and Nina and Kat jumped up and joined her. Briley leaned back in her chair and focused on Leah, noticing that Leah's attention was on her.

Leah placed her hand on Briley's forearm. "You don't have to stay with me if you want to join them. I know how competitive you are."

This is exactly where she wanted to be. "I'm not good at darts. You know I don't like to lose. Why put myself in that position? Besides." She adjusted her glasses. "Your company isn't unpleasant."

"Is that so?" The smile that played at Leah's lips sent shockwaves through Briley.

"Yes." She tapped her fingers on top of the table, but didn't dare to turn from Leah's gaze.

"Relax, Briley. This isn't the first time we've had dinner or spent time together." She patted her forearm before pulling back. "Your friends seem nice."

"You just make me nervous." Briley emptied her beer. "They are. I got lucky in that department. I wouldn't trade them for anything."

"I've had people like that over the years. They are hard to come by, and you should hold on to them if possible."

A sadness shaded her words that Briley hadn't heard before. She decided to change the subject and shifted in her seat so she faced Leah fully and placed her elbows on the table. "What's the one thing you've never done that you want to?"

Leah ran her finger along the lip of her glass. "I'm not much of an adrenaline junky, but I have always been curious about skydiving. Evan has almost got me convinced that it's something we should do. A bonding experience." She shuddered. "Almost."

God, could this woman be any more endearing. "Beth and I skydived about five years ago. It was scary as fuck, and not something I will ever do again, but I don't regret it. I can't explain the feelings of free-falling. Fear, dread, and immense exhilaration. It was an incredible experience."

"You almost have me sold, but it's going to take more than a pretty face to convince me."

"Well, what would it take?" Briley leaned forward, but jumped back when a hand landed on her shoulder.

Kat slipped her arm around her shoulders and eyed them both. "Nina won both games. What a surprise."

"Already." Briley laughed nervously. "That was fast." She shredded her napkin into tiny pieces. Her heart still pounded, and Leah still stared at her.

"It's getting late." Kat patted her shoulder. "We should be going."

Leah glanced at her watch, then picked up her purse. "I didn't realize it had gotten so late."

"Me either." Briley grabbed her things and followed behind them. Nina wrapped her arm around her shoulders and whispered in her ear. "I like her."

"Really?"

"Yes."

Outside the restaurant, Nina and Ashley hugged Briley and Kat goodnight, told Leah they would see her next time, then walked in the opposite direction.

Briley slipped her hands in her pants pockets and walked beside Leah. She managed to stay upright when Leah slipped her hand through her arm and pressed up against her. At the truck, she opened the door for Leah.

Leah winked at her. "How chivalrous."

"Yes, well." Briley shut the door and climbed into the backseat. At home, Briley walked Leah to her door. "Dinner was good."

"It was." Leah reached forward and straightened Briley's collar. "I enjoyed myself." Leah leaned back against the front door.

Briley rocked back on her heels. "Me too. I'll start on that list of places to go and then we can get going on it."

"I look forward to it."

"I should go." Briley pointed to her house. "It's getting late."

Leah nodded. "I'll see you tomorrow morning for breakfast."

"You will."

"Good. Good." Leah pushed away from the door and for a moment, Briley thought she was going to kiss her, but she only dug the key out of her pocket. "Goodnight."

"Goodnight."

When she walked through the back door, Kat

was waiting for her. "What's wrong?"

Briley flopped down in a kitchen chair and accepted the cup of tea Kat handed her. She recounted what happened on the porch with Leah. "I wanted to kiss her and I think she would have let me, but I don't want to mess this up."

"I think you should let her make the first move."

"I know. It's just, I've never felt like this before." Briley slipped her glasses off and rubbed her eyes.

"No one ever said it would be easy. From my calculations, you're up two to three and it's Leah's turn up to bat."

Briley slipped her glasses back on. "That's where we are at?"

"I'm the coach. I should know."

She rolled her eyes. "If you say so."

Kat took both of their empty cups and set them in the sink. "I do. I'm sure you'll see her tomorrow."

"Gee, what gave you that assumption?"

"Don't be a smartass. After all, tomorrow is another day." Kat called as she walked away from her and down the hallway.

Briley got up and glanced out the kitchen window at Leah's house. She still intended to make a list of all the places she wanted to take her, the dance and the Encampment being at the top of it. She took a deep breath, turned away from the window, and locked up the house. For the first time in a long time, she felt ready for the unknown and whatever the future held for her. She just hoped that future included Leah.

Chapter Fourteen

Briley crept down the hallway the next morning, so as not to wake Kat. After all the food she ate yesterday, a run was definitely in order. After a quick peek out the kitchen window to make sure Leah wasn't out and about, she opened the kitchen door and walked out, making sure the door shut quietly behind her.

The first mile went surprisingly fast and as the world started waking up around her, she did quite a few double takes at all the smiles, waves, and looks she received. Which was odd...even on a good day.

She had a feeling it wasn't her three-year-old cut off sweat pants and ratty t-shirt she wore that affected these people. By mile five, her legs were starting to tremble, and the looks she was receiving only continued to intensify. When Cara, a teenager that lived a block from her house, ran past and high-fived her and a teenage boy she didn't know practically cut her off to fist bump with her, she had a feeling she wasn't in Kansas anymore.

At the turn to her house, she slowed to a walk to catch her breath. As she pulled her water bottle from her belt, Kevin, the neighbor no one wanted to be alone with, tipped his hat and told her how damn lucky she was to have such a fine woman like Leah. Suddenly, it dawned on her what was happening. She saluted him, because he preferred that greeting, and fast-walked past his house.

The gossip mill from the church the day before must have speed raced around her neighborhood for everyone to think that she and Leah were an item. The riverfront and Midway didn't help matters either. A slow smile graced her lips until she realized that everyone around town thought that they were an item. What was she supposed to do now? The last thing she wanted was for Leah to be uncomfortable.

She was never so glad to see her house before in her life. Only two more neighbors had made any type of gesture in her direction. One had given her two thumbs up and the other one had, to the best of her knowledge, tried to attempt some obscene gesture with his hands, but only ended up looking like an idiot. She'd smiled and waved at him, which only seemed to piss him off even more. Next month she would throw an extra cookie in his basket when she handed them out.

Her steps faltered when she noticed Leah's kitchen light on and saw a shadow pass by her window. She hurried through the back door, slammed it shut, and leaned back against it with her eyes closed.

"If you would have woken me, I would have run with you."

Briley grabbed her chest and jumped a foot off the floor. "Christ, give a girl a warning first." She hunched over on her knees and steadied her breathing before raising up and glaring in Kat's direction. Kat grinned at her and handed her a cup of tea. "Thank you."

"What has you so jumpy? Could it be? I don't know." She snapped her fingers. "The fact that suddenly you and Leah are married with two point five kids and a cat."

"What? Don't be stupid."

"I received four calls this morning about it." She rolled her eyes. "Four, Briley. About you and Leah. Good grief. I had planned to sleep in."

"Shut up. Those busybody people at the church sale yesterday don't know how to mind their own business."

Kat rubbed her chin. "Seems to me everyone thinks you're a good match."

"What?" Briley adjusted her glasses and sat forward.

"After the church thing, the riverfront, and dinner last night, I feel we are on the right path." Kat squeezed Briley's hand.

"I think so, too." She jumped up and poured her tea out, opting instead for a cold glass of milk.

"Last night, she only had eyes for you." Kat drew her into a hug. "Do you know what will make you feel better?"

"No."

"Banana nut muffins."

Briley instantly perked up. "Those do sound good, but you'll have to scavenge on your own. I have breakfast plans with Leah."

"I'm sure I can manage on my own."

"I'm sure you can. I'm going to take a quick shower, then I'm going to head over."

"Don't linger on my account. Go. Your girl is waiting for you."

Briley stepped out of the shower, dried off, then dressed in a pair of jeans, a blue tank top, and her pair of work boots. After breakfast, she was joining Brandon at a property they were considering buying.

With a wave at Kat, Briley walked out the

backdoor and headed to Leah's. The door opened to a smiling Leah before she even knocked.

"Right on time," Leah said. Without thinking, Briley kissed Leah's cheek, then stiffened. That wasn't what she had intended to do. Although Leah had often kissed her cheek, this was the first time Briley had crossed that line. They both stood stock still, just staring at each other, until a smile blossomed on Leah's face and she motioned to the table. "Sit down."

"Right." Briley refrained from touching her and took a seat at the table. Laid out in front of her was fruit salad, scrambled eggs, bacon, whole wheat toast, and strawberry jam.

Leah set a glass of orange juice in front of Briley. "Freshly squeezed."

"No." Briley feigned shock.

"Yes." Leah grinned. "Nothing's too good for you."

"I hope you didn't go to any trouble?"

Leah reached across the table and picked up Briley's hand. "It was no trouble." She pulled her hand back. "They were on sale at the grocery the day before yesterday. So, fresh squeezed. It's not something I would get used to, though," Leah added with a wink.

"I'm flattered, and you don't have to do anything special on my account. Breakfast with you is always a reward in itself, no matter what we eat."

Leah shook out her napkin. "You're a smooth one, Briley."

"Only for you."

"You're on a roll this morning."

"I do have my moments." They ate in silence with occasional glances toward each other. Briley tried to keep her focus on the food in front of her, but Leah looked exceptionally good this morning. Her hair was put up off her face, highlighting the sharp planes of her jawline. A jawline Briley wanted to trail kisses along.

"You're staring." Briley jerked her eyes up to be met with the amused one's of Leah, but kept quiet. "I'm flattered, Briley, but you have to work today, so you need to finish eating."

"I'm sorry."

"Briley, it's okay. No harm done. Eat."

Fifteen minutes later, they were both finished, and Briley stood beside Leah, washing their dishes. Briley dried the last plate, wiped her hands, then turned to Leah, who was leaning against the wall, looking at her. "Breakfast was good."

"I'm glad you liked it."

Briley stuffed her hands in her pockets. "I should get going."

"Yes." Leah glanced out the window then quickly back. "I…there's something I wanted to ask you."

"Go ahead." Briley rested her hip against the island. "You can ask me anything."

Leah ran her fingers along the countertop. "I know what I said the first time we had dinner together, but…I." She sighed. "I was wondering if you would accompany me to the dance."

What? Had she heard her correctly? Briley's heart thudded in her chest. Did Leah just ask her out? She needed clarification. "Like a date date or a friend date?" Please let it be the first choice.

With each step Leah took in her direction, the more Briley felt like she was having a heart attack. When Leah placed the palms of her hands on Briley's chest, Briley damned near did have a heart attack. "Not a friend date. Over the last few weeks, it's come to my attention that I like having you around. I'm still unsure about a few things, but I would hate to keep you at a distance and someone else scoop you up. I would regret not taking the chance."

"So, you like me?" Briley wrapped her arms around Leah, resting them on the small of her back, holding her gaze.

Leah leaned into her further and slipped her arms around Briley's neck. "Yes. I like you. I would still like to take this slowly. I'm enjoying what we've been doing and would like to continue that, but with the promise of more."

The words Briley wanted to say were stuck in her throat at the feeling of Leah wrapped around her. Leah was offering her a chance at everything she wanted. "I would like that." She rubbed their noses together. "I like you."

"I know." Leah raised up and kissed Briley on the cheek. "You should be proud of yourself. If it wasn't for you kissing me on the cheek when you came in, I wouldn't have worked up the nerve to ask you out."

Briley lifted Leah up and held her tightly. "Let me just say for future reference you always smell amazing."

"Noted and catalogued."

This was a feeling she didn't want to lose. Briley held her for a moment longer. Leah felt so right in her arms. "As much as I don't want to, I really do need to go."

Leah placed a kiss on Briley's neck. "I know."

"Okay." Briley lowered Leah, then took a step back. "Work. I need to go to work." She pointed out the window toward her truck.

"Yes, you do." Leah opened the refrigerator, took out a plain brown paper bag, and held it out to Briley, who readily took it. "One of the many perks of dating me."

Briley blinked at Leah's words. Dating. They were dating. "Is this lunch?" At Leah's nod, Briley looked in the bag, which held a sandwich, a container of applesauce, a granola bar, banana, and a spoon. "This is awesome." A post-it-note was attached to the inside, but she wanted to wait to read it.

"It's not a big deal."

It was a huge deal. Briley swept an arm around Leah and drew her into another hug. "Yes, it is. Thank you." She kissed her cheek. "Though, you did forget something."

"Oh, really?"

At the door, Briley turned back toward her. "Stickers. You should have sealed the bag with stickers. You do know they make superhero ones."

Leah chuckled. "That is also noted."

"Just to be clear. We're dating?" Briley pointed from her to Leah.

"Yes."

"Only each other, right?"

"Yes, Briley. Only each other. I'm not a fan of sharing."

"Me either." Leah's smile was almost Briley's undoing. If she didn't have to work, she'd carry her into the living room, cuddle, and watch movies all day. She'd just turned the doorknob, when she turned back around. "The dance isn't until next week." Leah nodded. "Would you like to have dinner with me tonight? Nothing fancy. We can order in and relax."

"I would love that."

At Leah's lightening quick response, Briley puffed up. Nice. "Yes, all right, then. Seven?"

"It's a date."

"It's a date." Briley couldn't keep the smile off her face even if she tried. Which she didn't. Once inside her truck, she looked at her lunch bag, then back to Leah's house. Did that just happen? Leah had asked her out. Then she asked Leah out. She drummed her hands on the steering wheel. First work, then play.

Chapter Fifteen

Briley paced the finished kitchen of their newly flipped house. It was set to go on the market the following week, and already had quite a buzz around it. Nevertheless, her thoughts all day had been on Leah and their date that night. She could tell Brandon wanted to ask what was up, but he didn't and she didn't volunteer any information. If she was to start talking about Leah, she might not be able to stop.

She jumped when a hand landed on her arm. "I've called your name three times," Brandon said. "What's up?" He held his hand up. "Don't try and deny it. I've known you long enough to know when something's on your mind."

After taking a deep breath, Briley recounted everything that had happened up till this point. "So." She stuffed her hands in the back pockets of her jeans.

A large grin flashed across his face. "I think it's awesome."

"Really?"

"Yes. I can tell by the way you're acting that you really like this woman."

"You have no idea."

"I would like to meet her. Bring her to our potluck next month. Besides, this way I can get Mary off my back about setting you up."

Briley cringed. Mary was well known in the neighborhood for being a matchmaker. Not a very successful one, but a matchmaker none-the-less. "I didn't know she was still doing that." Rumor had it she had quit last year after a particularly bad match ended badly.

"Oh, yeah. She'll be happy for you, but sad her 'operation: find Briley a girlfriend' is over."

"Her search might not be over. She can work on setting up Kat." Kat deserved it for all the shit she'd given her over the past few weeks.

Brandon threw back his head and laughed. "I'll let her know."

They stood side by side, looking out into the open space of the living room. "I don't think we'll have a problem selling this place," she said. It would make someone a beautiful home.

"I also have my eye on another house, but the details haven't been worked out yet. I don't want to get your hopes up, so I'll let you know when I know. Hell, my hopes are already up and it's going to be heartbreaking if we don't get it."

"That good?"

"Even better." He chuckled and shook his head, before squeezing her shoulder. "Go. Get out of here. It's almost six, and by the time you get home and shower, it will be time for your date."

"My date." She was still in a daze about how everything happened. "Leah and I are dating."

"Oh, my friend. You have it bad. Happy looks good on you."

"Happy feels good. I'll see you tomorrow."

"Don't do anything I wouldn't do," he called after her.

The drive home was quiet and quick. Just the way she liked it. Breezing in through the front door, she acknowledged Kat with a nod, skipped to her room, tore off her clothes, and jumped into the shower. As the water beat down on her, the nerves that had been building all day seemed to vanish. Tonight was a date, their first official date, even though the times they've been spending together Briley would classify as dates.

It was going to be awesome. They needed to discuss each other's boundaries, but she hoped Leah would be comfortable with cuddling on the couch. Leah seemed like the type to be a hugger, but it was always good etiquette to work out these details beforehand.

Thirty minutes later, she was dressed in a pair of gray Bermuda shorts, and a white and blue striped short-sleeve Henley. After running a brush through her dried hair, Briley decided to put it up off her neck. She slipped her feet into a pair of sandals and walked out of her room and toward the kitchen. Kat was waiting for her with a hug and a cup of tea.

"Sit. Drink. You have fourteen minutes before you have to be over there." Kat pushed Briley into a chair, then sat down opposite her. "Nervous?"

"Not really. More like excited."

"I got that from the forty-six text messages you sent me today."

"It's what I wanted and now that it's here, it's almost hard to believe." Briley blew on her tea and took as sip.

Kat nodded. "Believe it. I see the way she looks at you. I knew it was only a matter of time. You realize I am an all-star coach, right?"

"Any pointers tonight?"

"I got you this far. You can take it from here."

Briley finished her tea and stood up. A quick glance at her phone told her she had four minutes.

"Don't wait up."

"Didn't plan to. Really, Bri, have fun."

The walk to Leah's took less than a minute, and she had barely knocked on the door before it was opened.

"Come in."

Leah wore a long red skirt, with flowers scattered around the bottom and a black silk tank top. Her hair was down and curled around her shoulders.

"I think I'm underdressed," Briley said.

"Don't be silly. You look great." Leah took Briley's hand and lead her toward the far side of the kitchen, then motioned for her to take a seat, but not before kissing her on the cheek. Leah rummaged through a kitchen drawer and pulled out several take-out menus. "Do you have a preference?" Leah picked up a pair of glasses that were laying on the counter and slipped them on.

Briley about fell off her stool when Leah looked up at her. She'd never seen her with glasses on before, and they made her look twice as enticing. Leah must have noticed the look on her face because a sexy smile graced her lips, and she shook her head.

"Briley, focus. Dinner. Do you have a preference?"

"Not pizza." Briley separated the pizza and Chinese ones from the rest. "How about Mexican?" She slid the menu toward Leah. "They do really good takeout."

"Evan and I have eaten there a few times. I miss him. We talked last night, but it's not the same."

"He'll be home in a little over a month and a half. The time will fly."

They spent the next few minutes deciding on what to eat, then Leah phoned in their order. "Thirty to forty minutes. Whatever shall we do until then?" She set her phone on the counter, walked around it, then slipped in-between Briley's open legs. "Do you have any ideas?"

Oh, how she didn't want to ruin the moment, but she needed to know their boundaries. "Actually, I do. Can we sit in the living room?"

Leah cocked her head, slipped her glasses off, then set them on the counter. "Is everything okay?"

"Yes," Briley hurried to say. "There are just a few things we should discuss first." Leah led the way into the living room, where they both took a seat on the couch. A few feet apart.

"Briley, if you've changed your mind."

"No. No." Briley scooted over and picked up Leah's hand. "Is this okay?"

"Yes."

"I'm big on consent and just wanted to know where your boundaries lie." Leah relaxed before her eyes, squeezing Briley's hand.

"Go on."

"So, we're taking this slowly and continuing to do things like we have been?" Leah nodded. "I'm not ready for sex yet; are you?"

"Not yet, no. I want to get to know you better before we take that step. I've had a sex-only relationship and hated it. That's not what I want with you."

"Good. Me too. Not the sex-only, but I want to get to know you better too."

"What else?"

"Is touching okay? You seem comfortable with hugs. What about cuddling or holding your hand? Those types of things?"

Leah moved and sat down right beside Briley.

"I'm okay with hugs and cuddling. Right now, I would like to keep our hands outside of our clothing, but whatever skin is on display, I don't see any reason not to touch it."

Briley took that as an invitation, lifted her hand, then traced her fingertips down Leah's arm, stopping to caress her wrist. "Like that?"

Leah shivered. "Exactly like that."

"What about kissing?"

Leah tangled their fingers together, lifted her free hand, and traced Briley's jawline. "Kisses are fine. I'm not opposed to a make-out session, but we can work up to that. Who knows? You are hard to resist." Leah leaned forward and Briley met her halfway. Their first kiss was brief, but intense. Leah pulled back and ran her thumb over Briley's bottom lip. "Are you okay with taking it as slow as I would like? I don't want to call all the shots."

"I'm okay with that. I really like you and deep down I know this could be something special. I don't want to jump into anything we're not ready for. We can take all the time we need."

Leah kissed her again and lingered for a second longer. "I could get used to that."

"Well, we are dating now, so you can do that anytime you want."

"You can as well."

"I wouldn't leave that an open invitation. I'll be hugging and kissing on you all the time."

Leah smiled. "I really don't mind, darling."

At the term of endearment, Briley had to ask. "Do you like nicknames?" Briley tried to tug her hand back, but Leah kept a firm hold.

"Depends on what it is." She played with Briley's

fingers.

"You called me darling, which I like, by the way," Briley was quick to add.

Leah eyed her warily. "Do you have one in mind?"

"Butternut," Briley blurted out.

The smile on Leah's face vanished. "Butternut?"

Briley tried to keep a straight face, but failed. "No, but it can't be worse than that, can it?"

Leah slipped her free hand around the back of Briley's neck and pulled her, until they were face to face. She lifted both hands, cupped Briley's face, and kissed her slowly.

They were both breathing hard when they parted, and Briley rubbed their noses together. "So, no foods? I just want to make sure."

"You have more?"

"Sure. Cupcake, Muffin, Peachy. Leah, you're my green bean." She batted her eyes at her.

Leah threw her head back and laughed. "I knew getting involved with you was going to be an adventure."

"Oh, tiny. You haven't seen anything yet." Leah sucked in a breath at the term of endearment. "No?"

"I like it."

Briley nodded, satisfied. She opened her mouth to speak when there was a knock on the door. "I'll get it. I asked you to dinner, so I'll pay." She led the deliveryman into the kitchen, settled the bill with a generous tip, shut and locked the door, then joined Leah at the island. "God, that smells good."

After the food was divided and they were seated, Leah spoke. "So, did you ask all your questions?"

"One more. What happened with the age difference you were worried about?"

"I decided it wasn't worth me keeping you at a

distance. It seemed silly to close that chapter before we even opened it. Any more?"

Briley was satisfied with that answer. "Those were all the questions I had for now. Well, I mean, I've been tested and I'm clean."

Leah took a sip of her beer. "I am as well."

"Good. Good." She fiddled with her glasses. "We're good."

"We are."

They ate in silence, but it was comfortable. Once the table had been cleared and the garbage boxed up, they settled onto the couch. Briley leaned into the arm of the couch and slipped her arm around Leah's shoulders, drawing her against her side. Leah turned the TV on and they settled on a wildlife documentary on the Discovery Channel.

If all they did for the next six months was cuddle on the couch and watch TV, she'd be satisfied. Well, with a few kisses and hugs thrown in occasionally. This was different from her start with Beth. "Being with you is easy," Briley said.

"How so?" Leah turned slightly and placed her hand on Briley's chest.

"It just is. When Beth and I started dating, it always seemed forced. Don't get me wrong, I was crazy about her, and it never felt wrong, it just never felt like this. Easy."

"I'm glad. I had to work at it with Kathy. I know what you mean about it being easy. You look like you want to say something." Leah touched the wrinkle on Briley's forehead.

"I want us to make it, you know?"

"I want us to make it, too."

Briley cupped Leah's cheek, and kissed her. "I

have all the confidence in the world that we'll prevail."

"Stronger together, Supergirl?"

"It is my motto."

"I wouldn't be opposed to a private showing of said costume."

The scandalized look on Briley's face made Leah giggle. "Well, well, Miss Daniels, I do believe that is a tad inappropriate."

Leah wrapped her arms around Briley's neck and brought their faces close together. "You don't fool me. I know what you're thinking."

"Enlighten me."

"You're thinking, if I show her my Supergirl costume, will I get a private viewing of her Captain Marvel costume?"

Briley chuckled and buried her head in Leah's neck. "You've got me, tiny."

"You better believe it. Now," Leah untangled herself from a protesting Briley, cuddled back into her side, and pointed at the TV, "don't distract me, darling."

"I won't." Leah was distracting enough without the kisses and touching thrown in and Briley wouldn't have it any other way.

Chapter Sixteen

The six days leading up to the Wednesday before the dance were one for the record books. She and Leah managed to have dinner three times, and breakfast a few times. They'd even worked out their schedules to have a picnic in the park. Even this morning, she'd awoken with a smile on her face. That was until she'd sat down at the kitchen table and one, realized Leah had to take a day trip, and two, Kat had said something about the dance. The same dance she didn't have an outfit for.

"I don't want to go shopping." Briley hid her face in her arms on the table.

"I thought you wanted to shine for Leah. Your girlfriend." Kat poked her on the arm.

Briley peeked one eye open and regretted it by the smug look on Kat's face. "Fine."

"That's the spirit."

Two hours and three stores later, Briley wished she hadn't listened to Kat's stupid idea. Her feet hurt, she was hungry, and they hadn't found anything either one of them had liked. "I'm hungry." On top of that, she'd only had one text from Leah all morning.

"All right. Food, then more shopping."

"Is it really considered shopping if we're not buying anything?"

"You seem to be forgetting I bought that new keychain in the first store. So, technically, we are shopping." Kat dug into her pocket and pulled said purchase out.

"Oh, I see."

Kat stopped walking and drew Briley to a stop. "Please, stop looking at your phone. You have plenty of battery left. If she needs you, she will call. You're acting a bit clingy."

"So, I shouldn't text her again?"

"Let's get some lunch. If she hasn't contacted you by then, shoot her another text."

"Fair enough."

Lunch was a simple fare of salads and iced tea. Briley had offered to pay, but Kat had looked horrified and paid the bill. "I may have quit my job, but I'm not broke and the freelance is paying all right. You worry too much."

"All right." She texted Leah then slipped her phone in her pocket. "Okay, we have two more stores downtown, then we would have to hit the bigger box stores, and I don't want to do that. I also want to take you by Turn the Page."

"So, it's either these stores, or we wear something we already have? What's Turn the Page?"

"Correct, grasshopper, and it's a locally owned children's books and comic store." Kat held the door open at yet another upscale, downtown boutique. As Briley's eyes scanned the area, she could see potential. Dresses were scattered throughout the entire layout. The dresses in front didn't interest her, but they were well made and pretty. She hoped there was something more to her taste near the back.

"Good afternoon, ladies. Is there something I can help you with?"

The sales lady was well dressed and not overly

cheery. Briley could work with this, but before she could get a word out, Kat beat her to it.

"We need dresses for the dance."

The sales lady, whose tag read Linda, smiled at them. "Is there a certain style you want?" She led them past the dresses in front and to a showcase near the back. "These are always a popular choice."

In the end, Kat went with a black lace, fit and flare dress and Briley didn't go with a dress at all. She picked a two-tone crepe, black and white, wide leg jumpsuit. They both selected a new pair of heels. As they each paid for their purchase, Briley's thoughts strayed to what Leah would wear.

"Earth to Briley."

"What?" Kat held out her bag for her and she took it, slinging her outfit over her shoulder. "I'm ready."

At the stoplight, Kat rubbed her hands together in the passenger seat. "We're going to have so much fun tomorrow night. You with Leah and me with whoever I want."

"I know you told Leah that the woman you were dating wasn't serious, but are you okay?"

"Bri, it was just one of those things. I had already decided to move and shouldn't have gone out with her when she asked, but she was cute and I said yes. But, the life change meant more to me than she did. Let me put it this way. Can you see spending the rest of your life with Leah?"

"Yes."

"I couldn't with Sarah. That simple. Nor with anyone else I've dated."

At the next stop light, Briley asked the question she'd been dying to. "Have you decided what your next career move is going to be? I know the freelance accounting you're doing is bringing money in, but I also know you hate it. There's nothing on the horizon?"

"I'm working on it."

"That's all I get?"

"For now."

Briley pulled into the parking lot adjacent to Turn the Page and shut the truck off. "Kat, you're going to love this store. One part children's book store, one part comic book store, and the owners are super friendly."

"Well, what are we waiting for?"

Once in the store, Briley waved at the guy behind the counter, then pulled Kat toward the large opening in the middle of the room that led to the comic book section. Thousands of comic books lined large cases that took up most of the room, and shelves along the walls held action figures, t-shirts, and one section was set up with board games. Dozens of large-scale posters of superhero movies hung on the walls. A life-size cutout of four different superheroes stood in each corner of the room and several different cardboard cutouts of ships hung from the ceiling. From the Death Star and USS Voyager, to Prometheus, and an F-302.

Kat scanned the space, wide-eyed. "This is awesome."

Briley grabbed her arm. "I know. Make sure and take a good look at the children's part, because it's awesome too. Let's browse."

"You don't even like comics."

Briley squeezed her arm. "No, but you do. If they don't have anything you want, they can always order it. That goes for children's books too."

"Do you come here that often?"

"A couple of times a month." Briley pointed to a room off the back. "They have board game and video game tournaments twice a month and give away prizes. They've only been opened for a year, but it's quite popular. It doesn't look it now, but once school lets out, this place will be packed."

Kat rubbed her hands together. "Let's do this."

Briley left Kat scanning through the comics, as she perused the action figures. After twenty minutes, she joined Kat.

They both turned when a woman walked up to them, dressed in a pair of Levi's and a Tardis t-shirt. "Hello, I'm Ainslon. I own the store and hope I'm not interrupting, but I have a survey you can fill out. We're going to be adding a few things to both sections and wanted to get our customer's opinions. For example, we are thinking about a life-size Tardis." She pointed to her shirt. "Or, something Harry Potter related, like the cupboard under the stairs or a Hippogriff or a Centaur. Justin, my co-owner, and I have our picks, but we want to get feedback first. Take your time, and if you fill it out and turn it in, you'll get a free comic."

Kat grinned at her. "Excellent, Ainslon."

"I'll leave you two alone." She winked at Kat and walked toward the children's section.

"She's cute," Kat commented.

"She is," Briley agreed.

"Bri, do you have a pen?" Kat accepted the pen Briley handed her. "Briley, fill yours out too and you can get me a comic with your voucher."

Briley rolled her eyes, but did as she asked when her phone rung. "It's Brandon, I have to take this." She walked a few feet away before answering. "Hey, Brandon. What do you need?"

He chuckled. "You. Remember that house I was telling you about? Well, it's ours if we want it. It's off

Sixth Avenue, across from the Wagner's crossing sign. It's being sold as-is, but, well, when you get here, you'll see. I'll text you the directions." She watched Kat walk into the other room to pay for her items.

"All right, we'll be there in fifteen minutes."

"Later, gator."

Briley joined Kat at the checkout. "Everything okay?" Kat asked.

"Yes, Brandon found a potential property and we need to check it out."

Once in the truck, she ignored Kat's grumbling from behind the wheel, searched for listings online of the house he was talking about, but quickly gave up. They would be at the house soon enough. "Must not be on the market yet," she mumbled.

"Bri, help a girl out," Kat huffed.

"Turn left at the next light, then another left at the stop sign. His truck is a white Ford."

At the final turn, Briley got her first look at the house and her heart skipped a beat. Nothing compared to seeing a potential house for the first time. A classic two story Victorian stood on a corner lot. Before she even got out of the truck, she knew they had to have it.

Brandon stood in front of the house with his arms spread wide. "What do you think?"

She loved it, but would hold off showing it. "What are the numbers?"

With a grin, he whipped a paper out of his back pocket. "Built in 1935. The foundation is solid and the previous owners had a new roof put on three years ago. Plumbing and electrical was updated fifteen years ago."

She turned to find Kat, but she was talking to Mary, Brandon's wife. She took the paper from Brandon and they walked around the house. "Needs new windows and siding."

"Yes."

The house was beautiful, and would be their biggest project to date. "Let's go back to your truck and look at the numbers." They both ignored the other women when they walked back to them. Brandon picked up his clipboard.

"What's the asking price?" She crossed her fingers, hoping that it was reasonable.

"Two hundred and forty-nine thousand."

She stiffened.

"What?" Kat asked, looking from one to the other. "Is that bad?"

"That's a bit low, isn't it?" Briley worried her bottom lip. In fact, it was extremely low. What the hell did the inside look like?

"The owner is ready to sell, and quick. But, it is an as-is sell."

"When does it go on the market?"

"Monday."

"What are the comps in the area?"

"Three houses sold in the last two months. One for four hundred, one for three hundred seventy-five, and the third sold for close to four hundred fifty thousand. This is an up and coming neighborhood and this house is on a corner, but still not much traffic."

"How did you find out about it?"

He grinned. "My grandpa knows the lady that's selling. She's ready to move on with her life. She's moving in with her son and his family. The house has already been cleaned out. My grandpa was in the house less than six months ago and he said it was beautiful. So even though it is an as-is sale we lucked out by him knowing her. I can't guarantee it still looks like he mentioned, I think it's a pretty good guess."

She punched him on the arm. "You should have started with that." Briley turned to him and smiled. Even without looking at the inside, she knew they had to have it, and she trusted Brandon's grandpa. He wanted them to succeed and wouldn't set them up for failure. "Make the call."

"That's what I'm talking about." He made a fist and lifted it in triumph.

Kat tapped her on the arm when he turned away to make the call and motioned for her to follow her. "You're buying it?"

"Yes. It's a fantastic deal. Even if we have to replace all the flooring and drywall."

"Wow."

"First a fantastic outfit and now this. This day can only get better."

Nearly an hour later, they were all sitting on the front porch when another truck pulled into the driveway and a young man stepped out and handed them the key to the house. Brandon grinned at her, and handed it to her. "Ready?'

"Let's do this." The final paperwork wouldn't be ready until Monday, but at least they would get a peek inside now. No turning back.

Briley took a deep breath, slipped the key in the lock, and turned the handle. Her breath left her chest when she got her first look at the inside. "Oh, my God." She took a few steps in and heard Brandon suck in a breath. He grabbed her by the shoulders and pulled her back against his chest.

"Damn, Briley." He laughed. They started out exploring the layout.

Waxed hard wood floors shined back at them

from every inch of the house. Polished wood trim surrounded every doorway and window. In the kitchen, the counters would need to be replaced, but the hardwood cabinets could be refinished and last another fifty years. The three bathrooms would be complete guts and the wall between the kitchen and living room needed to be taken down to open the space, but the house was beautiful and well maintained.

Kat whistled. "This house is amazing."

"It is. We hit it out of the park with this one."

"If we put a hundred thousand in it and sell for close to five we'll make our biggest profit to date," Brandon said.

"This is going to be awesome. Can you imagine what Nina and Ashley will do when they get their hands on it? Man." She ran her fingers through her hair.

Mary slid her arm around Brandon's waist. "I hate to break this up, but we need to go. I promised my parents we'd have dinner with them tonight." Brandon grimaced, but kept quiet.

"Right," Briley said. This project was going to be so much fun. A ton of work, but fun.

Brandon was quiet as they made their way to their cars. "So, Briley. How's it going with Leah?"

"Good. Really good."

He placed his arm across her shoulders. "That's what I like to hear."

"She said yes to the potluck." Before she'd left her house the night before, she'd asked, and Leah had been excited to meet more of Briley's friends.

"We can't wait to meet her. Kat," Mary slipped her arm through Kat's arm, "you're welcome to come as well. I don't know you nearly like I should."

"Oh, okay. Sure. Who says no to food?"

On the way home, Briley was starting to get antsy, not having received a text back from Leah. When she pulled into her driveway, she noticed Leah sitting on her front porch, talking on her phone. She looked longingly at her garage, then sent a glare in Kat's direction. Ever since Kat decided to move, her precious 2017 black Corvette Stingray Coupe 1LT had taken up residence inside Briley's garage.

"She's almost brand-new, Briley. Leave her be."

"I don't know why she outranks my truck, just because she cost more." They climbed out and Briley locked up her crew cab truck and patted the hood. Kat walked to the garage and placed her hand on the door. "Lucille is sensitive and deserves to be pampered. Rosie," she pointed at Briley's truck, "is a work truck. She can handle the elements."

They were locked in a stare-off when Briley felt an arm wrap around her waist and she relaxed. "Kat, the car is impractical. You have to recognize that."

Kat narrowed her eyes. "What I know is neither I nor Lucille deserve this abuse." Kat took three steps forward, leaned down, and kissed Leah on the cheek. Leah smiled, but Briley growled. "Now, now, Briley. No need for that. I was just saying hello."

Leah tightened her hold on Briley. "Have you two eaten dinner?" They both shook their heads. "How about ordering in? My treat. Anything but pizza."

"I'm game," Kat said.

"As if I would ever say no to you." Briley lightly kissed Leah's lips.

"Bri, give me your keys. We forgot our garment bags. I'll take those in, and meet you both at Leah's house."

"Sounds good." Briley and Leah strolled down

the sidewalk side by side, hand in hand. On the porch, Leah turned to her. "Garment bag?"

"We bought new outfits for the dance."

Leah slipped her arms around Briley's neck and pulled her down into a kiss. "I bought something new for the dance also." She pecked her lips. "I would have texted, but it was a long day. I'll try to do better in the future."

"I hope it didn't seem like I was bothering you. I was just worried."

"It felt good for someone to worry about me." She ran her fingers down Briley's cheek. "Let's head in and wait for Kat."

"Too late, I'm already here." Kat pulled them both into a hug. "You crazy kids. Let's not give the neighbors a show. In we go."

Briley held the door open for them and smiled at Kat and Leah laughing. The day just kept getting better and better.

Chapter Seventeen

An hour into the dance, Leah still hadn't arrived. Briley had asked her if she needed a ride, but she declined, saying she would meet them there. She'd already danced with a number of people, but was just as content to stand back and watch everyone else participate since the one woman she wanted to dance with hadn't arrived yet.

She finished her punch, then threw her empty cup in the garbage. After the first sip, she was sure Kevin had spiked it. Her suspicions were confirmed when she caught his eye and he gave her a thumbs up and a cheeky grin. Great. That's all she needed, to be wasted on top of everything else.

"So," Kat said, sidling up to her. "Still no Leah."

"That's quite the observation, Kat." Her eyes strayed to Brandon and Mary doing some weird dance. "I just don't know what could be keeping her. She said she would be here."

"And I'm sure she will." Kat slipped her arm around Briley's waist and scanned the surrounding area. "What about that blonde you danced with twice?"

"She asked, but I declined. It felt weird to be dancing with someone besides Leah."

"I understand." Kat handed her another cup of punch.

The cup had just touched Briley's lips when her eyes landed on Nina as she made her way toward them with a guy Briley didn't recognize. "Nina's headed this way."

Kat looked around until her eyes spotted Nina. "Wow. Blue's a good look on her."

The navy-blue sheath dress hugged her in all the right places and showed off her curves to perfection. Her blond hair lay loose around her shoulders. Briley pulled Nina into her arms for a quick hug. "You look fantastic."

"You flatter me. You as well." She motioned for the man to join her, then she placed her arm around his waist. "This is Trevor. Trevor, this is Briley and her sister Kat."

He shook Briley's hand. "I've heard a lot about you. You as well," he said to Kat. He was taller than Nina was, almost as tall as Kat, and good looking. His dark hair and beard were nicely trimmed and his suit was tailored to fit him. Briley could see why Nina was attracted to him, but she would withhold her judgment until she got to know him.

"I haven't heard anything about you." Briley took another sip of her drink, and Nina rolled her eyes.

"It's still new, and need I remind you that I am just now hearing about Leah?" Nina frowned when Briley turned away from her. "Where is she at?"

"Not here yet."

"Bummer."

"Don't look now, Bri," Kat said, "but there is a woman checking you out." She pointed to their left. "Ask her to dance."

Briley rolled her eyes but turned in that direction and all the air felt like it was knocked out of her chest. The long red dress Leah wore looked like silk, and draped her frame oh so well. All coherent thought vanished when Leah walked up to them and slipped her hand into Briley's. It didn't help Briley's nerves when Leah did a slow appraisal of her body.

"Sorry I'm late."

"Don't be silly." Briley adjusted her glasses. "You look amazing."

"You as well, darling."

"You remember Nina, and this is Trevor."

"It's nice to see you again and meet you."

Leah turned so she was facing Briley. "Well, Briley. What about that dance?"

"Whatever you want." Briley let her lead her onto the dance floor, and didn't bother to look back because she could feel everyone's eyes on her. Having Leah wrapped in her arms was a feeling she never wanted to end.

As soon as the first song ended, an upbeat one started. Briley laughed and twirled Leah around the dance floor, then grabbed her hand and pulled her flush against her and enjoyed the way their bodies molded together. After the third song ended, Briley led her off the dance floor and got them both a cup of punch. This was her third glass and she knew she would have to take it easy. She did not intend to get drunk tonight.

"Here's your punch, my lady."

"Thank you." Leah took a sip and cringed. "It's got a distinctive taste."

"You could say that. I'm not sure what Kevin spiked it with. I'm eighty-five percent sure it's nothing poisonous."

Leah stopped with the cup an inch from her lips. "You had me there for a minute."

Briley didn't correct her, because she didn't think Kevin would try and kill everyone. At least he hadn't thus far. They both finished their punch and Leah grasped her hand to pull her back onto the dance floor when a voice behind them spoke.

"Actually, I do believe this dance belongs to me. Doesn't it, Briley?"

"One dance." Briley slowly turned around and Nina reached for her hand.

"Well," Leah said, and turned to Trevor. "How about a dance?"

"I would love to."

She walked slowly to Nina and smiled. "Your guy doesn't mind you dancing with me?"

Nina snorted. "The moment any man thinks they can dictate what I do is the day I drop him. I really like him. A lot. I trust him, and I don't mind him dancing with Leah. You're not jealous?"

"Nope. It sounds serious with Trevor." Briley twirled her around. "How long have you been dating?"

"A few months, and I…I never felt this way. He's gorgeous, right?"

"He is."

"So, you and Leah. I'm happy for you."

"Thanks."

"Oh, Briley." She wrapped her arms around Briley's neck. "I love you and only want what's best for you. Do me a favor."

"I'll try."

"Live in the moment with Leah. Have fun."

"That's what I'm doing."

"Good." She pulled Briley off the dance floor toward Leah. "She's all yours."

Nina kissed Briley on the cheek, then walked back onto the dance floor where Trevor took her in his arms. Briley turned back to Leah. "Another dance?"

"Show me what you've got."

Song after song, they danced. Briley had never felt as alive as when she was in Leah's arms. Quite a few people had asked to cut in, but Leah had always declined their offer. Forty-five minutes later, Briley excused herself to use the restroom. When she returned, she hurried to Leah when she noticed Haley talking to her. She hoped to God Haley wasn't giving Leah the shovel talk.

"Haley, you look great." Briley slipped her arm around Leah's waist.

"You as well." Haley never took her eyes off Leah. "Leah, remember what we talked about."

Leah stepped forward and drew a surprised Haley into a quick hug. "Enjoy the rest of the dance, dear."

Haley coughed. "You as well." As she walked away, she threw a pointed look at Leah, then disappeared through the entrance door.

"I hope she was friendly." Briley stepped around Leah and drew her into a hug, resting her clasped hands at the small of Leah's back.

"You have a lot of people that care about you." Leah placed her hands on Briley's chest. "Her being one. She was harmless."

"No shovel talk?" Briley bit her lip.

Leah laughed and kissed Briley on the lips. "Oh, no, there was a shovel talk. A quite convincing one, in fact. Did you know that the wooded area behind the church belongs to the church?"

"I did," Briley said, slowly.

"She also mentioned that no one would find my body if it was to go missing, behind said church."

Briley cringed. "Sorry."

"Don't be. It was cute. It still wasn't as intimidating

as Kat's."

"What? Kat's?"

"Now hers was quite convincing. They love you, Briley. It didn't bother me."

"Do you want to dance some more, or go?"

"Let's go." Leah leaned into Briley. "Since you've been so good tonight, you can walk me home. I took a cab, and I know Kat drove her car so she could impress anyone she met tonight."

"Let's walk this way." Briley pointed toward their left. "So I can tell Kat I'm leaving." Their neighborhood was only a couple blocks over and would be an easy walk.

"Sounds good."

Leah took a firm hold of Briley's hand as they said their goodbyes to Kat. Silence met the first ten minutes of their walk.

"It's a beautiful night." Leah stepped in front of Briley and walked backward. "Did you have fun?"

Briley had to give her kudos. She didn't know how she walked backward in her three-inch heels. "I'm still having fun." She rushed forward and lifted Leah into her arms, bringing their bodies flush. "You're breathtaking."

"You do know how to make a woman feel good."

"It's so easy with you. The words just come and I don't censor them. It's quite freeing."

"I like it." Leah closed the distance between them and kissed her.

Briley bit Leah's bottom lip, smiled, and rested their foreheads together. "Let's get home." She took hold of Leah's hand. Thirty minutes later, they were curled up on Leah's front porch on her swing.

"We'll have to do this again." Briley moved

Leah's hair so she could look in her eyes.

"Yes, we will." Leah leaned against her. "We need to take the next month and spend as much time together as possible. Evan will be back before we know it."

"Is he having fun?"

"Loads. He always enjoys spending time with Kathy and his stepmom, and his little sister, Griffin."

"Griffin is an unusual name for a girl."

"Kathy wanted to name her after her dad, and Lilith agreed."

Briley sighed and kicked the swing into motion. "Did you ever want more kids?"

"At one time I did, but I'm happy with the two I have. I was surprised Kathy wanted more kids, but Lilith did and Kathy agreed. Do you want kids?"

"Yes. I don't want to give birth to one, but there are other ways to become a mother."

Leah intertwined her fingers with Briley's. "There are."

Briley stared at their fingers for a long time. She tightened her hold and leaned back on the swing. "As much as I'm enjoying this, it's getting late and I have to work early in the morning. The turnovers for the Encampment won't make themselves."

"Do you need any help?"

"I will never turn down help."

"What time?"

"Five would work."

"Sounds good." Leah untangled herself from Briley, stood up, then offered Briley a helping hand. Leah kissed Briley on the cheek. "Goodnight."

"Night." With reluctance, Briley pulled away, walked down the porch steps, and only glanced back once.

She climbed the steps and unlocked the kitchen door. Once inside, she made a cup of tea and settled down at the table. After her third sip, she heard Kat arrive home, so she got up and made her a cup of coffee.

"Bless you," Kat said, when she walked in the backdoor and accepted the cup. "Did you have fun?"

"Did you?"

"Yes."

Briley eyed her. "Did you meet anyone?"

"No one I want to call." Kat jumped up and plated two turnovers for them when Briley sat down at the table.

"Do you need my help in the morning?"

"Nope. Leah is coming over to help."

"Oh, thank God. I love you, but I did not want to get up early to help you."

"Not to worry. My girlfriend will help me." Briley finished her turnover and carried her saucer to the sink. "I'm turning in. Goodnight." She kissed the top of Kat's head.

"Night."

Forty minutes later, Briley was nestled under the covers when she received a text alert. A smile graced her face when she saw it was from Leah, wishing her sweet dreams. Yes, Briley had a feeling everything was going to be just fine.

Chapter Eighteen

Briley groaned when her alarm went off the next morning. The glowing numbers taunted her as she rolled over in bed and swung her legs over the side. She only worked the Friday of the Encampment and she needed to get the turnovers ready.

She had to assemble seven hundred and fifty, but over the years, she'd got her time down to the last second. It was two AM and the booth she set up at wouldn't start selling them until eleven o'clock. For the nine hours she would give up, she'd make an easy four to five thousand dollars that would go directly into her savings account.

She didn't bother changing out of her sweatpants and tank top, or brush her hair. She just put it up in a messy bun, brushed her teeth, washed her face, and made her way to the kitchen where she stretched and flipped the Keurig on.

The night before, she had taken her two giant tubs of apple pie filling out of the freezer, along with her pie dough, and put them in the refrigerator to thaw out. A few weeks back, she made the dough, cut it down to size, stacked each piece between parchment paper, layered them, then froze them all.

She sipped her tea and ran through the list of things she would need to do that day. When she was ready, she placed everything on the table, and sang along to the radio as she filled each piece of dough, then sealed them shut. It was a calming process and allowed her to clear her mind. As her cooler filled up, she would haul it into the utility room, right off the kitchen, and place each turnover in the large upright freezer to set up. After three hours, her back was starting to ache, but she was a third of the way done.

She'd just unloaded her latest batch into the freezer when there was a knock on the back door. Leah. Holding in her excitement, she shut the freezer, dropped the cooler by the table, and swung the kitchen door open.

A grinning Leah stepped in and kissed Briley on the lips. "Now, that's a good morning greeting I can get behind."

"I thought you might." Leah snickered. "You have." Leah pointed at her forehead. "Here. Let me." She grabbed a paper towel and reached toward her. "Hold still. You have flour on your face." Briley gulped but allowed Leah to wipe it off. "All gone."

"Okay." Briley coughed. "So, coffee?"

"Please. Then you can show me what to do. I'm a quick study."

"All right." After she fixed Leah her coffee and another tea for herself, Briley went through the process a few times, so Leah could get the feel for it. Briley smiled as Leah struggled with sealing the turnovers. "Here, let me."

Stepping up behind Leah, Briley wrapped her arms around her waist, molding their bodies together. Her breath hitched when Leah leaned back into her, placing her gloved hands atop Briley's. She closed her eyes, enjoying the moment, only to snap them open a moment later when Leah squeezed her hand. After getting her bearings, she moved her arms, reached forward and scooped up a bit of pie filling with the spoon, depositing it in the middle of the piece of dough. "Like this." Her hands trembled a bit, as she applied enough pressure to Leah's hands to properly seal the turnover. When Leah caught on, Briley took a step away. "Think you have it now?"

"With a demonstration like that, I believe I do." Leah ran her thumb along Briley's cheek. "We have plenty of time for cuddling later. Right now, we need to get these finished." They spent the next thirty minutes in silence, getting a rhythm until Leah spoke, making Briley jump in her chair. "Do you do this every year? You never said."

She shook her hands out and took a sip of tea, before glancing her way. "Yes. I enjoy it. I make them during the Encampment, the Fall Festival, and Christmas Festival. It's a quick ten to fifteen thousand dollars for all three."

Leah's eyes widened. "That's a lot of money."

"If I worked all three days of the festival, I could make a lot more, but one day is enough for me. With these events, most people that work them, this is their yearly salary and they can make a lot of money, especially at the Encampment. Since I own my business, all this money will go into my savings account. I would love to travel for a year."

"Traveling is so much fun, even when I was working. I would love to take Evan for a summer, but that's usually when he spends most of his time with Kathy, since I have him the rest of the year."

"Is there any place that stood out to you?"

"Let's see." She tapped her finger on her lip. "You know, you would think it would be someplace exotic, but I love going to Disney World. It's so much fun, especially seeing Madison and Evan's face's light up the first time we went. Even now, they enjoy it just as much as I do. Madison and Bryan are planning to take their kids for the first time next year. I can't wait."

"That's awesome. The first time our parents took us, the characters freaked me out, but it's not something I'll ever forget. Memories are everything, considering the older we got, the more our mom pulled away from us."

Leah placed her flour-dusted hand atop Briley's and started playing with her fingers. "That must have been hard."

"We got used to it. I think it has to do with our dad passing away. Even though Kat looks like Mom and I take after Dad, every time she looks at us, she sees him. It took her years to grieve properly and she clung to Candace, our cousin, for support."

"Still, it must be hard. My kids are my world." Leah patted her hand one last time before pulling away. "Any time you want to talk about him, I'm here."

Forgetting for a moment that flour covered her hands, Briley swept Leah into her arms. "Thank you. Not now, but later, we'll talk."

"Any time." Leah tangled her hand in Briley's hair, pulled her down, and kissed her. "Don't think you're off the hook for hugging me with flour all over your hands."

"And what are you going to do about it?" Briley swiped her finger across the tabletop where there was a bit of loose pie filling and dabbed it on Leah's cheek. "You seem to have something on your cheek." Leah chuckled when Briley licked her cheek, before bringing their lips together. "You taste good."

"I wonder why." She placed her palms on Briley's

chest and pushed her away. "We need to finish this."

"As you wish." They each put on a clean pair of gloves and after another hour, they were down to their last few. "Wow. I can't believe we're almost done." She whistled. "Thank you so much for your help." After they transferred the last ones to the freezer, Briley poured them each a glass of milk. "Since it's still early, what would you say to making some blueberry muffins?"

Leah tilted her head, a slow smile working its way onto her face. "That sounds like a wonderful idea."

"You have to help me, though." She placed her cup on the counter, then rubbed her hands together.

"I think I can manage that. Especially if it's as hands on as your last approach."

Briley blushed. "Since I'm in charge, you have to do everything I say." She gulped when Leah took a step in her direction and ran her finger down her neck.

"Oh, you're in charge, are you?" She eyed her up and down, then smirked when Briley started to fidget.

"Yes. Yes, I am." Leah was going to be the death of her. "Sit back down; I'll get all our ingredients. Have you ever made them before?" She wiped her hands on her apron. Time to get back on solid footing.

"No, I'm not much of a baker, but I love to cook."

Briley went through each step, with Leah executing each one like a pro. Briley narrowed her eyes and asked her again, but she insisted she didn't bake much. "Don't over stir. Lumps are fine for muffins." After dusting the fresh blueberries with flour, she dumped them in the batter. "Just a couple of turns, then we'll fill the cups."

Briley took over and filled the muffin tins, tapping them on the counter once they were full and slipped them into the oven and set the timer on her phone. "Now we wait." She turned back to Leah, who proceeded to stick her finger in the batter bowl and tap Briley on her lips.

"Cute, Leah. Real cute." Briley reached for a rag, but Leah grabbed her hand, halting her progress.

Leah winked at her. "I can get that for you." Leah leaned toward her. Time seemed to stand still the closer she got. Briley's heart beat faster and faster. When she was a breath away, Briley caught sight of Kat out of the corner of her eye, leaning against the doorframe leading into the kitchen, just watching them. Briley jerked away from her.

"What's wrong?" Leah questioned, then looked behind her. "Good morning, Kat."

Kat held her hands up. "Don't stop on my account."

"Don't be a perv, Kat." Briley wiped her lips off then threw the dishtowel at Kat, hitting her in the face. "Coffee?"

"Yes."

A few minutes later, Briley joined Leah and Kat at the table.

"I am so glad you helped Briley, Leah. I did not want to get up at two AM."

"It's in the girlfriend handbook," Leah said.

Briley choked on her milk, and Kat patted her on the back. "I'm fine. It went down the wrong way." The knowing smirk on Leah's face told her she knew exactly why it happened.

"Leah," Kat said. "What's this handbook you speak of?"

After taking a sip of her milk, Leah answered. "It's the weirdest thing. Two days ago, I heard a knock on my front door. When I opened it, there was a manila envelope on my welcome mat. Inside was the girlfriend handbook. It was an eye-opening read. Chapter six was…" she bit her lip, "rather detailed."

Briley and Kat both stared at her when she took the muffins out of the oven. "She's a keeper, Briley." Kat patted her hand.

"I know. Believe me, I know."

"So, Leah, what was chapter six about?" Kat inquired.

"I would tell you but at the beginning of the book, it stated I could only talk about the contents with others that had received it. You've already stated you haven't."

"That's awfully convenient," Kat answered.

"It is." Leah placed a muffin on her plate, peeling back the paper and spreading a small amount of butter on it.

"I have ways of making you talk." Kat held up the butter knife.

"There's only one woman at this table that could make me talk." They both turned to Briley.

"I'm staying out of this. I don't care what chapter six was about."

Kat threw her empty muffin wrapper at Briley. "Party pooper."

"These are good, Briley." Leah wiped her lips.

"I'm glad you're enjoying them." After another muffin each, Briley hopped up when she heard the refrigerated truck pull into the driveway. She paid Doug two hundred dollars to transport the turnovers to the Encampment and unload them into the fridge that was already set up for her behind the tent they would be selling at.

"Hey, Doug. How you doing?" She handed him a

cup of coffee, which he accepted readily, and a muffin.

"I'm good. Thanks so much for these."

"You're welcome."

"I'm so glad you texted me earlier. That way I can get yours delivered, then pick up another delivery for the event."

"I had help this year."

Kat helped them both load the partially frozen turnovers that were stacked in moveable trays into the truck. After everything was loaded, Briley wrote him a check and handed it over, along with four more muffins.

"Have a good day, Briley."

"You too, Doug."

Briley pulled up a chair beside Kat and Leah. "I'm going to take a shower and get dressed."

"And I need to go change." Leah stood, kissed Briley on the cheek, and headed for the door. "Text me when you're done for the day and we can get together."

"Leah, you can explore with me, if you want to," Kat said.

"I would like that." They exchanged numbers, then Leah left.

Kat pushed on Briley's arm. "You can't take a shower if you fall asleep at the table."

"Shut up." She laid her head on the table anyway.

"You and Leah seem comfortable together."

"Extremely. I don't know how to explain it." Briley put her empty plate and cup in the sink. "It's awesome."

"I can tell. It's okay if I hang out with you and Leah afterward, right?"

"I guess."

"Golly gee, I don't want it to be a hardship." Kat

touched her hands to her chest and pouted.

"Yes, loser. We can all hang out together."

"That's better."

"I think today's going to be fun."

"Me too, Bri. Me too."

Chapter Nineteen

After scooping out the turnover from the large vat of oil, Briley gently dropped it in the bowl Mrs. King was holding out, then proceeded to top it with powdered sugar and whip cream. She wiped her brow, but it was a lot cooler today than they had expected. They'd been at it for almost three hours and were down to their last dozen or so turnovers. Along with the turnovers, Mrs. King also sold buffalo chili. They'd never sold out this quickly and she was looking forward to getting out from behind the booth earlier than usual.

"So, you and Leah, huh?" Mrs. King asked out of the blue.

"Yep."

"I'm counting on you two to make it, Briley. Don't let me down. I have to live vicariously through someone, and I choose you. It does an old woman's heart good to see love bloom."

"I...okay. Yes." Briley nodded. "I will be your person."

"Fantastic. I saw her and Kat earlier."

"I'm meeting up with them both later."

"How many turnovers do we have left?" Mrs. King asked.

Briley opened the freezer. "About twenty."

"Go. Go spend time with your sister and your girlfriend."

"Are you sure?"

"Yes, we can handle this."

Briley kissed her on the cheek. "Thanks." She slipped the check Mrs. King handed her in her pants pocket, slung her backpack over her shoulder, texted Kat to find out where they were, and then took off in that direction.

She smiled when she turned a corner and spotted Kat and Leah sitting across from each other under a shaded picnic table.

Briley plopped down beside Leah and thanked Kat when she pushed the other half of her sandwich and chips in front of her. Briley gave her a grateful smile before chomping into it.

"I expected it to take longer." Leah rubbed her hand in circles on Briley's back.

"It was a bigger crowd than expected."

"So, what do you two want to do next?" Kat asked.

"I would really—" Briley never got to finish her thought when someone spoke up behind her.

"Briley."

Briley stiffened at the voice, causing her to drop the rest of the uneaten sandwich back onto the plate. A voice she hadn't heard in years. A voice that even to this day sometimes haunted her dreams. A shudder passed through her at the touch on her shoulder and she turned her head when the woman stepped in front of her. A squeeze on her leg from Leah broke her out of her stupor and she turned and came face to face with her past. "Beth, I didn't know you were back in town."

"Just for the weekend." She looked from Leah to Briley.

Beth's smile grew wider the longer Briley stared.

She looked just as good now as the last time she saw her, with her black hair pulled in a ponytail. She wore a pair of tight jeans, and a black, form-fitting tank top. Beth's gray eyes bore into Briley's soul as they had done all those years ago. "I…"

Beth reached forward and picked Briley's hand up. "Spend some time with me? We can catch up."

That was the last thing she wanted, and she didn't want to abandon Leah or Kat, but maybe she needed this to move forward with Leah. Seeing Beth in front of her now made her realize they had a lot of unresolved issues.

"We three are going to explore," Kat chimed in, throwing a death glare at Beth.

"Kat," Beth said. "It's good to see you. I only want her for a few minutes."

"It's not good to see you," Kat said. It was no secret that Kat disliked Beth after what she'd done.

"Kat, please," Briley said. "Beth, if you could give me a few minutes with these two."

"Of course. I'll be right over there." She pointed to a large oak tree.

"Kat, I know what you're going to say, but I need this. We left a lot unsaid between us."

Kat looked uncertain. "I don't agree."

Leah surprised Briley when she spoke up. "I think you should talk to her." She tilted Briley's face until they were looking at each other. "I don't want anything standing between us. If this is something you need to do, then do it. I trust you."

"You're sure? I don't want this to upset you." She wasn't sure she would be so understanding if they were talking about one of Leah's exes.

"We're both adults and you know Kathy's still in

my life, for the kids' sake. Go, talk to your ex." She cupped Briley's cheek and pecked her on the lips. "I'm really okay with it."

Briley kissed the palm of Leah's hand. "Okay." Briley stood, kissed Kat on the cheek and whispered in her ear that she was fine, and slipped her backpack on. The walk to Beth was short. "After you."

Beth giggled and slipped her arm through Briley's and they walked away from the table. "It's been what? Almost two years?"

"Seems like a lot longer than that." She dared not look back, afraid of the look on Kat and Leah's faces, so she kept her gaze ahead of them. "How have you been?"

A sigh slipped past her lips. "Up and down. My girlfriend and I broke up a few months back."

"I'm sorry to hear that."

"I'm not. We just drifted apart. Kind of like us."

"Yes, like us," she spit out.

Beth slid her fingers down Briley's arm and gripped her hand, dragging her along the pathway until she found some space that wasn't overrun with tourists. "I know we haven't seen each other in a long time, I get that."

"I..." Briley pulled her hand back and ran it through her hair. Did Beth really expect them just to pick up where they left off? She would never do that. Besides, Leah didn't need to see Beth's hands all over her. It wouldn't sit well with her if Kathy had her hands all over Leah.

"You don't have to tell me if you don't want to, but it looks like you have something on your mind."

There was something on her mind. They hadn't exactly ended things on a good note. "You cheated on me," she blurted out.

Pain flashed across Beth's face, and she wrapped her arms around her chest. "I know, Briley." Her gaze flitted over the crowd. "They say you shouldn't have regrets, but," she shook her head, "I regret leaving angry that night, and I regret drinking too much, but I'm not making excuses. My cheating was all on me and I regret it every day. Hurting you, destroying us on a whim was the worst thing I have ever done in my life and I'm sorry. I loved you." She laughed and slipped her hands into her pockets. "I love you. It's really hard not to."

"Even after all these years?"

"Oh, Briley, you're so easy to love and it's even easier to keep loving you. Lord knows I've tried to forget you, or to move on from you, but nothing's helped."

Briley took a step back. The last thing she wanted to do was give her the wrong impression. At one time, Beth was her entire world, but that time had passed. She wouldn't deny the flutter in her stomach when she spotted her or the way her heart raced, and although a piece of her heart would always be reserved for her, it was a small part and not one she would ever revisit again.

"I know our time has passed. I guess I just wanted to see you." Beth shrugged. "To hear your voice. To touch you again." She reached between them and tangled their fingers together. A flash of pain shot across her face when Briley jerked her hand back. "Whoever she is, she better know how special you are and that you, Briley," she pointed at her, "you deserve so much more than the way I treated you. Does she? Does she know how special you are?"

The comfort of such a familiar feeling as being

in Beth's presence threatened to overwhelm. She felt nothing for her, but they had been together for five years. Beth's apology was two years in the making and not what she had expected today. It would be easy to fall back into old habits, but she would do nothing to cheapen what her and Leah shared.

"Hey." Beth tilted Briley's chin up. "What's wrong?"

"Thank you for saying what you did." She sighed and took Beth's hand off her. "I forgave you, you know, a long time ago. Things happen. Some we mean to and others disrupt everything you've carefully constructed. It was hard after you left, but as you can see, I dusted myself off and put myself back together."

"Who is she, the woman at the table?"

Briley stared unfocused on a spot past Beth's shoulder, and a smile blossomed on her face. "You don't know her."

"Does she know how you feel? Because I can't see any woman saying no to you if they knew."

"She does."

"So, you like this woman?"

"Yes."

"Was that a question or the answer?" Beth asked.

"The answer," she said confidently, and Beth smiled sadly and took a step back.

"You never looked at me the way you're thinking about her. You're falling in love with her and you don't even realize it." She cocked her head. "Or do you?"

"Is this really what you wanted to talk about?"

Beth laughed. "You deserve it, Briley." Beth rocked back on her heels. "Wow. Who knew a friendly hello would turn into something so deep?" She buffed her fingers on her tank top. "Anything else Doctor Beth can help you with?" She winked and Briley instantly remembered why she had fallen in love with Beth in the first place. They had so many good times, but as much as she had loved her, she could never continue a relationship with her after the cheating incident.

Briley laughed and took a couple of steps forward until they were almost close enough to touch. "I can't believe I'm going to say this, but despite everything, it's good to see you." Beth closed the distance between them and drew her into a tight hug, resting their foreheads together. "God, and you smell the same." Briley accepted this moment for what it was. A glimpse into a past she would always remember, but never repeat. She pulled back and kissed Beth's forehead.

"I'm a creature of habit. It's really good to see you, too."

"Yes." Briley pulled away from her and took a step back, then pivoted and walked away.

"Briley."

She'd know that voice anywhere. When Leah reached her, she slipped her arm around her shoulders.

"Everything okay?" Leah was relaxed, but Briley could hear the undercurrent of uncertainty in her voice.

She moved the hair out of Leah's eyes, before leaning down and kissing her sweetly. "Everything is perfect. I needed that closure with her. Thank you for understanding."

"I'm not an insecure woman, but I'll admit to being a tad jealous when you walked off with her."

"There was no need for that. I'm right where I want to be." She let her hands drop, then latched onto Leah's nearest hand, interlacing their fingers. "Where are you headed?"

"To join back up with Kat." A short distance

later, Leah spoke. "Some of these men really get into this dressing up, huh?" Leah pointed to a tall man with long dark hair and a beard, only wearing a loincloth. By the way he walked, there was no guessing that he didn't wear anything underneath of it.

"The Encampment wouldn't be the same without him. No one knows his name, but he's here every year." They walked past several tepees with small fires burning and several children playing with wooden swords. "It's not everyone's cup of tea, but it does a lot for our town."

"I wasn't bashing it, Briley. It's just different. I've never been to anything like this before."

"It's different, that's for sure."

After a beat, Leah asked, "Do you want to get some ice cream?"

Briley chuckled and squeezed Leah's hand. "I have never turned down ice cream."

"Ice cream, then I think it's time we had some fun."

That sounded like a good idea. "Fun with you and me or fun with a crowd? What did you have in mind?"

"Get your mind out of the gutter. How about bowling? You can invite your sister if you want to. Just a friendly competition."

"I can get behind that, tiny. Are you sure you're even strong enough to pick the bowling ball up?" It did sound good after a long day of ups and downs.

"Already smack talking, Briley. I see how it is."

"I like to win."

"That you do."

They were almost at the table when Briley turned around and walked backward, pointing down her body. "Are you sure you're ready for the awesomeness you're about to unleash?"

The laugh that erupted from Leah was a balm to Briley's soul. "Oh, I think I can handle you." She traced her finger down Briley's cheek.

"It's about time you two showed up," Kat hollered.

Briley put her hand on Leah's back and pushed her forward. Then did a double take when she noticed Nina and Trevor seated at the table. "Hey guys." She kissed Nina on the cheek and settled down across from Kat. "Leah wants to grab some ice cream then go bowling."

Before Kat could answer, Nina did. "That sounds like fun. I haven't been bowling in ages. If it's no trouble, Trevor and I will also join you."

"Of course." Leah sat down beside her. "The more people that come, the more fun we can have when Briley starts to lose."

"What?" Briley said.

"Oh, Leah." Nina high-fived her. "I like the way you think."

"I see how it is. My girlfriend and best friend ganging up on me. Fine." She turned to Trevor. "Are you any good at bowling?"

He grimaced. "Not really?"

"Fantastic." Briley clapped her hands. "Neither is Kat."

"I resent that statement," Kat threw out.

"On a good day, Nina has a fifty-fifty chance of beating me." She eyed Leah. "You're the wild card, but I think I can take you."

"You can try, darling. You can try."

This is what she wanted. Just spending time with friends and family. Competitiveness was in her blood, but she would take it easy on them tonight. After all, it was just bowling with friends.

Chapter Twenty

After the first game, Briley realized it was *not* just bowling with friends. The competition between everyone was more intense than the Mexican lasagna Mr. Balkin made a few years back that sent Briley and three other people to the hospital. She didn't know they had it in them, but she'd had a hard time staying atop the leaderboard and it was putting her in a foul mood.

Trevor had been correct in his own assessment. He was terrible, but was a good sport, and cheered Nina on. That's all that mattered and they did look good together.

"Your turn," Leah said, squeezing her shoulder and bringing her out of her thoughts. "Good luck, darling."

A quick glance at the scoreboard made her gasp. Nina had taken the lead. That would never do. She jumped up and blew on her hands. "Enjoy the lead, Nina, because it's about to be taken away."

"Promises, promises." Nina winked at her.

Briley picked up her ball, took a few steps toward the lane, and let it go. Automatically, she took two steps back. Her eyes were glued to the ball and she shimmied with her feet as it flew down the lane. She jumped up when she bowled a strike, turned around, and made a shooting gesture with her fingers. "Take that, Nina."

"Whatever. I'll catch up."

Kat stood and patted Briley on the arm. "Your lead won't last long."

"You only wish it won't," Briley shot back. She shook her head and sat back down by Leah, who curled into her side.

"I hope you're having fun. I know I am." Leah kissed her on the cheek.

"I always have a good time when I'm with you." Briley tried not to squirm at the chills that raced down her spine as Leah played with her hand. "Loads." She knocked on the table beside their chairs that was solid wood. "I'm winning, so there's fun in that."

"It didn't last long."

"What?" Briley jerked her head around to look up at the scoreboard, then down at Kat's look of triumph.

"Leah," Kat said, standing close to them. "Your turn."

"I'll be right back." Leah said.

As soon as she got up, Kat sat in the spot Leah had vacated and turned just enough to look at Briley. "I'm glad everything is working out with you two."

"Me, too. It feels like…" She adjusted her glasses. "It feels so good."

When Leah returned, Kat moved, allowing her to sit back down beside Briley. The feel of Leah's body next to hers had kept her mind muddled all night.

"Your turn, Briley."

"Already?" That was quick. She hopped up and approached the lanes. "So, Trevor." Briley heard Kat say as she approached the lane, but drowned them out. A strike would ensure her win and she loved winning. As soon as the ball left her hand, she backed up. When all twelve pins fell, she jumped up and high-fived Kat.

Briley ended up winning two of the four games

they played and was quite happy to get out of there near midnight. The drive home was quiet as Leah drove.

"I had a really good time tonight," Briley said when they reached Leah's front door. "We'll have to do it again. I have a feeling Trevor will be sticking around."

Leah hugged Briley tight. "He seems like a good man and a well-dressed one."

"That he is." She leaned down and captured the oh so tempting lips of Leah. The kiss quickly deepened, both lost in the moment. Briley's hands found purchase on Leah's hips and pulled her close. Before things could get heated, Briley pulled back with a gasp, and rested their foreheads together. "Wow."

"Wow, indeed." Leah buried her head in Briley's neck, then nipped her neck. "We have to stop."

"We should."

Leah took a step backward, grabbing Briley's hands and pushing her away. "Go home. We'll see each other tomorrow."

"I go to the nursing home at least twice a month to visit the residents. Most don't get visitors. Do you want to come with me tomorrow?"

Leah leaned back against her front door. "What time?"

"Nine." Briley took a step in Leah's direction, but she shook her head and held her arm out to keep Briley at a distance.

"You're dangerous, Briley." Leah ran her hand through her hair. "I'll see you tomorrow."

Getting her bearings, Briley turned and walked home.

Kat was waiting for her in the living room, and handed her a glass. Without asking what was in the glass, she downed it, and hissed as it burned the way down her throat. "Shit." She coughed.

"I've been thinking about what I want to do," Kat said after a few minutes.

It was about time. "What have you decided?" Briley kicked off her shoes and curled up in the corner of the couch.

"You ever watch the shows about tiny houses?"

"I binge watch them all the time. Brandon and I have actually talked about building them, but his interest isn't as strong as mine."

"That's what I would want to do. They're not for everyone, but there is a market," Kat said.

"In the last few years, the market in Garriety has grown eighty percent and they're in the process of changing a lot of city ordinance to allow more in."

Kat looked surprised. "Really? Tiny houses are something you would want to do?"

"Yes. I've done a lot of research. I'll get it together for you and you can compare what you've already come up with."

"That would be great," Kat said.

"Wow. It seems things are changing for both of us."

Kat slipped her arm around Briley's shoulders, pulled her close, and rested their heads together. "That's not a bad thing. Sometimes you just have to jump. I've never been as brave as you are being with Leah. I think it's time I start. Quitting my job and moving was the first step. It was hard. You make it sound easy."

"Easy. You're kidding, right? It's not going to be easy. Leah and I are both going into this with baggage and issues to overcome. Starting something is the easy part, sustaining it is going to take time, but time is something I'm willing to give. You might laugh, but I want the white picket fence and happily ever after."

"Briley, I think you're well on your way." Kat shook her head. "I love you."

"I love you too. Don't worry so much. Life is short, and she's hot."

Kat threw back her head and laughed. "Should have known you would find a way to include a Doctor Who reference." They fist bumped. "How are you feeling about things? Honestly?" Kat asked.

"Good. I'm feeling good."

"There is something else I wanted to talk about." Kat finished her wine. "I'm thinking about moving out." Kat tried but failed to keep a smile off her face. "I've been thinking about it for some time."

That was also a positive step. She didn't mind having Kat around, but had gotten used to living alone for the last two years and it was an adjustment. "I don't mind you staying with me."

Kat gave her a knowing smile. "Thanks, but I want a place of my own. If you could look for a house for me, that would be great."

"Where and what kind?"

"I like your neighborhood. If not this one, maybe somewhere around this area. As for style." Kat shrugged. "I don't know. I'm not really worried about the style."

"I can totally do that."

"I would love to have my own place by Christmas."

"Until a couple of months ago when you arrived on my doorstep, I never thought you'd move here."

"Me either." Kat kissed her on the head. "I missed you."

"I missed you too."

Kat untangled herself from Briley and stood. "All right. It's getting late and I was just waiting up to make sure you were okay."

"And for that, I love you." At the door to her room, Briley called Kat's name. "I'm really happy you're here."

"Me, too, Bri."

Chapter Twenty-one

Briley woke early with a pep in her step that she hadn't expected, considering how late she went to bed. In years past, she would bypass the second day of the Encampment, instead opting to take her leftover baked goods from the week to the nursing home for the employees. Today wouldn't be any different. It was still early, so she worked in silence for a couple of hours, preparing and loading everything into her truck.

After she hopped into the truck, she slipped into the driver's seat and started the engine. Leah settled into the passenger seat beside her, kissed her lips, then pulled her seatbelt on. It didn't take long to reach the first red light.

"Light's green, Briley."

Twenty minutes later, she pulled up beside the doors of the nursing home. Working as a well-oiled machine, Leah helped her carry the three boxes into the lobby. Briley informed her she was going to park the truck and would be right back.

When she entered the building again, she noticed Leah was talking with a group of three people and decided not to bother her. Instead, she made her way to Sharon, the day manager at the home. "Good morning."

"You as well. Everyone looks forward to you coming every month."

"I'm happy to do it. I'll help you carry this stuff to the break room, then I'll mingle. Everything is labeled as usual."

"Sounds good."

After everything was laid out, she and Leah quickly became separated again, but she didn't mind as she chatted with the usual suspects. After five games of chess, three of checkers and a half-hour of helping Mrs. Burlin with her puzzle, her eyes found Leah across the room. She smiled when Leah raised her hand in acknowledgement.

Leah excused herself from the man she was talking to and joined Briley. "Briley, how did you get involved with the nursing home?"

Briley motioned for Leah to follow her. They both leaned back against a wall away from the crowd. "When I first met Nina after I moved here, she asked me to join her, but I kept turning her down. I was busy and didn't really have the time to dedicate to any volunteer work. After a few months of her careful prodding, I finally gave in. Seeing all these people sad broke my heart. Sure, there are a few whose family visits them, but the majority only have each other." Briley leaned close to Leah. "See that woman sitting in the wheelchair by the window?" Leah nodded. "That's Hazel. She was married for sixty years before her husband passed away from a stroke. She has five kids, but four months after he was buried, her kids banded together and set her up here. They sold the house, almost all her possessions, and haven't been to see her for the past four years. I come here twice a month, sometimes more, because I can't stay away."

"That's the saddest thing I've ever heard." Leah wiped at her eyes and accepted the Kleenex Briley handed her.

"Sometimes, I still cry myself to sleep after a visit, but I can't not come. After nine years, they expect me and I may not be in control of a lot of things, but this I can do and I won't let them down."

Leah leaned sideways until their shoulders were touching. "I can't imagine the people you must have lost over the years."

"I talk to Nina. It's never easy. I used to play chess with Vern every time I would visit. It was a tradition, then one morning I woke up out of sorts. I can't explain it." She rubbed her arms. "When I walked in here, I just knew. No one had to tell me, it just felt different. Vern was a character and everyone loved him. It hasn't been the same without him, but life is a cycle."

Leah eyed her. "That's a good way to look at it, but that doesn't make it any easier."

"Oh, no. It really doesn't. It sucks."

"When we leave here, do you want to head to the park? Spend some time together."

Briley drew Leah against her side. "You mean like a date."

"No, Briley. Not like a date. An actual date."

"Your forthrightness is extremely sexy."

Leah buried her head in Briley's chest and chuckled. "I'll have to be more forthright then."

"Sounds good to me."

A few hours later found them both walking side by side along the river's edge, eating bowls of ice cream. Briley got her usual mint chocolate chip and Leah ordered rocky road. Their silence was comfortable as they continued walking.

"They have the best ice cream," Leah said, licking her spoon.

"They do." Briley finished her ice cream and held her hand out for Leah, who didn't hesitate to take it. Her hand was warm and reassuring clasped with hers.

Leah smiled and let Briley set the pace after they threw their trash away. "I can't believe we're really doing this. You. Me. When we first met, I didn't think it would be like this."

"No."

Leah shook her head. "No. It's even better than I thought it could be."

"We're just getting started. If I've already successfully wooed you, just you wait for the full-frontal assault. You won't know what it hit you."

"You have my complete attention. Well, until Evan comes home."

"When does he get home?" Briley held tightly to Leah's hand.

"Kathy is bringing him home a week before school starts."

"Nice."

"He loves spending time with his Ma and Griffin."

This is what Briley wanted all along. To just be with Leah. Enjoying her company.

"Did you have any pets growing up?" Leah asked after a few minutes.

Briley looked between their clasped hands and Leah's smiling face. "I had a cat. Mr. Whiskers. He died when I was seventeen and I haven't had another pet since. I've thought about getting another one, but haven't made my mind up yet. You?"

"I had a pet hamster when I was six and a Guinea pig when I was ten. After Harry, the Guinea pig, died, my parents let me pick a cat from the pound. Percy died a few years later. He was older when I got him, but he deserved a home just as much as a kitten did."

"They do."

"Evan's been asking for a dog."

Briley tugged on her hand to lead her down a different path. "Are you going to allow him one?"

"He's been wearing me down for the past few months. He'll turn seventeen two weeks before Christmas, and I'm going to take him to the pound to pick a pet out. I didn't realize we would be expanding our family so soon."

"He'll be so excited."

"I know and I feel he's ready. He takes excellent care of his little sister."

Briley grew quiet. "Do you ever wonder how we got here? I mean not just us, but every situation that people find themselves in. My mom and dad met at the circus. He wasn't even supposed to be there but changed his mind at the last minute. He said it was the best decision he had ever made."

"If you're asking if I believe in fate, I'm not sure, but I can't argue with it either." She shrugged. "Maybe we were meant to talk months ago, but it never felt right. There were plenty of opportunities."

"Just because we never talked, didn't mean we never communicated."

"That's true." Leah squeezed her hand. "If you're asking me if now is the right time for us, then I would have to say yes. It is…it feels right."

"It does." Briley smiled and tightened her hold on Leah's hand. It did feel right and that wasn't anything she wanted to argue with.

It didn't take them long to make a circuit around the park and make their way back to the truck. Briley grabbed a blanket out of her truck and laid it across the bed. After climbing up, and helping Leah up, they both laid back, looking up at the faint sprinkling of stars, smiling when Leah lay close to her and intertwined their fingers. If she moved her head just a smidge she could kiss her, but right now, the moment was perfect the way it was.

Briley was content to lay in silence, but after a few minutes, Leah lifted her free hand, pointed out several constellations, and told stories about each one. "When Evan was three, he took an interest in the stars and I learned everything I could about them. It was an experience for both of us. He loved it and I loved seeing his face light up. I could have made stuff up, but that felt like cheating. Madison never showed an interest."

"I would like to spend more time with him, if that's okay? I would with Madison as well, but she doesn't live here."

"Of course. Just to be clear, I've talked to both Evan and Madison about us and they're both on board. I believe Madison's words were, 'way to go, Mom.'"

"Smart girl. They're really okay with us being together?"

"They are."

Her kids' acceptance lifted a weight off Briley's shoulders. "That's good news."

"Madison wants to meet you before making up her mind completely, but she trusts my judgment and I have a feeling you'll both get along just fine." Leah raised their hands and kissed Briley's knuckles. "I can't promise I won't mess up, but maybe you can give me a nudge if I'm heading off course or I do anything that makes you feel uncomfortable."

"I can do that, if you do the same for me. I don't

plan on going anywhere."

"Me either."

Briley turned back to the sky, lifted their clasped hands, and brought them to her chest and cradled Leah's between hers. She lay quiet as Leah continued to speak about the stars and point out different things before they both lapsed into a comfortable silence. Briley was content just to lay next to her, when a kid screaming broke the moment. A quick glance at her watch showed almost two hours had passed.

"I guess it's time to go?"

"How about another date tomorrow night?"

Leah rose up and pulled Briley up with her. As soon as their feet hit the ground, Leah brought Briley down for a kiss that quickly became heated. "Yes."

"Yes." Briley knew she had a goofy grin on her face but couldn't help it. "Awesome."

"I'm dating a child."

"What? Where?"

Leah shook her head, then folded the blanket, before pushing it into Briley's chest. "Let's go home. I have some work to catch up on and you need to have dinner with your sister. Just because we're dating doesn't mean that you shouldn't spend time with her." Leah straightened Briley's collar. "I'm all yours tomorrow night."

"I like the sound of that."

"Impress me, Briley."

Briley brought her right forearm across her chest. "Challenge accepted."

Leah cupped Briley's cheek. "As it should be."

Briley reached up and squeezed her hand. "You have no idea what you unleashed when you decided to give us a chance."

Leah tilted her head and that signature grin broke out. "It's fun finding out, though."

"We have all the time in the world." Briley wrapped her free hand around Leah's waist, pulled her closer, and rubbed their noses together. "You haven't seen anything yet, tiny."

"I can't wait."

Briley pulled back, and opened Leah's door for her. "Onward home." Dinner with Kat tonight, then another date tomorrow night. Game on.

Chapter Twenty-two

Briley wiped the sweat off her brow, pocketed the rag, then pulled her phone out of her pocket. Her emotions had been from one end of the spectrum to the other trying to decide where to take Leah on their date. It eventually hit her that they didn't have to go anywhere in order to have a memorable night. They just needed to be with each other. Instead of overthinking it, she dialed Leah's number.

"Darling."

Chills raced up and down her spine at Leah's soft voice. "I'll be over at your house at six-thirty. We're staying in."

"Oh."

The surprise in Leah's voice set her heart racing, but she pushed on. "Yes and no need to dress up. Casual. Super comfortable."

"Our ideas of comfortable could be completely different."

"Well, I was going to wear sweatpants and a tank top."

Leah chuckled. "Will do."

"Don't freak out, I know exactly what I'm doing."

"I'll take your word for it and I'm not freaked. Quite the contrary, I'm looking forward to what you've come up with."

"I promise it won't disappoint, but if it does, I'm giving you permission to say I told you so later."

"How considerate of you."

"I have my moments." Briley looked up when someone in the side yard called her name. "I have to cut this short. I'm being summoned."

"Don't keep them waiting. I'll see you tonight."

"No keeping me away." The grin stayed plastered on her face for the rest of the workday, and even when she walked in the front door of her house. Kat looked up from the couch, where papers surrounded her, but didn't say anything.

Ever since Kat had mentioned the tiny house business, she'd been working non-stop on setting up the new business venture. It was good to see her motivated again.

Briley took her time in the shower and once out, dried off, then stared at her dresser. Without looking, she grabbed a bra and a pair of boyshorts out and slipped them on. Next, a pair of gray sweatpants, white tank top, Christmas socks, and a pair of sneakers. No makeup and she kept her hair down. Yep, super casual was the phrase that came to mind when she looked in the mirror.

Fancy dinners had their place, but eight times out of ten, it would just be them relaxing at home. There was no time to change her mind now. A quick glance at the clock told her she had less than fifteen minutes to be at Leah's.

In the living room, she opened the cabinet beside the TV and pulled out Rack-O, Sorry, and a deck of cards. She stacked them on the coffee table, ignoring Kat's pointed stare from where she sat on the couch, eating a cookie.

Bouncing on the balls of her feet, she shook her hands out, then made a beeline back to the cabinet and pulled out the first season of *Golden Girls*. With all her treasures in hand, she walked into the kitchen with Kat right behind her.

She laid her things on the table, took a basket out of the pantry, and put everything in it, along with a few cookies and brownies, then took a pint of vanilla ice cream out of the freezer. Satisfied with what she'd chosen, she picked up the basket, turned on her heel, and approached the door.

"Have fun," Kat called.

"I will." She bounded down the steps, took a deep breath, walked down the sidewalk, headed toward Leah's front door, and knocked. A few moments later, a smiling Leah opened it, dressed similar in a pair of cut off blue sweatpants and a black t-shirt.

"Don't just stand there." Once they were both inside, Leah dragged Briley to the couch, where they both sat down. "What have you got?"

Briley took a deep breath. "I can do fancy, but fancy isn't needed all the time. I want us to be comfortable with each other. Have fun. Do stupid shit. Just enjoy our time together."

"I want that, too."

"So, we've got three games." She held up the dvd. "*The Golden Girls* and dessert."

"Which we should put in the freezer."

"Nope."

Leah looked from the ice cream to Briley. "No?"

"Dessert first."

"Now that," Leah said, pulling Briley up, "is something I can get behind." Once in the kitchen, she grabbed two bowls and spoons. "What did you have in mind for dinner?"

"It's already been ordered and should be here by

     Shannon M. Harris

eight at the latest."

"Well then. Since this is your show, why don't you fix our dessert and I'll put the first dvd in."

As Leah walked by her, Briley pulled on her arm and gathered Leah into her arms. "You look quite fetching, tiny."

Leah feigned shock. "These old things." Her shock turned into a sexy leer, and Briley leaned down to kiss it away, but Leah turned her head at the last moment, so Briley kissed her cheek. "Time for that later."

"For the record, your ass looks fantastic in them."

"We've already established you're an ass girl, darling."

"Only yours." While Leah got the dvd ready, Briley dished up some ice cream and crumbled the chocolate chip cookies and brownies into it. Simple, but tasty. Leah was waiting for her in the living room, but she had pushed the coffee table out from in front of the couch and laid a blanket on the floor, where she already sat.

"I figured why not have a floor picnic while we were at it."

"No reason not to." Briley handed the bowls over, then plopped down beside her, grabbed the remote for the fireplace, and flicked it on low. The days may have been hot, but the night tended to run cooler. "Why not set the mood even more?"

"No reason not to," Leah repeated Briley's words, handed Briley her bowl back, then started the first episode.

Forty-five minutes later, their desserts were gone, and Leah was wrapped in Briley's arms, enjoying the show. "I'm probably Sophia, and even though Kat isn't a slut, she would be Blanche."

"Who am I?" Leah held tightly to Briley's arms.

"A combination of Blanche and Dorothy."

"You think?"

"Yes." Briley opened her mouth to say something when the doorbell rang. "That would be dinner." She reluctantly untangled herself from Leah, opened the door, then accepted their food. She carefully deposited everything on the coffee table, then grabbed two plates and silverware from the kitchen. Even from her spot in the kitchen, she could see Leah grab a piece of fried okra and put it in her mouth.

Instead of the normal take-out food, Briley had opted for good old southern cooking and no one did it better than Grandma Esther. With her bounty in tow, she sat back down and handed Leah her plate and the silverware. "The food's okay?"

"I didn't even realize they delivered. Evan and I have been a few times."

"They deliver two days a week."

"I'll have to remember that."

As the third episode played, they piled their plates with fried okra, collard greens, fried chicken, mashed potatoes, gravy, and a piece of cornbread. Dinner was a silent affair, but Briley enjoyed the fact that Leah savored the food just as much as she did. Two episodes later, the food was put away, the dishes washed, and they were just starting their first game of Rack-O.

Briley won the first game. "My grandma always enjoyed playing games with Kat and me when we would stay with her. This was our go-to game. It was hard after Grandpa died, but having us there helped some. We stayed with her as much as we could, or she would allow."

"My family was big on playing games growing up, also. I did the same with Madison and Evan. Evan and I still have game night a couple of times a month. I know he's getting older, but I love it that he still wants to spend time with me."

"You bet." Briley couldn't keep her eyes off Leah, even though it cost her the second game. The night was progressing just as she had predicted. It was rewarding when an idea came together.

Two hours later, the games were put away, the coffee table moved back, and they were snuggled together on the couch. Briley paused the show when Leah's cell phone started ringing.

"It's Evan."

"Take your time." Briley stretched out on the couch and closed her eyes. She didn't know how much time had passed, but she kept her eyes closed at the feather light touch that ghosted across her cheek and down her neck and didn't protest when her glasses were taken off.

She kept still even as the touch continued. After a moment of exploration, the touch stopped and Briley opened her eyes to see Leah sitting on the coffee table in front of the couch. A pleased smile on her lips, hair lightly damp. A quick glance at the clock told her it was eleven forty-five. She hadn't intended to fall asleep. "You know, a girl could get used to waking up like this." Briley stretched, then intertwined her fingers with Leah's and enjoyed the sensation of Leah's thumb brushing over the back of her hand.

Leah wore a knowing smile as she tilted her head. "You don't say." She squeezed Briley's hand.

With a racing heart, Briley rose, pulled her hand back, and placed both of her hands on Leah's cheeks.

Before Leah could even blink, Briley closed the gap between them, and her heart pounded as their lips met. At the first touch of Leah's lips, Briley knew there was no coming back from this. Before things could get out of control, Briley pulled away, but kept her hands in place, running her thumbs along Leah's jaw. "You always taste so good."

Leah gulped audibly.

Briley smiled. "I wanted to do that as soon as I walked in the door."

"I know." Leah grasped one of Briley's hands and kissed the palm. "You're not exactly a hard one to read."

"Oh, really?" The smirk on Briley's face vanished when Leah stood, took a step forward, and climbed on the couch, straddling Briley's lap. Briley tugged on Leah's waist and brought them flush together, locking her hands behind Leah's back. "Don't start something we can't finish, tiny." This felt right. She was ready, but this had to be Leah's choice.

Leah sat back with her hands around Briley's neck. "Is that a challenge? Because, I love a good challenge." She leaned forward and whispered in Briley's ear. "I want you, Briley. Do you want me?" She licked the shell of Briley's ear, then nipped it. Leah's grin when she pulled back was almost Briley's undoing.

Briley fought the urge to throw her on the couch and ravish her. This was their first time and she wanted it to be special. This was Leah, after all, and she deserved only the best. "Yes," she said, before lunging forward and capturing Leah's lips. The kiss was sloppy, and hurried, but perfect on so many levels. Briley tilted her head, slid her hand up Leah's back, and cradled her neck, as she deepened the kiss, pouring every pent-up emotion she'd built up over the last two months into it. When breathing became an issue, she backed off, and trailed open-mouthed kisses down Leah's jaw, then nibbled her neck, noting which spots along the way made Leah gasp for future reference.

Leah tightened her arms around Briley's neck. "God, don't you dare stop."

Briley growled deep in her chest and stood. Leah's feet hit the floor but she still clung to Briley and kissed her again. Briley grabbed Leah by the waist and lifted her up, her hands finding purchase on Leah's ass, and forcing Leah to wrap her legs around Briley's waist. She nibbled on Leah's ear and started fumbling toward the bedroom. Briley's heart pounded when Leah latched onto her neck and started sucking, causing Briley to fall backward into the wall. "Oh, sweet Jesus."

"Bed now." Leah nibbled Briley's ear.

Briley pushed off from the wall, entered the bedroom, and laid Leah on the bed. Leah giggled and moved to get comfortable. Briley grinned, then lifted her tank top over her head in an easy motion and threw it on the floor, along with her bra, before crawling onto the bed and hovering above Leah's body. Her arms settled on either side of Leah's shoulders and Briley moaned as Leah traced her eyes along Briley's chest, then she forced her eyes up to meet Briley's.

"Are you sure abo—?" Before Briley could even get the words out, Leah pulled her down and kissed her, trailing her tongue along Briley's lips. Briley moaned and pressed forward. Leah shifted underneath, sliding her thigh between Briley's legs, making Briley shiver even as Leah ran her fingers along her chest. "Christ," she moaned when Leah hit a sensitive spot.

Pulling back, Leah stared into Briley's eyes as her

fingers started at Briley's cheek, traced along her jaw, down her neck, along her shoulder, skimmed over her nipple, then moved along her side and settled on her hip. "Darling, we are going to have so much fun."

Briley's chest heaved and she got a wicked grin on her face. "You're a tad overdressed, aren't you?" Briley hissed when Leah ran her hands inside of Briley's sweatpants and cupped her ass.

Leah's lips quirked. "Then you should do something about that."

First, Briley grabbed the hem of Leah's shirt and lifted it over her head, then tugged on her shorts and threw them to the side, along with her own sweatpants and boyshorts. She lay down beside Leah, and traced circles on her stomach before latching her lips onto Leah's neck and kissing her way down her chest.

"Don't play games with me, darling. We both want this and we're both ready. Make love to me, Briley."

Briley felt as if her heart skipped a beat. Anything. She would do anything Leah wanted. With a tender smile, she settled her weight on top of Leah, then proceeded to do just that.

Chapter Twenty-three

With a groan, Briley rolled over in bed, covering her head with the blanket when it dawned on her what had transpired the night before. Instead of screaming, she pounded her fists on the bed and held back a squeal. It was then she realized she was alone in bed. Waking up with Leah in her arms would have been ideal but she wasn't about to complain. It had been both exhilarating and terrifying getting to hold Leah and be that close with her. The orgasms didn't hurt either.

She smiled as she stretched under the blankets, trying to work out the soreness of the night before. Leah may have been older than she was, but her stamina matched, maybe even surpassed Briley's. She would have to work on that. Briley lifted the blanket and hopped out of bed.

She grabbed a pair of Star Trek loungers and a tank top that was laying on top of the dresser, and smiled when she opened the bedroom door and the smell of blueberry muffins hit her full force. So, that was what Leah had been up to. Before heading to the kitchen, she used the bathroom, took a quick shower, found an unopened toothbrush and brushed her teeth, washed her face, and put her hair up in an unruly bun. She was in and out in less than ten minutes. The face in the mirror showed the same woman as the day before, but she was changed. There was no going back from this now.

She stopped at the entrance to the kitchen and leaned against the doorframe. Leah was standing by the stove, wearing the same sweatpants as the night before and Briley's tank top. It was a good look on her.

She greedily took Leah in. Her eyes trailed from her red painted toes, up her legs, and stopped on a well-defined ass that Briley had so much fun with the night before.

"I don't mind you looking at my ass, but breakfast is almost ready." Leah threw a wink over her shoulder. Briley rushed across the space between them, spun her around, and lifted her up into a hug. Leah giggled, tightened her arms around her neck, and kissed the underside of her jaw. "I take it you're happy to see me?"

"Uh-huh," she mumbled. "For a second, I was a bit disoriented when I didn't see you in bed, then I came to my senses and realized who in their right mind would leave all this sexiness behind if she could help it."

Leah threw her head back and laughed. "I'm afraid that you're stuck with me, darling."

"Is that so?" She kissed her cheek, watched as a myriad of different emotions cross Leah's face, and breathed a sigh of relief when Leah relaxed in her arms.

"Yes." Leah tightened her arms around Briley's neck.

Briley rested their foreheads together. "You make me so happy and last night was amazing. More than what I had ever wished for, tiny."

"Oh, darling, I know the feeling. I've been infatuated with you since the first time I saw you wearing those cut off shorts and holey t-shirt on your morning run almost a year ago."

"Well, now. Who knew I had so much game even then?" She buffed her hands on her shirt.

Leah leaned back, but kept her arms around Briley's neck, with a much too serious look on her face. "You don't see it, do you?"

Briley furrowed her brow. "See what?"

"You're amazing. Besides being gorgeous, you're funny, smart, loyal, trustworthy, and have a killer figurine collection."

"I…thank you. You make me feel amazing. I've always wished I was more like Kat, but I like who I am."

"I like who you are, too."

Briley squeezed her and lifted her up again. "I like who you are, too." The kiss that followed left them both breathless.

"Put me down." Leah pushed her away and took a step back. "I didn't slave over breakfast for it to get cold. Plenty of time for that later. You wore me out last night."

Briley snickered and raised her hand to tip her imaginary cowboy hat. "I do what I can, ma'am."

"I just bet you do." With a quick kiss, she sent Briley off to the table.

Briley couldn't keep the silly smile off her face as she took in Leah's bed head and make-up free face. She barely kept herself from picking Leah up and carrying her back to the bedroom or having her way with her on the kitchen table.

Leah started to fidget under her gaze and tucked a piece of hair behind her ear. "I know what I look like." She arched an eyebrow. "Which shouldn't illicit that look from you."

"Just try and keep this look off my face today.

Not going to happen." She reached out and grabbed Leah's hand. "You take my breath away."

"You really mean that, don't you?" Doubt crossed Leah's delicate features.

"I do and I'll make sure to tell you every day. Don't get me wrong, you always look amazing, but having you here, like this, in the kitchen, wearing my tank, eating breakfast with me, is everything."

"Still a charmer, I see." She winked.

"You haven't seen anything yet."

"Which I am looking forward to."

After the table was set with bacon, scrambled eggs, muffins, and toast, Leah sat down in the seat across from Briley. "I hope everything is okay?"

"It looks delicious."

They loaded their plates, and Briley was leaning across the table to capture the tempting lips in front of her again when the kitchen door slammed opened. They both jumped in their seats as Mrs. Hanlin stepped in, pulled the door shut, and set a basket of corn muffins on the table. Briley and Leah exchanged a look but didn't say anything.

"Good morning, ladies." Mrs. Hanlin looked from Briley to Leah. "I'm glad you two finally came to your senses and got a clue." She grabbed a plate and filled it with food before speaking again. "I hope you don't mind me barging in here like this?"

For the first time since Briley had known her, she looked nervous. Leah squeezed her knee under the table to snap her out of it. "Of course not, and you came bearing gifts."

"I know how much you like them."

"I do." Briley looked at Leah. "She's given me the recipe, but every time I make them, something is missing." She shrugged. "It's a mystery."

Mrs. Hanlin pointed her fork at her. "I just have the touch."

"Is everything okay?" Leah asked.

"Well, dear, I'm not getting any younger and who knows, my time might be up tomorrow, so I wanted to come and let you both know how much I love you. You both mean the world to me. I don't know if you're aware, but Mr. Balkin had a stroke yesterday. His son has decided he can't live on his own anymore and he's moving him into his house."

"I didn't know that. I hope he's okay," Leah said.

Briley reached across the table and fought back tears. "We love you, too. Anytime you want to talk, feel free to come over, or if you need anything, don't hesitate to call." She was only a few years younger than Mr. Balkin and the possibility that they would lose her anytime soon, or something would happen to her didn't set well with Briley. She may have been a busybody, but she was their busybody. Briley would make sure to keep a close eye on her.

"If you need something done, put Evan to work. The discipline will be good for him." Leah cut her corn muffin open and buttered it, took a mouthful, then moaned.

"Told you." Briley winked at her then got up, poured a cup of coffee, and placed it along with a glass of milk in front of Mrs. Hanlin. "Here you go."

"Thank you, dear. You girls are too good to me."

Briley ate her eggs as Leah and Mrs. Hanlin talked about her garden. When the conversation lulled, she addressed Mrs. Hanlin. "You can tell Mr. Balkin's son I might have someone who's interested in the house. As you know, Kat moved in with me a couple of months ago and asked me to start looking for a house for her."

"Oh," Mrs. Hanlin smiled. "That's wonderful news. She's such a good girl."

"It's going to be awesome having her close again." She squeezed Leah's hand. A warm feeling engulfed her when Leah smiled at her. She could get used to mornings like this.

Chapter Twenty-four

The next few weeks passed in a blur, from Kat putting the finishing touches on her business proposal and finalizing the sale of Mr. Balkin's house, to Briley and Leah working almost non-stop. Leah had hit her stride in her autobiography, which meant she and Briley didn't get to spend as much time together as they would have liked. Briley and Brandon had bought two more houses and were knee deep in renovations.

Today was the first day all three of them had the day off all week. Kat was going to join them for breakfast, but she had made plans for the rest of the day, leaving Leah and Briley to occupy themselves.

Briley had just taken the pan of banana muffins out of the oven when Leah opened the back door, walked in, and slipped her arms around Briley's waist. Briley braced her hands on the counter top and hung her head as Leah slid her hands under Briley's t-shirt and ran her fingers along the bare skin. "That feels good," Briley moaned.

"I know." Leah had just cupped Briley's breasts when a coughed jerked them both out of their haze.

"Don't mind me," Kat said, picking up her cup of coffee and walking off.

"Wait, Kat." Briley took Leah's hands out from under her shirt and kissed each palm. "Sit down." She placed a cup of coffee in Leah's hand and pushed her in the direction of the table. "Both of you. I'll finish breakfast."

Leah pecked her on the lips. "You're a doll."

"Leah, don't encourage her." Kat kicked the chair across from her out from under the table for Leah to sit down. "She'll get a big head."

"I think it's too late for that," Leah said.

"You could be right."

"You both do realize I am still in the room, right?" Briley set a plate of muffins on the table, along with a bowl of fruit salad and a plate of scrambled eggs and turkey bacon. "Dig in." She sat beside Leah.

"What do you have planned today, Kat? Briley never said." Leah stole a piece of bacon off Briley's plate.

"Shopping. Briley gave me a list of things I needed to buy for my house." Her face lit up at the last word.

"I didn't realize it was finalized yet," Leah said.

"Yesterday," Kat said. "Briley and I took a walk-through last night and for the most part, everything looks good. My first step is to renovate the master bedroom and bathroom. We made a list and I'm going to pick out what I like. We also sketched out the new layout for the kitchen."

Briley swallowed the last of her eggs. "I didn't know you were doing that today." She rested her arm on the back of Leah's chair.

"No time like the present. It'll be fun."

"Don't buy anything until I'm with you. We have to pick up a lot for the two houses we're working on and should be able to do a bundle lot. We'll throw in your items as well."

"Isn't that a bit dishonest?" Leah asked.

"I'll tell Jim what we're doing. He'll still give us a deal. You snagged an honest woman, tiny."

Leah reached up and latched onto Briley's hand that rested by her shoulder. "I'm starting to realize what a catch you are."

Kat groaned. "You two are gross." She winked, then stood. "Don't do anything I wouldn't do today. I'll see you two later."

"We'll consider your advice." Briley held Kat's gaze when the look on Kat's face grew way too serious for her liking. "Kat?"

"You two look good together and I'm really happy for you both."

Briley hopped up and engulfed Kat in a hug. "You freak me out when you're so serious."

"I'm just happy for you. I've never seen you like this before."

"It feels good."

"It shows." Kat kissed her on the cheek, before slipping out of her grasp and walking away.

With a sigh, Briley sat back down when she heard the front door shut and Leah plopped down in her lap. "I feel good, too."

Briley gave her a cheeky grin. "You'll feel even better shortly."

"Do tell." Leah slipped her arms around Briley's neck and leaned in close, licking her lips.

"How about you, me, and a bubble bath, for starters." She slipped one hand underneath Leah's shirt, caressing her back, then cupped her neck with her other hand, and pulled her forward into a kiss. Leah tasted so good. Briley deepened the kiss, bringing their bodies closer together. "You're driving me crazy." Leah tilted her head to allow Briley better access, and she trailed kisses up and down her neck.

"Your feeling is mutual." Leah cupped Briley's

cheeks. "The quickies we've had are satisfying, but I'm so glad we both have a free day." She ran her tongue across Briley's lips. "We have all day to play, but that bath does sound good."

There were no other words needed. Briley stood, Leah securely in her arms, and carried her down the hall to the master bedroom, depositing her on the bed. "Stay there. I'll get the bath ready." Once in the bathroom, Briley braced her hands on the sink, taking deep breaths to slow her breathing. It was confirmed, Leah was going to be the death of her.

When she renovated her home, she allowed herself the luxury of a large whirlpool tub. It was something she'd set her heart on, and wouldn't have backed down from. The price was costly, but well worth it. She hummed as she dropped a capful of soap into the streaming water. This was going to be awesome.

With a final look, she backed out of the bathroom, turned and stopped dead in her tracks. Leah was standing in front of the wall mirror, completely naked. She'd seen her naked plenty of times over the last few weeks, but this was different. Looking at her now, Briley couldn't believe Leah had chosen her. Full breasts lay atop a slim waist where several stretch marks were visible, a tight ass, and well-defined legs. At a cough, Briley raised her eyes to meet the amused ones of Leah.

"Like what you see?" She turned and planted her hands on her hips. They'd talked about Leah's insecurities the first couple of weeks they dated. Leah had been frank with her concerns and Briley had been honest. It didn't take long for Leah to realize how much Briley desired her.

Instead of speaking, Briley undressed, slipped

her hand in Leah's, who seemed surprised by her actions, and led her toward the bathroom. She cupped Leah's cheeks, kissing her softly. "Don't misunderstand my actions. I want you, and the sex is fantastic, but intimacy is more than sex. Right now, I want to take a bath with you."

Leah slipped her arms around Briley's waist and kissed her collarbone. "You're full of surprises, darling." Briley slipped in first, resting back against the tub. She took Leah's hand, helping her in, and gasped as she slid in between Briley's legs and leaned back. "Is this okay?"

"Perfect." Briley relaxed and slipped one arm around Leah's waist, who clutched onto the hand.

"I haven't taken a bath with someone in a long time." Leah ran her free hand down Briley's thigh.

"Me either."

"You and Beth didn't take baths together?"

Briley heard the note of jealousy in Leah's voice and smiled. "A few times. She didn't enjoy it. As for this tub, I had it installed a year after Beth and I broke up. So, this is the first two-person bath in this tub."

"Good, but for the record, I'm not a jealous person by nature."

"We all have our moments."

Leah sighed, then chuckled.

"What's funny?" This was absolute bliss.

"When I talked to Evan last night, he said that Kathy and Lilith were leaving early this morning to travel to a flea market a couple of towns over. He loves Griffin but was nervous about watching her all day by himself."

"I'm sure he can handle her."

"I wonder what they're getting up to."

Briley ran her hand along Leah's side. "Call him when we get out."

"I think I will, but this is our time together." Leah turned, straddled Briley's hips, ran her hands up Briley's chest, and settled them on her shoulders. Briley in turn gripped Leah's hips.

"Is there something I can do for you, tiny?"

"You're really okay with me being a mother and grandmother of two?"

"If you don't know that by now, I'm going to have to step up my game." She pasted a cheeky grin on her face.

"No, Briley. I'm serious. We've been having fun and I enjoy being with you, but it all seems too good to be true. Me. You. Everything."

Briley hadn't realized until this moment how unsure Leah was about them dating. "Leah, I care about you, more than I probably should, seeing as we've only been dating for a couple of months. I don't plan on going anywhere. I mean that. I want you and everything that entails." She tightened her grip on Leah's hips. "We're so good together. Will it be easy? Of course not. We'll fight. Have disagreements, and what not, but I'm not a runner. I never have been. What we have is something special. You're an incredible woman and I'm still shocked you want me."

"How can I not? You're everything I never knew I wanted. I will admit the age difference did give me pause. Though, you've never been bothered by it and I will take your lead on that. It doesn't feel like that big of a difference when we're together. I find myself thinking about you constantly. It's unnerving, but exhilarating at the same time. I've never wanted anyone as much as I want you. That's scary, right?"

"Terrifying because I feel the same way." She rose up, and pulled Leah against her. "Terrifying and beautiful. I don't scare easily, Leah. Nothing that could happen will run me off. I can promise you that."

"Nothing, huh?"

"Nope." Suddenly, this conversation had turned much too serious. Without blinking, she rose and dunked Leah under the water. A spluttering Leah's head shot out of the water, covered in bubbles. Briley doubled over laughing, then moved the suds from her face. "It's a good look on you." Leah tackled Briley, who fell back, head dunking under, only to come up a second later, full blown smile on her face. "I love that we can play together."

Leah smirked. "Oh, playing is what you want?"

Briley arched her brow. "If you think you can handle me, come and get me."

Three hours later found them dressed, and cuddled on the couch. After their bath, making love, then a shower, they decided to start in on the fourth season of *The Golden Girls*. Briley wrapped herself around a willing Leah, trying to focus on the show, but instead all her focus was on the woman in her arms. The woman she loved.

It was much too soon to say those three words, but she felt them. More so than she ever had before. Everything about Leah felt right. The moment was broken when her stomach protested its lack of food.

"What would you like?" Leah turned, and ran her fingers through Briley's hair.

"How about a grilled cheese?"

"And tomato soup?"

Briley made a face. "Chicken and stars."

"That's Evan's favorite also. Madison prefers

vegetable." Briley grumbled, but eventually they both got up and headed to the kitchen. As soon as the food was on the table, Leah's phone rang and she went to answer it. After ten minutes and still no Leah, Briley went looking for her. She found her sitting on the couch with her head bent, and the phone to her ear.

"Evan, calm down, sweetheart. Please…okay. Take a deep breath. Good. I'll be there as soon as possible, but it'll still take me at least four hours. Who's there with you?"

Briley sat down beside her and Leah grasped her forearm with her free hand. Whatever had happened was bad, judging by the haunted look on Leah's face.

"Okay. Put her on the phone." Leah wiped her eyes. "Helen, can stay with him? Thank you. I'm going to leave in a few minutes. Thank you."

Briley pulled her into her arms.

"Evan, please, baby, you have to calm down. Your sister needs you right now. I know." She closed her eyes and a sob broke lose. "I know. You don't have to talk to your grandmother if you don't want to." A pause. "I'll be there before you know it. Okay. I love you, too. If you need me, call me."

Briley didn't ask any questions when the phone call ended, only held Leah tighter when she sobbed into her chest. Leah grasped Briley's shirt.

"Kathy and Lilith are dead."

"What?" Oh, dear God. Poor Evan.

Leah accepted the Kleenex Briley handed her, but didn't back away from her embrace. "There was a pile up on the interstate. A semi lost control. They died on impact."

She didn't know what to say to that. 'I'm sorry' always felt like a slap in the face when her dad died.

"My poor baby. I've got to leave in a few minutes. He's scared and heartbroken."

"I can imagine. How are you feeling?"

"Numb. We haven't been a couple for years, but I loved her with everything I was at one point." She grabbed her phone from the coffee table and dialed a number. The conversation was short. "Madison and Bryan are headed there now. They'll make it an hour before me. Kathy wasn't her mother, but they got along and she'll be able to help her brother through this in a way I can't."

It hit Briley then that Madison had also lost her dad at a young age.

"Is anyone staying with Evan until Madison gets there?"

"Yes. Helen, she's Kathy's neighbor."

Briley pushed the hair out of Leah's eyes. "Do you want me to go with you?"

"No." Leah shook her head. "I know you're in the final stages of your flips. You have to be here."

"I do, but I would drop everything for you."

Leah traced Briley's jaw. "I'll be fine. I lost an ex, but Evan lost his mother. He's the one we should be worried about. Griffin is too young to realize what's happened." She scrubbed her hands down her face. "You'd really come with me?"

"In a heartbeat." Briley scooped Leah up and held her close. "If you need anything at all, don't hesitate to call me. Anytime. I don't care. You've hooked me, now you're stuck with me." Her joke had its intended affect when Leah gave a weak laugh.

"I need to go pack."

"I'll come with you."

"Okay."

An hour later, Briley watched a resigned Leah pull out of her driveway and drive off. She wanted to go with her, but, for the time being, would abide by Leah's wishes. If Leah had been too distraught, she wouldn't have had a say, Briley would have gone no matter what, but she wasn't. She didn't know what it was like for an ex to die, let alone two, but she did know what it was like to lose a parent, and Evan was going to need all his loved ones around him. Right now, that didn't include her. In time, she hoped it would.

Chapter Twenty-five

For the last ten days, Briley and Leah had talked every day, sometimes with Briley telling Leah a story to help her fall asleep. The funeral had been three days after they died. Now, Leah was having to deal with Kathy's irate mother, after the will was read two days ago, and Kathy left everything to Evan and Griffin. The house and property was to be sold, with all the proceeds being split between Evan and Griffin, and all their possessions put in storage until Evan, along with Griffin, could decide what he wanted to keep and get rid of.

Lilith had been an orphan and had no one to contest the will. On the other hand, Barbara, Kathy's mom, was not a happy camper. One, because Leah was named as executor of Kathy and Lilith's estate, and two, because they had left Leah as sole guardian of Griffin. To top it off, the only thing Barbara was given in the will was her own mother's jewelry that she'd given to Kathy when she turned twenty-one.

Leah had told Briley she'd agreed to be Griffin's guardian if anything had happened to Kathy and Lilith when Griffin was born, but she never expected it to come to fruition. To say Leah Harris overwhelmed was an understatement and Briley had to talk her down twice. Just from talking to Leah on the phone, Briley knew she was worn out, and fighting with Barbara was only making matters worse. On more than one occasion, she was ready to drive out there, but Leah insisted everything was fine.

She was brought out of her thoughts when Kat dropped a take-out bag on the table in front of her.

"Moping time is over. We're going to eat, then talk about our new business venture." A few days ago, Kat was approved for the business loan she'd been working non-stop to get. "She'll be home before you know it."

Briley drew her plate toward her. "I don't want to be selfish. I know things are going to change, but I've enjoyed our time together."

"And now you're not only going to have to share her with Evan but with Griffin as well."

"I'm such a shit."

"Bri, no." Kat grasped her hand. "It's going to be okay. She's going through a lot right now. She had to bury two people, deal with her son's grief, her ex-mother-in-law stirring shit, plus..." she squeezed her hand, "she's been granted custody of a toddler. Her ex's daughter. That's a lot to take in. On top of that, the selling of the house and cars and putting everything in storage. Things are changing, but they don't have to be bad."

"When you put it that way." Briley lifted her taco and took a big bite of it. Kat was right. It was a lot to take in. Instead of feeling sorry for herself, she needed to buck up and act like a grown up. The next time Leah called, Briley would be as supportive as possible. "What's on the agenda today?"

"Seeing as you don't have to work, I wanted to get your input on which building I should purchase and help me pick through the resumes that have been sent."

"Sure thing." Briley and Brandon both had decided to be a silent partner in Kat's business, but Briley would help Kat in any way possible. They all wanted this to be a successful venture. So far, Kat only wanted to hire one, maybe two carpenters to help her in the construction of the tiny houses. Kat planned to sub-contract the plumbing and wiring until she received her certification in those trades.

"Here." Kat slid over the folder with the properties when they were done eating.

Briley flipped through them and discarded two right off the bat. "That's too far away from the main roadways, and that one is too close to downtown. It would be a bitch to get a tiny house out of that property." She took three pieces of paper out. "These are good choices, but it would be better to see them in person. Two of these are with the same agency. Call them and see if you can set up appointments for today. Maybe they can fit us in."

"You didn't say anything about the price."

"Nope. They're all within your budget."

"But, this one is significantly lower than the other two." Kat pointed to one of the listings.

"True, but it might need a lot more work than the other two."

"You've already picked one out, haven't you?" Kat slipped everything back in the folder except for Briley's three choices.

"I have my favorite, but we need to look at them, and ultimately it's your choice."

Kat rolled her eyes. "I wanted you in on this for a reason. I trust you and you've already built a successful business."

"That's a good point. After you make your phone

calls, we'll go across the street and check on the progress of your house." The roof and siding had already been replaced, as well as the front porch and back deck. The electrical had been updated a few years ago, but the plumbing had to be completely replaced. The cost was extensive, but worth it in the end. It also allowed Kat to move her kitchen around the way she wanted it. Not to mention she wanted the small office beside the master bedroom knocked out to enlarge the master bath.

The scope of the project and the cost surprised Briley, but Kat got a fantastic deal on the house, and she'd padded her savings account quite nicely over the years. She joined Kat in the living room and sat down across from her in the recliner.

"The agent for the two properties can meet us at the first one in an hour and the other agent can't meet with us until three."

"Let's head over to your house, then drive to the first property."

"After you."

Forty-five minutes later, they pulled into the first property. A large metal building was situated on three acres of property right off downtown. The location wasn't ideal, but it was a nice plot of land. After the agent arrived and they walked the property, they both concluded this wasn't the one.

They both took a liking to the second property. From Kat's house, it would be a thirty-minute drive, but the land was ideal. A metal building was located on the edge of the four-acre property and two smaller buildings were adjacent to it. One of the buildings was a small bunkhouse, complete with a standard bathroom, and kitchenette. A twin bed was pushed up against the wall.

She pulled Kat off to the side. "You know, you can work this into the work offer."

"What? This place?"

"The craftsmanship of the building is on point. Invest a few hundred dollars and it will look good as new. Fresh paint, redo the flooring. Offer this place along with a salary. The other outbuilding you can turn into an office. It'll probably take closer to a thousand to get it the way you want it, but in the end, it will be worth it. Let's look at the main building."

Briley's eyes lit up when the large doors were opened and she got her first look inside. She had expected a dirt floor, but was pleasantly surprise to find concrete and concrete that was in good shape. Large beams ran across the ceiling and down the sides.

"Is the electrical up to date?"

"The building is only a few years old, and the entire building is wired along with being insulated. Instead of the standard sheetrock, the owner wanted plywood walls as an extra barrier. The building is also equipped with a heating and cooling system as well as a state-of-the-art ventilation system."

It was impressive and the price showed that. The ceiling was at least twenty feet tall. Kat grabbed her arm and dragged her away to a corner of the room.

"What do you think, Briley? It's perfect, right?"

"Yes, it is. You don't even need the other building for an office, since there's one in here, plus a bathroom. Whatever the owner wanted this building for, it was a serious venture. Do you have the paper for the other property with you?" Kat handed it over and they compared the specs. It was clear who the winner was, and it hadn't been Briley's choice. "I like it. With the size of the building, you could build two tiny houses at a time, and the land is large enough you could set four or five house out there comfortably."

"Me too." Kat looked as excited as Briley felt.

They walked back to talk to the agent. Kat allowed Briley to do the talking. "The property is amazing. The price on the other hand…"

The agent nodded her head and sighed. "You're not the first to be interested in the property, but the price has deterred people."

"Is there anything that can be done to get the price down? It's overpriced and I'm not just saying that. I've bought enough properties to know. It's overpriced by a lot."

The agent smiled. "What would be your ideal price?"

"Are you asking for a commitment right now?" Briley asked.

"Yes."

"I would feel comfortable and we're approved with a price at least thirty-five thousand off the asking price."

"Let me call my clients and see what they have to say. Do you mind if I ask what you want the property for? I know, Briley, you own Jacob Anderson."

Kat spoke up. "I'm starting a tiny home building business."

"I'll be right back," the agent said.

Briley and Kat leaned back against the wall, waiting.

"Do you think they'll come down?" Kat asked. "You were asking for a lot off."

"Are you nervous?"

"Yes."

Briley laughed. "It's hard to tell. Besides, I don't

expect them to come down that much. Fifteen off asking is a realistic price."

"That's still a lot." Kat ran her fingers through her hair.

"I thought you wanted this one."

"I do. It's just a lot. What if I fail?"

Briley cupped Kat's shoulders. "You won't fail. I won't let you. We've got this. There are plenty of people in your corner."

"I know."

They both looked up when the agent returned. "He wouldn't come down thirty-five, but he came down twenty."

Briley bumped Kat's shoulder. "I'll take it."

"Excellent. Let's go down to the office and I'll get your information."

While Kat filled out her papers, Briley called the other agent to cancel their appointment and had just ended the call when her cell phone rang. Leah.

"Hello, tiny."

"Darling, it's good to hear your voice. It's been a long day."

Briley sat down on the bench outside the real estate office. *Be supportive.* "It sounds like it. The last time we talked, you almost had the house cleared out. How's that going?"

"Good. The last of their things were put on the truck and it left for Garriety an hour ago. The only things left belong to Evan and Griffin and Evan has already loaded most of that in the Escalade. We're staying at a hotel for the next few nights and are leaving early Saturday morning to come home. Madison and Bryan left this morning, also."

"How are you?"

"Tired and sad. I didn't realize how much Kathy affected me until I had to say goodbye and pack up all her things. It was hard. Griffin doesn't understand. Barbara left this morning, also. We talked and even though she doesn't agree, she is going to abide by Kathy's will."

"How do you feel about that? You haven't said much about being Griffin's guardian."

"It's surreal, darling. Before the accident, I hadn't spent that much time alone with her. Now, my lap is the first one she crawls into. I don't know that I can do this, Briley. I'll be fifty-one this year. Evan will be seventeen and Madison twenty-five. My grandbabies are three and two, and now I have what amounts to another daughter. A toddler a little younger than Henry. I thought those years were over for me. I had planned on traveling after Evan went to college. Is being in my life really something you want? Because I'm quite the package."

"Don't be so hard on yourself. Do you remember me saying I wasn't running? Well, I'm not running. Granted, this isn't what I expected when I said it, but I'm here. Griffin is coming home with you and well, they made the internet for a reason. If I need to know something, I can just Google it."

"Briley, I can't ask you to put your life on hold for me. Not now. This is a huge undertaking. It won't be just you and me anymore."

Briley's heart beat fast in her chest. "No, it won't, but I'm here, Leah. I'm here waiting for all of you to come home."

"Maybe we should put a hold on the dating part of our relationship, and stick to being friends."

"That's...God." That's not what she wanted. She

buried her head in her hands, aware that she was starting to draw looks from people passing on the sidewalk. "Is that really what you want? Because if it is, I'll take a step back. But, if you're only saying this to give me an out, I don't want it. I want you and whatever comes along with that. Leah, I…I lo…like you. A lot. Like a lot lot." She wouldn't say those three words until they were face-to-face. "Evan is great, and I look forward to getting to know Madison and her family. Griffin is just icing on the cake."

Leah chuckled. "You've a way with words. Hold on, Evan just walked in. Stay with Griffin, I'm going out on the balcony to talk with Briley."

"Sure thing, Mom," Briley heard over the phone.

"Sorry about that," Leah said after a few minutes. "Evan dug through the car for the *Finding Nemo* dvd that he and Griffin are going to watch. He's doing better than I expected. It helped having Madison here with him. For three days straight, they went off together, and every time they came back, he seemed lighter. Madison made it clear to me that he still had a long way to go and for me to just keep an eye on him."

"I'll be here, too. I've been through what he's going through, as has Kat. If he doesn't feel comfortable talking with me, he can talk to her."

"You're a saint."

"Hardly." Briley nibbled her bottom lip for a moment. "Are you sure you don't need me to do anything for you before you get home on Saturday?"

"I'm trying to think. You can replace everything I had you throw out from the fridge, and Griffin has been eating some snacks I don't have at the house and I didn't expect Evan back for a few weeks."

Briley pulled up the note app on her phone.

"Name off what you want and I'll pick it up, plus the staples." Leah was hesitant, then started naming things. Applesauce, peach cups, fruit leather, cheerios, and a few things for Evan. "This might sound stupid, but you don't need diapers? Stuff like that."

Leah laughed. "I have plenty of diapers for now. When I get home, I'll have to stock up, but we're good on that front for now. I hope to have her potty-trained in the next six months."

Briley traced her fingers over the wood on the bench. "It'll be like I'm your own personal delivery person. At your service twenty-four-seven."

"At my service, huh? I miss you."

"I miss you, too. You'll be back in a few days and I'll be waiting for you."

"It's not going to be the same. I thought we had a few more weeks of it just being us and then Evan, but now there's Griffin."

"We can make this work. Please don't give up on us yet. Let's at least give this a try. I think we owe that to ourselves. I can even take Griffin to work with me if need be. I'm sure I can find a miniature hardhat somewhere." She'd start looking as soon as she got home.

"What am I going to do with you?"

"Love me," Briley blurted out, then cringed.

"Yes, I think I will."

It felt like all the air had been sucked out of her chest. Did Leah just say that? "A-awesome."

Leah laughed. "I have a few more minutes. Tell me what you and Kat have been up to."

Briley went on to recap their day thus far. "I'm really proud of Kat and what she's building. I think she's going to do well."

"I do as well. She's got a clear head on her shoulders and with you by her side, how can she fail?"

"Truer words have never been spoken."

"I can't wait until I get home to ravish you. I got so used to your kisses, I took our time alone for granted. That won't happen again," Leah said.

Briley felt like she was melting. "We all do that. The first opportunity we get, I'm going to rip off all your clothes. Well, maybe not rip off, but slowly remove, and lick you from head to toe."

"I look forward to it."

"Me too, tiny. Me too."

Chapter Twenty-six

The radio blaring out at them filled the ride to Marketplace the following Saturday as Briley pulled into the semi-full parking lot. She held up her fist and Kat bumped it. "Let's do this." Thankfully, the service area was empty of other customers.

"Can I help you?" the man behind the counter, whose nametag read Dave, asked.

"I need to pick up my order, Dave," Kat said.

"I'll need your ID." Kat dug in her purse for her wallet and handed over her driver's license. "Thank you." Dave handed it back. "If you'll wait, I'll go get someone to bring it out to you. The bed is in large boxes."

"I have a truck." Briley flopped down beside Kat on one of the three chairs situated across from the counter.

"This is exciting. Everything is coming together," Kat said.

"I know and it's a good thing your guest room is finished. That way we can put everything in there. The contractors told me they would be done with the master bath and kitchen by next Friday. So, barring any disasters, you should be able to move in next weekend."

"Thanks, Bri, for all your help. You've made this whole experience a smooth one."

"You're welcome." A moment later, her phone

rang. "Hello."

"Briley, we just got home."

Briley glanced at her watch. It was almost eleven-thirty. "You made good time."

"They both slept most of the way. I may just take you up on that offer of a nap."

"I aim to please."

"That you do and you're good at it." Briley could hear the smile in Leah's voice. "It's good to be home."

"I bet. Oh, they're bringing Kat's stuff out now, then we're stopping by the store. I'll see you in forty minutes or so."

"We'll be here."

Briley slipped her phone in her pocket and accepted the clipboard, comparing the items on it to the items on the long cart. Everything checked out. She handed the clipboard to Kat, who signed it and handed it back.

"We'll follow you," one of the workers said.

It only took a few minutes to load everything. Halfway home, Briley pulled into the parking lot of the grocery store. While Kat hunted down the items on her list, Briley headed back to the deli counter. "Good afternoon, Alice."

"Briley, how are you?"

"Good. Can I get five chocolate chip cookies and," she clicked her tongue, "five peanut butter cookies." She hadn't baked in the last few days and she wanted a few treats to take with her.

"Sure."

After Briley had her cookies in hand, she went in search of Kat. She had just passed an aisle when she did a double take. Garriety was home to an excellent minor league baseball team, The Meerkats. The team was aptly named after the world-renowned meerkat exhibit that the Garriety Zoo housed. A few of the players had set up a large table at the front of the store, selling jerseys and other odds and ends. How had she missed that when they first came in?

Briley gnawed her lip in thought, then headed toward the table. A smile ghosted her face when she took in the small jerseys. Surely, Leah wouldn't get mad.

"Briley, I know you have a couple of jerseys, but I will not be opposed to you buying another one," Kevin said. He was the Meerkats' shortstop.

"Not for me, no. I may need help though. I need four. An adult small, two larges, and I need one for an average sized two-year-old." Kevin handed over the adult sizes and his wife, Brenda, held up the other one. Briley almost swooned at the small size. "Will you be here tomorrow?"

"Yes," Brenda said.

"They are gifts. I'm confident the adult sizes are correct but if the small one is wrong, I can exchange it, right?"

Kevin nodded. "If you have your receipt. Oh," he said, and grabbed something under the table. "We have new hats and new stuffed mascots." He grinned and held up the hat and a stuffed meerkat with a jersey on.

The black hat sported a smiling meerkat logo and bright red piping along the edge. But the stuffed animal was the cutest thing she'd ever seen. "I'll take two mascots as long as they're safe for kids and I'll buy four hats if the players that are here sign one of the hats."

"You got it. We're doing a signing next Saturday."

He passed the hat to the next player. "You'll be able to get the rest of our signatures then."

"Will do."

"There you are," Kat said, stopping the cart beside Briley. She glanced at the jerseys and chuckled. "Getting them started young."

"Of course. Us Meerkats have to stick together."

"Damn straight," Kevin said, and high fived her. "Brenda, throw a few of those posters and some coupons in the bag for Briley."

"Already done."

Briley signed the receipt and accepted her credit card back and her bag. "Thanks, guys."

"Briley, have a good day."

"You, too." Briley handed the bag and her keys to Kat, then took possession of the cart. "I'll pay for this and you can head to the truck."

For once, Kat didn't argue. "All right."

Briley breezed through the line and was out the door faster than she expected. After depositing her bags in the truck, she handed off her cart to an older gentleman. Briley sighed when she sat down and slipped her seat belt on.

"Don't get tired now. We're just getting started," Kat said. "Are one of these jerseys mine?"

Briley kept her eyes on the road. "Yes."

"Really?"

"Why do you act so surprised? You're one of us now."

At the stoplight, Briley turned to Kat and voiced what had been on her mind for the past few days. "I don't know what I'm doing, Kat."

"Nobody does, and if they say they do, they're lying. Ashley has a kid."

"She didn't adopt her until she was six."

"Close enough."

It wasn't but she would roll with it. Twenty minutes later, she pulled into her driveway, turned the truck off, then stared at the house. When Kat tapped her on the shoulder, she looked towards Leah's house, where Leah stood with her arms crossed, staring at them.

"Briley."

She turned to Kat and swallowed. "I don't..." She shook her head.

"It's okay. She's waiting for you. You want this, don't you?"

Briley took a deep breath. "Yes. More than anything." She knew she told Leah she was ready for this, and she was, but it was still scary.

"Let's go." They both stepped out of the truck at the same time. Briley grabbed the jersey bag and a few of the grocery bags and Kat grabbed the rest. Kat was the first one on the porch, with Briley not far behind. Leah held the door open for them. As soon as she walked through the door, the change was evident. Griffin was asleep on a blanket on the floor and Evan was standing in the kitchen. They both set their bags on the kitchen table.

"I'm Kat." Kat held her hand out to Evan. "Briley's sister."

Evan accepted her hand. "Good to meet you."

"You, too. I bought the house across the street and need to unload the truck. Why don't you help me and we can give them some time alone?"

"Kat," Briley said. "That's not necessary."

"It's all right, Briley." Evan drew her into a hug that was so quick, she didn't even have time to be shocked. "I'll help Kat."

"Oh, okay." Briley ran her fingers through her hair.

Briley watched them until the front door closed behind them, then took her first look at Leah. There lay a heaviness that wasn't there before and she looked dead on her feet. Briley tucked a stray piece of hair behind Leah's ear. "Hello, tiny."

Leah clung to her and rested her head on Briley's shoulder. After a few minutes, Leah kissed Briley on the neck, then raised her eyes to meet hers. "You are a sight for sore eyes. I look a mess."

"You don't." Briley rested her clasped hands at the small of Leah's back. She looked like she'd lost some weight. Weight that she didn't need to lose. She was already so skinny. "You will always be beautiful to me." Briley kissed Leah's forehead then held her tighter.

"It's been a long couple of weeks," Leah whispered.

"You're home now, and you have me."

Leah nuzzled her nose in Briley's neck. "I hope you know how much I appreciate you."

"Well, you might change your mind when you see what I bought," Briley said, trying to lighten the mood.

Leah pulled back enough to look Briley in the eyes. "What did you do?" She arched her brow.

"Nothing bad, I assure you. I know you and Evan have been here for over a year, but I never saw you wear a jersey and I had to take care of that."

"Jersey?"

Briley squeezed Leah, then leaned forward, drawing Leah into a kiss. "What you do to me." Leah closed her eyes and smiled as Briley ran her fingers along her jaw, snapping her eyes open when Briley stepped away from her, and watched as Briley grabbed ahold of the bag on the table. "Are you aware that Garriety has a minor-league baseball team?"

"I was not."

"I figured. While we were at the grocery store, the team had a table set up, selling merchandise. I picked up something for you and your kids. Because, frankly, if we're going to continue dating, I have to know you're a supporter. I probably should have mentioned that before now."

Leah crossed her arms and tilted her head. "You expect me to wear the jersey?"

"Yes." Briley looked offended. "We have to support our team. Now," she clutched the bag in her hands. "We are sometimes made fun of because of our mascot, but the team is damn good."

"Oh, God." Leah planted her hands on her hips, but a smile played on her lips. "How bad is it?"

Briley looked properly offended. "Not bad at all. I find the mascot adorable. Seriously." She whipped a hat out and slipped it on her head. "Who doesn't like meerkats?" She grinned at Leah, who had a blank look on her face.

"A meerkat?" A smile blossomed on Leah's face.

"Not a meerkat. *The Meerkats.*" Briley pointed at the hat and winked at her. "Now." She pulled out a poster. "They gave me a few posters for buying so much. I don't know if Evan likes baseball, but they are having a signing next Saturday. I'm going and if he wants to get his poster or something else signed, he can come with me. The whole team will be there. It's like a mini festival." She fumbled in the bag. "Of course, Griffin and you and Kat can also come." She handed

Leah a poster, then set the bag on the table and pulled out the two adult jerseys.

As soon as Briley faced Leah, she felt a pair of warm lips settle on hers. Surprise quickly turned into desire. Briley clutched the jerseys in one hand and slipped her other arm around Leah, who deepened the kiss. "Wow." Briley licked her lips as Leah took a step backward. "What was that for?"

"For being you." She pecked her lips again. "Now what else do you have?"

"Okay," Briley said, still a tad dazed, and handed over one jersey to Leah, setting the other one by Evan's poster. Leah held the jersey up to her chest. "You are going to look awesome." Leah laughed and pulled the jersey on over her t-shirt and Briley felt herself falling just a little more. This woman amazed her. Briley snapped a quick picture. "Yep. Awesome." She clapped her hands and pulled a hat out of the bag. "I got Evan a jersey and a hat. I hope the jersey is the right size. Oh, you get a hat also."

Leah lifted Evan's jersey up. "It is. Briley, you didn't have to do this."

Briley nibbled on her bottom lip. "Well, there's more."

"More?"

Briley nodded and reached into the bag with both her hands. "Are you ready? I'm not sure you're ready for this, because I wasn't. Ready?" Leah nodded and Briley pulled the small jersey out and held it against her chest. Leah reached out and ran her fingers along the logo. "Cool, huh? If it doesn't fit, they're still going to be at the store tomorrow, I can exchange it."

"It's perfect."

Briley smiled and handed it over, then reached

into the bag one last time. "I was assured this was safe for kids. If you thought the jersey was cute, wait until you see this." She pulled out the stuffed meerkat in a flourish. "Have you seen anything cuter? I haven't. If Griffin likes it, the zoo has an amazing meerkat exhibit. We could take her, and Evan, of course."

"You're amazing, darling." Leah took the toy and jersey out of Briley's hands, laid them on the table, then slipped her arms around Briley's neck, playing with her hair. "We haven't been together that long. Most people would have cut and run. I'm glad you're not. I want you to stay. I like what we have, and I want to explore it more. Us. Explore us. Before, I had a grown daughter and an almost grown son; now I have Griffin. This isn't what you signed up for."

Briley tugged her closer. "I signed up for you and everything that comes with that. You're not giving yourself enough credit. Put simply, you're amazing and anyone would be lucky to have you. I know I am and I don't plan on taking that for granted. Will it be easy? No, but I don't expect it to. I didn't buy any of this to get in your good graces." Leah placed her finger over Briley's lips.

"I know, and that's what makes it so special." She sighed and played with the hair at the nape of Briley's neck.

"Okay then." Briley glanced to where Griffin lay asleep, then at the door, before whispering in Leah's ear. "We don't have enough time to fool around, do we?"

Leah shook her head. "That's a dangerous thing to say, darling."

"I can be quick."

"Not that quick. We should be able to carve out

some time just the two of us this week."

"Since Evan knows about us, I'm not opposed to sleepovers."

"That is also noted." Leah rested her forehead on Briley's chest. "You make it sound so simple."

Briley tightened her arms around Leah. "No, it's not, but what is, is our plan going forward. I just know what I feel for you and I don't want to run or hide from it. But, I will follow your lead. You sell yourself short. You make me feel, Leah. So much."

"You make me feel, too. Don't doubt that."

"I won't and if we don't get a lot of alone time in the next few weeks, well, I am a champion cuddler." She rested Leah's forehead. "I am not opposed to more strenuous activities either. I'm quite creative."

"Briley, I hope your wooing doesn't include having sex with me in your truck." She looked appalled.

"It's a nice truck. I could throw some blankets in the back, drive you out to some rural road, and we could look up at the stars. Plenty of pillows and snacks. Just you, me, and the night sky."

"That actually sounds romantic."

"Right. We've got this. We do."

"Are you scared?"

"Yes, and that's okay."

Leah leaned up and kissed her again. "We should probably check on Kat and Evan. He's been quiet all day."

Briley didn't mind the change in subject. In fact, she was grateful for it. She ran her hands down Leah's arms when she took a step back and picked up one of Leah's hands and kissed the palm. "It's not a bad thing if they're talking." She pulled Leah by the hand into the living room and stopped beside Griffin, who was dressed in a pair of pajamas that had bear cubs all over them. She was a gorgeous baby. "How long has she been asleep?"

"About ten minutes before you got here. You don't have to whisper. I found out she's a heavy sleeper."

Seeing the little person in the flesh in front of her was all too real. She watched, captivated, as Griffin's chest rose and fell. This was happening. The woman she was in love with was going to raise another child. Briley wasn't sure what she was supposed to feel, but at that moment, a surge of protection washed over her for the little person.

"I know what you're thinking," Leah said. "And it's okay. I thought the same thing. Seeing her makes it all real."

"She's so little and vulnerable. I'll protect all of you as long as I can."

"We'll protect you, too. Stronger together."

"You betcha."

They walked out onto the porch, where Kat and Evan were sitting on the steps side-by-side. Kat had one arm wrapped around his shoulders and they were staring into the yard. Briley and Leah sat down on the porch swing, watching them, but keeping quiet so as not to disturb them. It didn't take Kat long to notice them.

"Thanks, Kat." Evan jumped up, and kissed Leah on the cheek. "I'm going to my room."

"All right. I'll holler for you at dinner."

"Okay."

Kat stood and approached them then leaned back on the railing. "He's a good kid. We talked, but I'm not going to tell you what we talked about, but Leah, I have a feeling he's going to be okay."

"He's been so quiet."

"I know. We all grieve in our own ways, and this is just his coping mechanism. Don't push him and he'll talk to you when he's ready."

"Thank you."

Briley opened her mouth to say something when a wail broke the silence.

"I'll get her," Leah said.

"I take it, it went well?" Kat asked, when the front door shut behind Leah.

"Yes, it did."

Kat slapped her on the shoulder. "I'm happy for you."

"I'm happy for me, too."

"That's the Briley I know and love. This means no more moping, right?"

"Yes."

Kat grinned. "Happy looks good on you."

Briley shook her hands out. "Let's get in there and see if Leah needs any help."

"I think I've earned a cookie." Kat smacked her lips.

"I believe you have."

Leah was sitting on the couch, holding Griffin, who had calmed down. Kat sat in the chair by the fireplace and Briley sat down beside Leah.

"As soon as I picked her up, she fell back to sleep," Leah said.

Briley lifted her hand and raked her fingers through Griffin's soft black curls. If this was their start, she couldn't wait to see how everything else played out.

Chapter Twenty-seven

Instead of going to the park as they'd planned, Briley and Kat helped Leah move the bed out of the guest room and set up Griffin's things in there. With the four of them working together, they also moved Evan's bed, dresser, and desk to the finished basement apartment. It was equipped with a separate entrance to allow him a bit of freedom.

Evan had asked and Leah had agreed to allow him to move down there. He would be going to Garriety University in the next couple of years, and his plan was to still live in the apartment. Especially now that he had his little sister to think about.

Three hours later, Kat flopped down on the couch. "Since I was put to work, am I getting fed?" She said, eyeing Leah and Briley. Evan snickered from beside her on the couch.

Evan picked up a squealing Griffin and bounced her in the air. "We are hungry."

"I'm so hungry I could eat a horse," Kat said, rubbing Griffin's stomach, causing the child to giggle.

"Well, what does everyone want?" Leah asked, rolling her eyes, and sitting on Briley's lap.

"I vote Chinese," Evan said.

Briley pulled Leah against her chest. "I second that."

"Sounds good to me." Kat relieved Evan of Griffin and peppered her face with kisses.

"I'll order." Leah walked into the kitchen to place their order.

"So, Briley," Evan said. "What are your intentions toward my mother?"

Briley flipped Kat off, who was outright laughing. With the way Evan was regarding her, he may have phrased the question in an attempt at humor, but his face told another story.

"I care for your mom very much, Evan. I don't plan on going anywhere."

"Well, you do live next door."

"True. Let me clarify. I've never felt this way about anyone before. Your mom is special to me, and I'm not going anywhere."

"Griffin's not something you signed up for."

"She's not, but any relationship is about learning, growing, and compromise. I don't run when things get hard, or when the unexpected pops up. I'm terrified, but I don't think that's a bad thing. Do I know where our relationship is headed? No, but I know where I want it to. Getting to know Griffin is an added bonus. I don't really know you either, and I've never talked to Madison. It's a curve ball, but I'm a fan of baseball."

He stared at her for a long minute. "Mom deserves only the best."

"I agree." Briley kept her eyes on Evan, even though she could feel Leah's eyes on them.

"Mom said something about the Meerkats signing next Saturday," he finally said. "Thanks for the goodies."

"You're welcome." Briley was glad for the change in subject. "Yes, Saturday. The team will be there and we can get your poster and jersey autographed, if you want."

"I love baseball, but have never been to a minor league game before."

"You're in for a treat. I'm a season ticket holder and when it comes time for me to renew, I have the option to buy more season tickets. If you and your mom want, I'll add you two onto my plan. I'm already adding Kat. Kids five and under get in for free."

"Yes, we want that." Evan accepted Griffin back, who cuddled into his chest, clutching her meerkat in her tiny hand.

"Evan," Leah said, then turned to Briley. "That's generous of you, but we can pay for our passes." Briley shot her arm out and grabbed Leah's hand, pulling her onto her lap and kissed her cheek.

"My treat." She buried her head in Leah's neck.

"Evan," Kat said. "Get used to it. They do that all the time."

"I don't mind. It's actually pretty great."

"Yeah," Kat conceded, "It is."

After dinner, Kat left to go home, Griffin was asleep in her new room, and Evan was downstairs.

A quick glance at the clock above the fireplace confirmed it was only ten o'clock. Leah was asleep in her arms. She hated to wake her, but Leah would sleep better in her own bed.

Leah blinked a few times, then stretched. "What time is it?"

"Ten. I hated to wake you, but you'll sleep better in your own bed." Briley gave her a hand up.

"I'm going to wash my face. Don't leave. I'll get a second wind."

"Okay." Briley stepped into the kitchen, poured them each a glass of milk, and set out two chocolate chip cookies on the table.

"Those look good," Leah said. Before she sat down, she kissed Briley on the cheek. "You know," she said, after taking a drink of milk, "you could have told me I looked like shit."

Briley coughed on the drink she just took. "What? You look great. Tired, but great."

"How diplomatic of you."

"Just eat." Briley bit into her cookie. "Griffin still asleep?"

"Sound. I will warn you. She didn't always, but sometimes when she would wake up, she would crawl into bed with me. Evan said she used to do it with Kathy and Lilith."

"She's tiny, like you. I think I can handle her." Briley lifted her hands up.

Leah rested her elbows on the table. "That same tiny person kicked Evan out of bed when he slept with me one night." Leah pointed her fork at her.

"Well, I think I'm made of tougher stuff than Evan and I can handle you just fine."

"You can, can you?" Leah wiped her lips and pushed the plate away from her.

Briley made a muscle with her arms. "I'm a certified tiny handler."

"You're something all right."

"You like me."

"I don't think there was any doubt about that." They were both quiet while they finished their cookies. "I'm not sure I'm ready for this, darling. I never thought another child was in the cards for me."

Briley picked up Leah's hand and ran her thumb over the knuckles. "I would be worried if you weren't freaked out. I'm freaked out and she isn't my kid, but you're not alone. I'll be here. I am here."

"Briley, I think we both know where this relationship is headed. If things work out for us, at some point, she will be your kid. More so than Evan and Madison."

She knew that, but hearing Leah say it made it real.

"I scared you."

"No. Just thinking it and hearing you say it made it real." She licked her lips. "I'm not sure I'm ready to be a mother, but I think that's a role I could grow into."

"I think so, too. Do you think things are moving fast for us?"

"On one hand, it may seem like that, but we've been dating for almost three months, and before that we lived next to each other for ten. I know those don't really count, but it's fact. Kathy and Lilith's deaths were unexpected, and not something you can plan for. All relationships have bumps in the road."

"This is a bump?" She drew Briley's hand to her chest.

"I'm not trying to make light of their deaths."

"I know that."

"It's just." Briley sighed. "No one can plan for these things. I'm not about to throw away what we have because of the unexpected. I'm expecting a lot of unexpected for us and I'm ready." Briley picked their trash up and threw it away. As she started to turn back to Leah, she noticed a Bose system, for the first time, in the corner of the kitchen. "Is this wired through the whole house?"

"No, just the living room and kitchen. What are you up to?"

Briley hooked her phone up and found the song she was looking for. Before hitting play, she stepped toward Leah and held out her hand. "May I have the honor of this dance?"

A smile broke out on Leah's face and she placed her hand in Briley's just as the opening lines of *Small World* by Idina Menzel filtered through the speakers. Briley held Leah's hand to her chest and slipped her other one around Leah's waist. They swayed around the kitchen in complete sync with each other.

Briley kissed Leah's cheek, then loosened her hold and dipped her. Leah's laughter cut through Briley's soul and solidified the love she felt for this woman. Leah wrapped her arms around Briley's neck and gazed into her eyes. Briley leaned forward and captured Leah's lips as the final notes of the song played.

"I've underestimated your pull over me, darling. Now that I know what it feels like in your arms, I don't want to be anywhere else." She closed her eyes. "I'm not sure I'm supposed to feel happy right now."

"There is nothing wrong with feeling happy." Briley ran her hands down Leah's arms and grasped her hands, taking a step back in the process. Leah opened her eyes. "I would love to take you to bed and make love to you, but with the threat of a little one walking in, sex can wait. Just holding you tonight while you sleep will be enough." Briley shook her head. "I don't take that for granted. I know how hard it is to let one's guard down. You've allowed me this gift and I will cherish it. Sex with you is mind blowing, but allowing someone to see your tears, your anger, your sadness, your fears, is an intimacy all on its own."

"You take my breath away. Why couldn't we have spoken when I first moved in?"

"Things happen in their own time."

Leah walked back into Briley's embrace. "You're smooth."

"I only speak the truth."

"You're too good to be true."

"Not the case. If you were to make a list of pros and cons about me, I would have plenty of cons. I tend to procrastinate. I'm impatient, stubborn. I really like sweets, but only exercise because it's a tradeoff."

Leah silenced her with a kiss. "I wouldn't write anything in the columns. Across the page, I would write, I could fall in love with her."

Briley's heart started pounding and her stomach flip-flopped. "Well, ditto." Leah chuckled against her cheek, then kissed her neck.

"Your eyes give you away." Leah smoothed the wrinkle between Briley's brow. "That's not a bad thing. It's a reassurance. I still can't believe you feel anything for me."

"Oh, Leah. I feel everything for you." Briley glanced at the clock. "How about one more dance?"

"One more dance."

Chapter Twenty-eight

With a groan, Briley swatted at her nose. She kept her eyes tightly shut when a giggle reached her ears and she realized there was light pressure on her chest. She could feel Griffin's hair tickling her face. It all came flooding back to her. Sometime in the middle of the night, the little one had climbed into bed with her and Leah.

Leah had tried to apologize but Briley had only smiled and waved her words off. There was nothing to apologize for. Briley had laid on her side facing Leah, who was also lying on her side, and Griffin settled in between them. When Briley pictured her future, this wasn't it. Not by a long shot, but being here, in this moment, she wouldn't change a thing.

She cracked one eye open and Griffin leaned in closer to her.

"Hi." Briley opened her eyes and noticed Leah was sound asleep. She placed a finger over Griffin's lips then slid out of bed, and set Griffin on the floor. She led the girl out of the bedroom and toward her room. "Come on." Griffin hesitated. "We've got this."

After changing Griffin's diaper, and doing her business, Briley washed both of their faces, brushed her teeth, then helped Griffin with hers. She'd Googled everything she could think of so she wouldn't screw this up. "Let's go make breakfast." Briley picked her up and carried her down the hallway. In the kitchen, she plopped her in her high chair then rummaged in the fridge and brought out the blueberries, then plucked a banana off the counter and held them toward Griffin.

Griffin scrunched up her nose and bounced in her seat, making grabby motions to the banana. "Good choice." She bopped her on the nose. "Plus, I'm thinking eggs, and…"

"Sausage."

Briley turned to see Evan shuffling in, hair sticking up at odd angles. "Good morning."

"Morning," he grunted.

While Briley mixed the batter for the muffins, Evan poured all three of them some milk.

"I miss talking to them."

Briley turned from sliding the muffins in the oven and sat down across from Evan. "You can still talk to them."

He shook his head. "That seems so—"

"I know, but it helped me when my dad died."

"Kat told me."

"I still talk to my dad sometimes. It really does help."

"Maybe." He downed the rest of his milk, then filled the glass back up.

"Help me finish breakfast."

They worked side-by-side, scrambling the eggs and frying the sausage. "There is no right way to grieve," Briley said.

"It's okay not to cry." He sounded so sad.

"Yes, it is. I cried all the time, but Kat didn't. My mom shut herself away from us. It's different for everybody and that's not a bad thing."

He shrugged. "I don't know. Taking on Griffin is a huge responsibility."

"Your mom is on board with this. She really is. If she wasn't, she wouldn't have agreed to it in the first place."

Evan tilted his head toward the hallway. "Mom's coming."

Just as the words left his mouth, Leah walked into the room in her pajamas.

"We made breakfast, Mom."

Leah kissed his cheek, then Griffin's, then Briley's. "Everything looks good."

After eating, Evan excused himself and took a protesting Griffin to get dressed.

When the leftovers were put away and the dishes washed, Leah sat down in Briley's lap.

"Darling," Leah said. "You did invite Kat to go to the park, didn't you?"

"Yes, but hand me my phone and I'll send her a text." Kat answered back shortly. "She'll be here in a few minutes."

An hour later, everyone gathered in the living room. Kat had on her backpack and held Griffin in one arm, who looked colorful in a blue t-shirt and denim cover-alls that depicted a lion on the front. Briley had her backpack on and Evan had a firm grip on Griffin's stroller. Briley had already made one trip to the Escalade to deposit the cooler.

Briley lifted her phone and took several pictures, some with Kat, Griffin, and Evan making funny faces. "Everyone ready? I know I am."

"Let's ride," Evan said, leading the charge out the door.

Before Leah could walk through, Briley wrapped her arm around her waist and pulled her away from the door. "You look beautiful," she whispered in her ear.

Even wearing something as simple as a pair of green capris and a black tank top, Leah never failed to take her breath away.

Leah wrapped her arms around Briley's neck. "You're easy to please," she said, giving her a coy smile.

"Well, look at you. How can I not be?" Briley kissed her on the tip of her nose. "Seriously." She ran her free hand down Leah's arm. "You look beautiful."

"Thank you." Leah rose on her tiptoes and placed a soft kiss on Briley's lips. "You do as well."

Briley took the opportunity to attach her lips to Leah's neck and sucked at the spot right below her ear. Leah's arms tightened around her neck and she moaned. With a final kiss to Leah's lips, Briley pulled back. "They're probably wondering where we are."

"Your sister is good at distracting them. But," she let her hands slip to Briley's shoulders, then down her arms, where she clasped their hands together. "This isn't over yet."

Briley smirked, opening the door for her. "Promises. Promises."

By the time lunch rolled around, Briley was exhausted. All three of the adults ran after Griffin, but Leah had bowed out ten minutes ago. She reclined on one side of the picnic table they had claimed and Evan had met up with a few of his friends to play basketball.

"Briley." She turned slowly from Leah to Kat. "Griffin and I are going to explore." Kat motioned with her head in the direction of Leah. "Spend some time with her. I've got this." She nudged Griffin with her shoe. This caused the child to giggle.

Well, Briley guessed that settled that. Not that she was complaining. "Have fun," she called after them. If the way Kat was interacting with Griffin was any clue, Kat would probably be a mom in the next few years. She was a natural.

They'd decided on the smaller park, and even though almost all of the twenty picnic tables were full, it didn't seem that crowded. She knew most of the people here, but they'd stayed to themselves, opting on spending a quiet time with their family, like she was, instead of making the rounds and talking.

She made a detour to the Escalade and grabbed a blanket that lay in the backseat. She folded it and dropped it onto the concrete beside where Leah lay. The good thing about this park was that a few picnic tables were set on concrete and had a roof built over top of them to keep the sunlight out. They were lucky enough to snag one.

Leah was laying on her back with one arm covering her eyes and the other dangling by her side. Her head was resting on a folded hoodie and her sunglasses were on top of the picnic table. Briley was close enough to her that she rested one arm around Leah's stomach and ran the fingers of her other hand through Leah's hair. She didn't really want to disturb her but wanted to let her know she was there.

The emotions that flooded her when she was with Leah were almost too much. It felt like she was on the run and always dodging some obstacle in her way. The rush was intoxicating and addictive. It scared her far more than she wanted to admit. Leah held so many cards that made Briley afraid of coming on too strong or pressuring her into something she wasn't ready for. Everything was still so new. She rested her head on the arm around Leah's stomach and watched Leah's chest rise and fall steadily.

It felt like her heart was held in a vice grip, and

every time she thought of Leah ending what they tentatively had, it squeezed a little tighter. There was no denying their chemistry, but Briley wanted so much more than just a sexual relationship with Leah. She wanted everything. She closed her eyes, but kept running her fingers through Leah's hair. In the distance, she could hear Griffin and Kat laughing. It would kill her if she lost Leah. If she lost this.

"I can hear you thinking."

Briley smiled but didn't open her eyes, just enjoying the feeling of being with Leah. She sighed, then felt fingers run along her forehead then through her hair. "I didn't mean to wake you."

"You didn't."

Briley opened her eyes to see Leah staring at her. Her heart started pounding in her chest, as it always did when they were this close. God, she loved her. There was no denying that. She ran one of her fingers along Leah's eyebrow.

Leah's features grew soft, as did her voice. "I've told you before. Your feelings are written in your eyes, Briley."

She had. "Does it scare you?" 'As much as it scares me,' was left unsaid.

"Yes." Leah swallowed, but never averted her gaze from Briley.

"It terrifies me." Briley sighed.

"Oh, Briley." Leah tangled their fingers together, then looked up at the sky. "You have your whole life ahead of you."

She understood where Leah was coming from but was so tired of dealing with the age difference. Instead of telling Leah it didn't matter, she would continue to show her. "You make it sound like yours is over."

"Not over, but it is starting again. I love my grandkids, but I never thought I would be raising another child their age. I'd planned on traveling again when Evan went to college. If I was lucky, meet someone and travel with them. I'm not sure if you've noticed in the living room, but since our brunch with Mrs. Hanlin, I took your words to heart. I have a large mason jar that I've been filling with places I want to visit. Now, it's going to be at least sixteen more years before I can even touch that jar. I hope I don't sound bitter because I'm not."

"You don't. This isn't something that anyone expects. I don't blame you for being a little selfish or upset. It's okay to be upset and angry. Not at Kathy or Lilith but at the circumstances. No one will fault you for that." She ran her fingers down Leah's jaw, tracing her lower lip, and yelped when Leah nipped it. "No one, and if they do, that's their problem."

Leah opened her eyes. "Sixty-seven, Briley. I might not even be alive. Then what? Where will she go?"

Briley sucked in a breath at her words. "Don't talk like that. I could die tomorrow. Yes, the older you get, the closer death is, but dying of old age isn't a given, as we both are well aware. I'll be fifty-one. So what? You'll still be the sexiest woman at Griffin's graduation and the sexiest woman I've ever laid eyes on and you won't be alone. If for some God awful reason we don't work, Evan will be beside you." Leah looked at her disbelievingly and Briley hurried on. "You don't have to believe me. Not yet, but it's true. I'll show you. You make me weak in the knees, and it's still hard to formulate words around you. I get this weird fluttering in my stomach that I've never felt before. My heart feels like it's going to burst out of my chest every time you smile at or touch me. And your kisses are mind-blowing. The sex is the best I've ever had. I want you to be happy with me."

"You seem to be doing okay on the word front now." Leah grabbed Briley's hand and kissed the palm.

"I guess what I'm trying to say is," she gulped, "in for a penny, in for a pound." She knew Leah liked her, and they had agreed to give them a chance, but there was so much more to them than that. "Look, I don't want to scare you away, but you need to know I'm here for the long haul. I feel for you, Leah. A lot. You won't scare me off. I'm here and I'm not going anywhere. Whether it be as your friend or your lover, you don't have to worry about me leaving. Worry about Brandon and me screwing up a flip, or me messing up a recipe or spending too much on my hobbies or spending too much on your kids. Or Kat and I getting into trouble. I've had to bail her out a couple of times. I have a bad habit of leaving wet towels on the floor and I squeeze from the middle of the toothpaste tube. I love, love to put sour cream on my pizza, and I hate mushrooms. We have so much time to find out about each other and we will have plenty of time for worries. I just want to assure you that you don't have to worry about me suddenly leaving. I'm sure I'll get overwhelmed. No doubt I'll mess up. We all do. Probably say the wrong thing to you and your kids. I may even leave if I get angry enough, although I never have in the past, but if I do, I will always come back." She traced a heart on Leah's chest. "It's too much, isn't it?" she asked, without looking at Leah's face. Stupid. She should have waited.

"Briley." Leah's voice was soft.

Briley shook away her morbid thoughts and turned to Leah. "I'm sorry."

Leah pushed Briley's hand off her chest and sat up, patting the spot beside her for Briley to take. Briley reluctantly got up, placed the blanket on top of the table, then straddled the spot beside Leah. Leah mimicked her position and ran her hands along Briley's thighs without breaking eye contact. "Don't ever be sorry for sharing your feelings with me. It's such a good look on you. I can't help but believe you when you say you won't leave, but I also can't help but wonder if it's all too soon. I know we talked about this yesterday, but…I don't know."

"Maybe it is too soon." She tapped her fingers on the picnic table. "It's crazy, but a good kind of crazy. Don't you think? You don't have to be scared alone. We can be scared together. I'm not talking about moving in or getting married. That will come later if that's something we both want. All I'm talking about is spending time together. Just being together. Like we have been. Making something together. I'm all in for that. And let the record show, I'm okay with the kids that you have. I don't want any more."

Leah scooted forward and pulled Briley into her arms. "You always know the right thing to say. I'm scared, but I want this. You. I really do. I *want* us to make it."

Briley tilted Leah's chin up so she could look at her. "We're going to be amazing."

"You're so sure of yourself. So sure of us. It's refreshing. I've never had that before. I'm not sure what to make of it." She kissed Briley's lips. "It's not going to be easy."

"Who said it had to be? Anything worth having

is worth fighting for."

"Yes, it is."

A blinding smile broke out on Briley's face and her stomach filled with knots. She couldn't believe this was really happening. It felt so unreal. To have everything she wanted in front of her. Leah grabbed her hand out of the air and tangled their fingers together. Briley marveled at the softness of Leah's skin. She was pulled out of her thoughts when Leah spoke.

"Kiss me, Briley."

Briley didn't hesitate to pull Leah close and kiss her with slow deliberation. She wanted to savor the taste and texture that was all Leah. When Leah moaned, Briley deepened and lingered the kiss. She wanted Leah to feel everything she felt. This kiss was different from the rest. A promise of more to come.

Leah nipped Briley's lip before she broke the kiss. Her breath sounded hard and fast. With eyes still closed, she let out a low moan. "Wow." She rested her forehead against Briley's and ran her hands up and down Briley's sides. It was a feeling, no matter how long they stayed together, that Briley would never take for granted.

Chapter Twenty-nine

Briley settled down on the couch as Leah put Grif to bed. She'd wanted kisses from Briley and she'd been more than happy to oblige, but left story time to Leah. Today had been a good day. An eye-opening day. She was ready for Leah's moods to shift. It was a huge life change to suddenly take custody of her dead ex-wife's daughter. She closed her eyes, and laid her head back against the cushions even when the couch dipped beside her and a finger traced along her brow and down her jaw.

"What's that smile for?" Leah asked.

"You." Briley pulled away from Leah when she leaned in for a kiss. "None of that right now. If we start, it's going to be hard to stop and I have other plans. At least for now. Later is a different story."

"Really? Well, what are these plans?" Leah danced her fingers along Briley's thigh, and Briley grabbed them.

"You deserve to be pampered and I have the perfect solution."

"Do tell."

Briley leaned closer until their noses were touching. "A foot massage. Lay down and put your feet in my lap and relax."

A contented sigh escaped Leah. "That's sounds amazing." She did as she was told and laid back on the couch with her head on a pillow and her feet in Briley's lap.

"Just relax. I've got this." Briley slipped Leah's socks off, picked up the lotion, and started on her left foot. Each of Leah's moans sent shivers down Briley's spine, but now wasn't the time for that. This was about Leah's comfort. "What was your favorite gift at Christmas when you were young?"

"When I was growing up, my parents didn't have a lot of money. When I was eight or nine, there was only one thing I wanted. A camera. All my friends were asking for dolls and clothes, make-up, but I wanted that camera. I had a specific one in mind, but knew my parents would never be able to afford it. When it came time to write Santa a letter, the only thing I put on the list was a camera. I know my parents probably didn't think I heard them later that night, but they were talking about other things they could get me instead of the camera. I was disappointed but I would have never shown them that. They worked hard, and four or five years later, that hard work paid off for them, but that Christmas, money was tight. I went to bed Christmas Eve and promised myself I would not be upset when I saw the gifts under the tree. I woke up Christmas morning and crept down the stairs, scared of what was there. My parents were already up and they smiled at me when I saw only one gift under the tree. I don't know how they did it, and I never asked, and they never told me, but they got my camera. The one I wanted, with lots of extra film. Over the years, of course, they got me more expensive gifts, but none ever meant to me what that camera did. It was a fantastic Christmas."

Even as the story brought tears to her eyes, Briley continued with her massage. "That's a beautiful story."

"What about you? You can start on the other

foot." Leah wiggled her toes to get her point across.

"Let's see." She dug her fingers into Leah's heel. "I was twelve. Like you, all my friends wanted clothes, and stuff like that, but I had seen this chemistry set at a store. That is what I set my heart on. My parents were skeptical because I had never shown any interest in chemistry. Even Kat tried to talk me out of it, but when I have my heart set on something, I go for it."

Leah chuckled. "No, not you."

"You're sassy, tiny." At Leah's glare, Briley hurried on. "I woke up Christmas morning and there was my chemistry set. Not even wrapped, just sitting under the tree. Granted, I only played with it one time, but not because of my parents' reasoning. Kat and I had researched different projects we could try, both of us hopeful I would get it."

"Oh, no."

"Oh, yes. That Christmas I got my chemistry set and my mom got the new kitchen she wanted. I can't remember what Kat and I mixed together. If we had stuck to what was in the box, we'd been okay, but Kat and I never really played by the rules. I mean, it wasn't a big fire, but it ruined quite a few cabinets. It was a great Christmas either way. We all had a good laugh years later." She patted Leah's feet, then lay down beside Leah on the couch. It was a tight fit, but they made it work. Briley buried her head in Leah's neck, and Leah wrapped her arms around Briley's neck. "This is nice."

"It is."

"Favorite Halloween memory."

Leah settled her head on Briley's chest. "When I was a kid?" Briley nodded. "I don't know. One year I dressed up as Robin Hood. That was fun."

"I was six and I dressed up as the Pink Ranger. It

was awesome. I believe Kat dressed as a pirate. She was going through a pirate phase, and my parents let her run with it. She won the costume contest at school. I didn't talk to her for like two weeks after that."

"Yes, I have learned you're quite competitive. It's incredibly sexy." Leah kissed Briley's neck. "I do have a question though."

Briley held her closer. "Shoot."

"What *did* happen to my inflatable turkey last Thanksgiving?"

"What? That's not important." Briley fiddled with her glasses and avoided her gaze.

"I will ask again, but for now I'll drop it."

"You're too good to me," Briley mumbled into Leah's neck.

Leah turned in Briley's arms so they were facing each other and traced her finger along Briley's cheek. "Our lives are never what we expect, are they?"

"I think that's true to a point, but there are always unexpected occurrences. I like to think we, as individuals, do a good job of weaving our own paths. Tragedy is not something we ever expect and it can break your heart."

Leah didn't say anything and Briley wasn't going to push her. They lay still and Briley welcomed the silence. It was almost twelve-thirty. "It's almost one and I know how early Grif gets up."

Leah groaned and buried her face in Briley's neck. "I know it's short notice, but I have a favor to ask. You can say no. Don't feel obligated to say yes."

"Go on." Like Briley would ever say no to her.

"I have a doctor's appointment tomorrow and I need to run a few errands with Evan. It should only be a few hours."

"Kat and I'll watch her. Don't worry," Briley was quick to answer.

Leah pulled back to look her in the face. "Are you sure?"

"Yes." Briley kissed her lips softly. "I'm sure. I mean, how much trouble can she get up to in a few hours?" Leah looked skeptical. "Really. Two adults against one toddler. What could go wrong?"

"Briley." Leah chuckled, and kissed her cheek.

"What?" What had she missed?

"Just make sure you keep an eye on her. It's not about trust. I trust you with her, but she can get into a lot. A lot. Don't let her size fool you. Don't underestimate her."

"You make it sound like she's going to destroy the house."

"Okay." Leah kissed her. "You've got this."

"I do." Warmth flowed through her when Leah snuggled closer. "I mean, really," she mumbled. "How much trouble can she be?" She groaned when Leah snickered.

"More than you realize, but enough of that. I do believe it's time you took me to bed."

"When the lady speaks, I listen."

Chapter Thirty

The next morning, everyone had a leisurely breakfast. Kat had come over early and helped Briley cook.

Kat lifted her cup and took a sip. "How long are you going to be gone, Leah?"

"A few hours. I pray for less, but anticipate more."

It was as if no one had any faith in her. Briley rolled her eyes. "We've got this, Kat. Grif is tiny." She eyed Grif, who was sitting on Evan's lap, eating a banana.

"You're awfully confident," Evan said, wiping his sister's hands off.

"Is there a reason I shouldn't be? Leah hinted that she could be a handful, but she's been okay the last couple of days."

Kat ran her fingers through her hair. "And Leah and Evan have been with us, too. It's the first time she'll be alone with both of us."

"It'll be okay." Maybe the more she said it, the more she would believe it. With a kiss to Leah's lips, Briley sent her off for the day. Leah shut her door, and Evan shouted good luck out the window as Leah backed out of the drive. Briley shoved her hands in her pockets and walked back into the house. Grif was sitting on the floor, staring at them with a frown on her face.

"We've got this." Briley and Kat looked at each

other then at Grif, who was standing up with her tiny fists clinched by her sides.

Kat took a step in Grif's direction and she took a step backward. "You sure you've got this?"

"No doubt about that. Leah and Evan will be gone for a few hours. I have the perfect game plan, but I do have to make a quick run to the store," Briley said.

"What?" Kat jerked around.

Briley waved her hand in the air. "You'll be fine. I'll be gone twenty minutes tops."

"Fine. Go."

Briley kissed a frowning Griffin on the cheek, then hurried out the backdoor. Twenty-five-minutes later, she walked back into the kitchen. The house was quiet. Eerily quiet. After setting her bags on the table, she tiptoed into the living room and spied Kat and Griffin asleep on the couch. It was too cute not to capture and she took several photos with her phone.

Kat opened her eyes, but Briley held her hand up, indicating she needed five minutes. Walking quickly into the kitchen, she cleared the table, laid a large piece of craft paper over the top of it, then lined up everything she'd bought on top of the craft paper.

Instead of baking cookies, she'd bought four dozen pre-made sugar cookies, shaped like different animals. Some as meerkats. A dozen different sprinkle containers were lined up side by side, and a dozen different icing containers were set up on the other side of the table. She didn't know much about kids, but she did know baking and decorating. Who wouldn't enjoy decorating cookies and eating them?

That should take up a couple of hours, then a bath and nap time. Briley nodded, proud of her decision.

Briley swept into the living room, and stood by

the couch as Griffin started to stir. Wide eyes looked at Kat then at Briley. Before the tears could start, Briley picked up a fussy Griffin, carried her down the hall, and changed her diaper.

"Don't you feel better?" She wiggled her fingers like claws as Griffin giggled, then tickled her belly. Griffin made grabby hands. "What?"

Griffin grabbed Briley's nose. "Nose."

"That is my nose. You're such a smart girl." Briley kissed her cheek, and scooped her up in her arms. "I have a treat for you."

"Juice."

"You want some juice?"

Griffin bobbed her head and played with the collar of Briley's shirt. Kat held her phone up and took several photos of Briley and Griffin then followed Briley into the kitchen. Griffin's eyes widened when she took in the table.

"Cookie." She tried to jump out of Briley's arms, but she kept a firm hold on her.

"That's right. We're going to decorate them. Kat, can you get her a small cup of juice?"

"Sure."

Briley sat down at the table and settled Griffin in her lap, keeping her hands away from the cookies. "Juice first, then cookies."

When the juice was consumed, Briley set Griffin in her booster seat, and let her loose on the icing and decorations. It was messy, but so much fun. Briley couldn't remember a time where she'd laughed as much. She made sure to take tons of photos, and even managed a video or two.

An hour and a half, and twenty-six decorated cookies later, Griffin had icing all over herself, as well as Briley and Kat. Neither one minded since the smile never left Griffin's face. Most of the cookies weren't edible, but Briley had made sure to save a few that she and Kat decorated for Leah and Evan to eat.

Since not all the ones Griffin decorated could be eaten, Briley had set the majority aside to turn into ornaments. Surely, Leah would want to keep them; she knew she wanted a couple for her tree. Closer to Christmas, she would make some dough for the specific purpose of using them for ornaments, but for now these would do.

"While you give her a bath, I'll get this stuff put away," Kat said.

"Then lunch?"

"What do you want?"

"Let's keep it simple." Briley set Griffin on her feet. "Sandwiches, carrots sticks, milk. I think Leah had some blueberries left, also."

"I'll make it."

"Thanks." Briley pretended to be a giant lobster and chased a squealing Griffin down the hallway and into the hall bathroom. Before Briley could even ask, Griffin was undressing. "You like taking a bath?"

"Yes."

When the temperature was to their liking, Briley lifted Griffin up and into the tub, and gave her a few toys to play with. While Griffin occupied herself, Briley looked in the mirror. Staring back at her was an icing dotted face. She lifted her phone, took a picture of herself then one of a smiling Griffin, and sent them both to Leah.

It didn't take them long to clean up, and to Briley's surprise, Griffin didn't make a fuss when bath time was over.

They met Kat in the kitchen, where lunch was a quiet affair while they watched an episode of Sesame Street. Griffin seemed to be entranced with Big Bird and Briley made a mental note the next time she was in town to pick something up for her.

Their pleasant time together ended after lunch when Griffin ran around the living room, evading both her and Kat. How could someone so small run so fast? At that point, she was ready to tear her hair out, but Kat saved the day with yoga.

Watching both Kat and Griffin go through the poses was the cutest thing Briley had ever seen and she took a video and photos to show Leah. She'd already decided to start scrapbooking to preserve all the memories she was making. She knew it wouldn't always be this easy, but for now, she would take it.

Before bath time, Leah had sent her a text, informing her they would be later than expected, but Briley had assured her everything was fine. By the third rotation of the yoga poses, Griffin had decided she'd had enough and climbed into Briley's lap on the couch, curled up, and fell asleep. Kat, who flopped down beside Briley, followed her, hiding a yawn behind her hand.

"The little thing wore me out," Kat said.

"Me, too."

"It was nice, though." Kat looked at Griffin with a dopey grin on her face.

"Yes, it was." Briley kissed the top of Griffin's head and held her more securely.

"It looks good on you."

"What's that?"

"Motherhood."

"I'm not a mom, Kat, but I will admit that while

kids were never in the forefront for me, I don't mind this."

"Mom is going to freak."

"Mom's already decided she's spending Christmas overseas."

"I know." Kat rubbed her hands on her thighs. "The same as last year."

"This year's going to be different for us. We'll be with Leah, her kids, and grandkids."

"Different isn't bad."

"No, it isn't. It's awesome." Briley turned toward Kat to ask her a question, only to clamp her mouth shut when she noticed Kat was asleep.

She'd just closed her eyes when the slamming of a door grabbed her attention. Leah and Evan's voices carried into the house and she would have shot her a text message to keep it down, but her phone was in the kitchen.

Leah walked in, saw them, then quietly shut the front door, set her bags down, and made her way to the couch. She kissed Griffin on the head and Briley on the lips. "Tough day?"

"No, but as you can see, she wore us out."

"Thank you for the photos." Leah ran her fingers through Griffin's hair.

"You and Evan have a good day?"

"We did." Leah took her phone, then brought up a picture of an icing covered Griffin. "Not as good as yours."

"Just different good."

"Did you have anything in mind for dinner?" Leah asked.

"Whatever you want is fine. I'll be lucky if I don't fall asleep in my food."

Leah chuckled. "Why don't you and Griffin go take a nap in my bed? I'll wake you when dinner's ready." Leah shook Kat's shoulder. "You can go with them."

"Where?" Kat rubbed her eyes.

"You can either take a nap with them in my bed or here on the couch."

"As long as you have an extra blanket, I'll stay here."

Leah helped Briley and Griffin up off the couch then sent them to bed with a kiss. As soon as Briley's head hit the pillow, she was fast asleep with a squirming two-year old curled into her chest.

Chapter Thirty-one

Three hours later, Briley and Leah sat down for dinner. Kat had taken Evan out for dinner under the guise to get to know him, but Evan had been quiet all afternoon and Kat knew he needed someone to talk to. They left with the promise to be back no earlier than eleven. Griffin was tucked in bed after two bedtime stories and several kisses.

Leah lifted her glass of wine. "You were excellent with her today, as I knew you would be."

"Never doubted, huh?" Briley touched their glasses. "What was all the 'she's trouble' talk?"

"She's not all sunshine and kisses, Briley. She had a complete meltdown when we were packing up Kathy's house. *I* almost had a breakdown taking care of her breakdown."

"We had our moments, especially after the cookies, but Kat was wonderful and wore her out with yoga."

"I'll have to remember that. The cookies were a nice touch, also."

Briley smiled. "It *is* what I do."

"It's not the only thing you do."

Briley fanned her face. "I do declare. Miss, are you flirting with me?"

"If you have to ask, I'm not doing it right," Leah huffed, then drank the last of her wine.

"Never fear, tiny. Your lines will always draw me

in." Briley made a heart shape with her hands. "Right in the feels."

"Dork."

"I'm your dork."

Leah sighed. "If you must."

"I must."

"So, does that make me yours?"

Briley pushed away from the table and stood. Once she reached Leah, she extended her hand, which was quickly taken. Briley pulled a willing Leah into her arms. "Yes, it does make you mine, but not in a possessive, creepy, stalkerish way. In the healthy, compromising, partnership relationship way, then yes. Yes, it does."

"I can live with that." She racked her fingers through the hair at Briley's neck. "Evan and Kat will be back in less than an hour. Let's curl up on the couch."

"That's sounds like a fantastic idea." Briley flopped down on the couch, resting against the arm, and pulled Leah into her arms.

"Tell me something no one knows about you. Not even your sister."

After a moment, Briley answered. "That's a tough one. Kat and I share almost everything. First, I should say I do not like horror movies and I have an active imagination. Brandon and I had just bought our third house to flip. I was apprehensive about it. There was just something about the house that creeped me out. Every time I entered, dread filled me. Even after the house was finished, I still had a creepy feeling. It was late the night before open house when Brandon and I both left. Brandon was headed straight home, but I stopped at the store. He called me and said he had left his notebook at the house and asked if I would go pick it up for him. Well, I didn't want to, but I had never told him about my fears of the house. I sat in the driveway for fifteen minutes before I worked up the nerve to get out. I needed to feel grounded, so I called Kat and we talked while I went in the house and grabbed Brandon's notebook."

"What happened?" Leah squeezed Briley's thigh.

"Nothing. I was still creeped out, but talking to Kat helped. I never saw anything or heard anything. It was just a feeling I got. Even years later, if I'm not comfortable about a house, I speak up. I don't think I can go through that experience again."

"Did you ever find out why you felt like that about the house?"

"Do you believe in ghosts?"

"I can't say that I do, but I do believe spirits still linger on earth. If we can see them, I don't know. I never have, but that doesn't mean someone else hasn't."

"I still get an eerie feeling every time I drive by it. A family of five bought it a week after we put it on the market and are still there. It's stupid."

"No, Briley, it's not. Our feelings never are. My dad always told me to trust my gut. Your gut was telling you something was off. There is nothing stupid about that and nothing stupid about your feelings."

"Now your turn."

Leah was quiet for so long Briley thought she might had fallen asleep. "I caught my dad cheating on my mom one day on summer break. I was seventeen. I never told him or her. It changed the way I looked at him. I didn't talk to him for weeks after that. He couldn't figure out what was wrong and my mom tried to talk to me, but I blew her off. I never told either of them I knew. You're the first person I've ever told."

She tracked her fingers down Briley's chest.

"Jesus, that must have been hard." That blew her story out of the water.

"It was. It knocked him off the pedestal I put him on. I eventually talked to him again, but things were changed. My trust in him for me was still there, but my trust in his trust for other people was skewed. If that makes sense."

"Perfect sense. He and your mother had issues, but he still loved you."

"I think the only reason my mom stayed with him was because of the money. I vowed to only marry or be in a relationship for love. Not money."

"Well, then we know this is going to last. Because I live a comfortable life, but I'm not rich."

"Do you know what I enjoy about being with you?" Leah gazed up at her.

"I am all ears."

"Even when we're not talking, just cuddling, I feel so comfortable and safe with you."

Briley gave a quick nod. "I concur." She leaned forward and captured Leah's lips, but the hand pushing her away stopped her from deepening it.

"I'm not strong enough to say no to you tonight."

"You don't have too. I can stay tonight." Briley kissed her cheek, then drew Leah into her arms. "I love holding you just as much as I love kissing you. You always smell so good."

"Well, I'm glad my hygiene practices are working."

"Whatever you're doing, keep doing it."

Leah raised up and threw one leg over Briley's legs, straddling her and resting her hands around Briley's neck. "I don't know why anyone lucky enough to have you in their life would let you go."

"I feel the same way about you." Briley slid her hands under Leah's shirt and caressed the smooth skin.

"I would like to take the kids fishing before school starts." Leah pulled back to look in Briley's eyes. "Is that something you'd be interested in?"

"Fishing with you and your kids. Most definitely. Though, I should warn you. I was a four-time winner of Little Miss Bass in my hometown."

Leah smothered a smile. "Oh, I see. Competitive even then."

"What can I say? When you've got it, you've got it, and I do."

"Is this the point where I should swoon?"

Briley gave a mock scandalized look. "Yes, yes, it is. I am an all-around go-getter and winner."

Leah leaned forward and whispered in Briley's ear. "And if I was to say my dad and uncle were champion bass fishermen that took me with them all the time, what would you have to say to that?"

"I would say…" Briley tightened her hold on Leah and reversed their position, depositing a giggling Leah on the couch before resting on top of her and peppering her face with kisses. "I would say that we'll have this fishing trip well in hand." Briley kissed her again. "You make me happy."

Leah smiled and slid her hands up Briley's sides. "You make me happy too." She grabbed the front of Briley's shirt and pulled her down for a kiss right when the front door opened and Evan and Kat walked in.

"Told ya, Evan," Kat said.

Briley watched as Evan took his wallet out and handed Kat a ten-dollar bill.

"Really, Kat," Briley said, sitting up and helping Leah do the same. "You bet on us?"

"Why not?"

"Mom," Evan said. "Happy looks good on you."

Leah jumped up and engulfed him in a tight hug. "Thank you, but in the future, we'll try to be more careful."

"It's all right as long as I don't walk in on you two in a more delicate situation."

"I can guarantee that won't be happening," Briley said. "Considering the little feet running around."

"I'm going to bed. Night all," Evan called out, then continued on downstairs.

"I guess that's my cue to leave, also."

"Kat, make sure this one stays out of trouble tomorrow."

"Leah, as much as I like you, that's not a promise I can keep. Briley, we're leaving early. You're taking me out for breakfast."

"All right. Bright and early. I can do that."

Briley wrapped her arms around Leah from behind. "Ready for bed?"

"Always."

Briley would make sure tomorrow she and Kat went someplace she could buy a new fishing pole on their self-imposed sister day. She may have been Little Miss Bass when she was a kid, but she hadn't been fishing in almost twenty-five years. No time like the present to start back in.

Chapter Thirty-two

So, tell me again why we're at Bass Pro Shops?" Kat asked when Briley pulled into the parking lot.

Briley put the truck in park and pulled the key out. "I told you I need to buy a fishing pole."

"For your fishing trip with Leah?" Kat looked skeptical.

"And the kids," Briley added.

"Fishing." Kat patted the dashboard and Briley nodded. "What are we waiting for?" They'd woken early and had breakfast at a local diner, then sat by the river and watched the boats pass by. Kat had picked Turn the Page for another visit and Briley had sprung Bass Pro Shops on her.

"It's not that I don't like fishing," Briley said.

Kat arched her brow. "Bri, you don't like fishing."

"Come on, Kat." Briley ran ahead of her and stopped her with a hand on her chest. "I couldn't say no. She was so beautiful and she wants us all to go together."

"God, you're whipped."

Briley straightened her glasses. "You say that like it's a bad thing."

"Let's get this fishing pole." Fifteen minutes later and they were still standing in front of the fishing poles. "Just call her and ask what kind of fishing pole you need."

Briley planted her hands on her hips. "That feels like defeat."

"Oh, good grief. Then Google it." When Briley showed no move to do anything, Kat snatched Briley's phone out of her hand.

"Kat, don't."

"Leah, hi, it's Kat. Briley's good. Listen. Briley was too chicken to call you, but she left me no choice." Kat paused. "I know, but that's how she is." Kat chuckled. "You'll learn. What kind of fishing pole does she need? She dragged me to Bass Pro Shops and we don't know what to buy." Kat rolled her eyes. "True. Okay. I'll do that. Thanks." She handed the phone back to Briley. When she didn't take it, Kat wiggled her hand. "Here."

"Why did you do that?" Briley grabbed her phone. "We could have figured it out."

"She laughed and said she thought it was cute. You were cute. Quit freaking. Although, she did say she might have found something she can beat you at besides air hockey. And before you say it, no, we cannot go fishing today."

"I wasn't." She bounced on her feet. "Okay, I was."

Kat called over a worker and explained what they needed. He led them to a section and pointed at several poles.

Briley scanned the shelf and was drawn to the purple and black one. She picked up the Bass Pro brand Megacast rod and reel baitcast combo. The worker helped them pick out the right length.

"That's one of our most popular models. Are you going to be needing anything else?" he asked.

Kat waved him off. "No, her girlfriend said she'd take care of the rest."

"Have a good day," he said, walking off.

"You as well." Briley grabbed the pole and held it securely in her hand. "Let's look around."

"As long as we're here, I'm going to look at the hiking boots."

"I saw a few flannel shirts when we came in that I liked."

"Lead the way."

Two hours and several hundred dollars poorer, they huddled back into the truck. "Well," Briley said. "That was pretty productive."

"I agree, but I'm getting hungry."

"Your wish is my command. How about that new biscuit restaurant?"

Kat turned slowly to look at her. "Biscuit?"

"Almost every dish is centered around biscuits. My mouth is watering just thinking about their biscuits and gravy or their chicken biscuits. So good."

Kat punched Briley on the arm. "That sounds awesome. Why am I just now hearing about it?"

"Oh, it is and I don't know why." She put the truck in drive. "Don't hit me again."

Less than an hour later, they were seated and waiting for their food. They had both ordered the biscuit and gravy platter, with a chicken slider. Kat had opted for the sweet tea, and Briley, water.

"Everything okay, Bri?"

"It's going to be weird not having you around."

"I'm just moving across the street. Besides, you've spent the last few days with Leah. You probably didn't even know I wasn't there."

Briley flinched. "I've been neglecting you."

"No." Kat touched her hand. "I was just kidding. I'm looking forward to my first night in my house."

"Saturday?"

"That's the plan. The rest of the furniture I ordered will be delivered Friday morning. It's exciting." Kat rubbed her hands together.

Briley lifted her glass of water and clinked it with Kat's. "To being a first-time home owner."

"And business owner."

"That too. How are you doing, though? I might have fallen in love, but you've moved halfway across the country, bought a house, and started a new business." Briley frowned at Kat staring at her with wide eyes. "What?"

Kat leaned forward and rested her elbows on the table. "Do you realize what you just said?"

"Moving, buying a house, starting a business."

"Fallen in love."

"Huh?" Briley sipped her water and tried to remember exactly what she'd said. "Oh."

"Yes, oh."

"It just slipped out."

"That's a good thing. You're dating now. I believe you jumped around the kitchen telling me she's your girlfriend. This is just the next step."

"When the moment's right, I'll tell her, but I think it's a fine line I have to walk with everything that's going on with her."

Kat patted her hand. "You'll work it all out. Don't overthink it. You'll know when it's time."

Briley moaned when their plates were set in front of them. "Love talk later. Right now, let's focus on our food."

"Damn straight." Kat took a bite of her food. "Oh, my. These biscuits are so good."

"I know." She picked up her chicken biscuit and took a big bite. The flavors danced on her tongue and the flaky, buttery layers of the biscuit were a thing of beauty. "Wow. They always outdo themselves."

Kat pointed to the little card in the middle of their table. "That chocolate biscuit looks good too."

"It is." When the restaurant first opened, Briley had eaten the dessert for three days straight. "I'll have to bring Leah here," Briley mumbled around a mouthful of gravy.

"You do that."

After their plates were cleared, Briley motioned the waitress back over and ordered two loaded chocolate biscuits and two more to go.

"Really, Briley."

"What? Leah likes dessert and the kids will love it."

"I'm sure they will." Kat reached across the table and grasped Briley's hand. "I know I've said it before but I am really happy for you."

"It feels good."

"When we get home, deliver the dessert to Leah, then come home. I've already picked out the movie we're going to watch." Kat thanked the waitress when their dessert was set in front of them. "This place is heaven."

"Of that I'm sure."

Since the restaurant was in the city, it took them a little over twenty minutes to get home, but it was still only a little after eight. Briley knew Griffin would be in bed, but she knew from experience the dessert kept well over night in the fridge.

"Go, give her the dessert, but don't be long," Kat said.

"I won't."

Leah had the front door open even before she

could knock.

"I can only stay a few minutes, but I brought you and the kids dessert." She handed over her biscuit bag.

Leah lifted the bag so she could read the name of the restaurant. "Evan has been hounding me to go to this one."

"I've what?" Evan said, coming up behind her, until his eyes latched onto the bag. "What's in the bag?"

"The best dessert you've ever had," Briley said.

"Sweet." He took the bag from Leah.

"There's one for both of you. I figured you both could save Griffin some of yours."

"Sure thing." Evan winked at her, then bounded into the kitchen.

"The dessert is awesome, but so is the food. We'll have to go sometime. Be prepared. They're usually is a bit of a wait time, but it's worth it." Briley rubbed her stomach.

"You look nice," Leah said, reaching forward and straightening Briley's collar.

"Thanks." She stuffed her hands in her pants. "Why is this weird?"

Leah lifted her brow. "I don't know, but we can easily remedy that." She grabbed Briley by the collar, pulled her forward, and kissed her. "Much better." She smacked her lips.

"Yes, yes, it is." Briley lifted her up, and kissed her again. "You taste like strawberries."

"Ice cream."

With one last brush to Leah's lips, Briley set her down and backed away. "I would stay if I could."

"No, go spend time with your sister, and I'll enjoy my biscuit."

"It is so much more than a biscuit. You'll be

blown away." Briley mimicked explosives and Leah laughed.

"Goodnight. I'll see you tomorrow."

"Was there really any doubt about that?"

As soon as she walked through her backdoor, Kat handed her a glass of wine

"Let's get this party started."

"After you, my liege."

Kat laughed and patted the spot beside her on the couch. For the first time in a long time, Briley felt content with all areas of her life.

Chapter Thirty-three

The following Saturday, Briley paced in front of the couch with her hands clasped behind her back, with a glance thrown at the occupants sitting on said couch. "I know I've been over the game plan twice, but I just want to make sure you all get it."

Leah, who sat on one end of the couch with Griffin in her lap, rolled her eyes. Kat lifted a throw pillow and threw it at Briley, hitting its mark, and Evan sat back with a contented smile on his face.

"You've taught us well, Briley," Evan said. "Let us make you proud."

"This," Briley pointed at Evan, "is the commitment I expect from you two." She looked from Leah to Kat.

"Go. Go." Griffin clapped her hands together.

"In due time, Griffin." Briley ruffled her curls. "Now, I'm glad everyone dressed per my guidelines."

"Like we had a choice," Kat threw out.

"It was number one on your list, Briley. In capital letters outlined in a glitter marker." Leah shifted Griffin on her lap.

"Which was a nice touch," Evan added.

"Thank you, Evan. At least someone appreciates all my hard work getting us to this point. You're dressed properly; all the items on our list have been checked."

"Twice," Kat said.

"With all three of us watching." Leah shared a

look with Kat.

Briley grinned, knowing she was starting to irritate both Kat and Leah. It was fun, but a quick glance at the clock let her know they would need to leave in ten minutes. Today was the Meerkats' fan appreciation day at the ballpark. On top of the players having a signing, there were games set up, demonstrations with the players, food trucks, and a local band was set to play.

Briley took a few pictures of the couch, then slipped her phone back in her pocket. Everyone was wearing their jerseys, and had shorts on. She and Evan were wearing their ballcaps, and Griffin held tightly to her stuffed meerkat. "Let's do this."

"Bout time," Kat grumbled, shoving Evan back when he shoved her.

"Take her, Briley." Briley lifted Griffin into her arms and accepted the kiss she freely offered. "Do I get a kiss?" Leah slipped her arm around Briley's waist.

Briley grinned. "You get all the kisses."

"There's time enough for that later," Evan called out from the front door. "Let's go."

"The boy has spoken," Briley said.

"Then we must listen," Leah said.

Almost thirty minutes later, they were standing in front of the stadium. Leah gripped Griffin's hand tightly. "It's bigger than I was expecting."

"That's why," Briley said, opening the passenger door, and lifting out a backpack, "I bought this. It has a leash on it that any one of us can hold, but it will allow her the freedom to walk around."

"Madison has one of those for Henry," Evan said, taking it from Briley's hand and helping Griffin into it. She stood still while he adjusted the straps, and he slid the handle onto his hand. "I'll take first go."

Briley adjusted the tote on her right shoulder, then offered her other arm to Leah, who planted a kiss on her cheek, before taking her arm. "Kat, get a picture of us."

"Sure."

"Thanks." A moment later, Briley received the photo Kat had sent. She and Leah hung back while the other three walked ahead of them. "I'm writing this down on the calendar as a date."

Leah squeezed Briley's arm. "Have you written all of our time together down?"

"Yes. It helps me keep everything balanced in my life. I can look at the calendar and know when I've spent too much time at work and not enough with you or Kat and now it will allow me to set up some time that Evan and I can spend together, and Griffin, of course. And it reminded me tomorrow is nursing home day."

Leah squeezed her arm. "You surprise me every day, Briley."

"I hope that's a good thing." Briley waved at a few people she recognized.

Leah pulled her to a stop. "It's a very good thing." Leah leaned into Briley's personal space. "I hope I do that for you?"

"More than you know." Briley tucked the hair behind Leah's ear. "It's the little things. Knowing you care enough to make me lunch, and put cool stickers on the bag, is everything. The way you look at me is indescribable. Plus, all the post-it notes I find everywhere that you leave for me makes my heart sing. I've kept them all. Just knowing you've thought enough about me to take the time to write a note and put it in my lunch, or in my purse, or on the bathroom mirror…I've never had that before." She frowned. "I don't do those things for you."

Leah smoothed the crinkle between Briley's brow. "The foot rubs, spontaneous hugs and kisses, the impromptu dance sessions, the way you look at me, the way you treat my kids. Briley, I don't need fancy nights out, or expensive gifts; all I need is you."

Briley hugged her tightly, and felt an overwhelming surge of protection run through her. Leah was someone she could spend the rest of her life with. A woman she wanted to spend the rest of her life with. Briley moved her head so she could whisper in Leah's ear. "I love you, Leah." Leah didn't answer, but she fisted her hands in Briley's jersey. "With all that I am."

Leah buried her head in Briley's neck. "Oh, Briley." Leah looked up into Briley's eyes. "I love you, too."

A smile split Briley's face. "Yeah?"

"Yeah." She ran her finger down Briley's cheek. "I couldn't not love you."

"As it should be." She grinned and rubbed their noses together. "I love you."

"I love you."

"You two love birds done?" Evan asked.

"Evan, I told you it was something you'd have to get used to," Kat said.

Briley and Leah turned their heads at the same time. Kat had Griffin on her shoulders, and Evan had his arms crossed.

"How much did you hear?"

"Enough," Evan said. "I'm happy for you both, but the longer we stand in the parking lot, the shorter the fun we'll be able to have inside. Let's move." He clapped his hands.

"We're coming." Briley groaned.

"What's wrong?" Leah asked after they turned away.

"I had this whole date planned out where I was going to wine and dine you then tell you I loved you."

"I'm glad it happened today. Like I said, you're spontaneous and I love you for it."

Briley chuckled. "I see what you did there."

"We're good together. Let's enjoy our time with our family, then tonight you're all mine, Briley. From head to toe."

"Try and keep me from holding you tonight."

"Holding, huh? I can think of a lot more ways we can occupy our time and Evan wanted to spend a little one-on-one time with Griffin. I think it would be good for them. He's been missing Kathy and Lilith something terrible the last couple of days. So, Briley, how about we have our own sleepover at your house?"

It would be the first time they'd spent alone at Briley's house. "I think that sounds like the best thing I've ever heard."

"Another bath would be nice."

"Done."

Leah chuckled and pecked Briley on the lips. "Let's go catch up with everyone. I'm pretty sure it will only get better from here."

"I can guarantee that."

Chapter Thirty-four

A week later was date night with Leah. They hadn't had very many formal dinner dates and she wanted to make this one special. Even though Leah said she didn't need fancy, Briley knew that's what she deserved from time to time. More than once during the week, Briley had been fidgety and voiced her concerns something would go wrong, but Leah would always shut her up with a kiss. It was a good plan on Leah's part.

"Are you listening, Briley?" Kat said over the speakerphone.

It seemed like a good idea at the time to call Kat to help with the nerves she was feeling, but so far, it was a bust. "I'm listening."

"What did I say?"

"I…something about flooring."

Kat snorted. "I was talking about maybe buying a ferret."

"Oh," Briley frowned at the phone. "Are you sure? I could have sworn you were talking about flooring."

"I think you have Leah on the brain."

A goofy grin crossed Briley's face. "When am I not thinking about her?"

"I can hear the smile in your voice. There is nothing to be worried about. You've gone out countless times. Why so worried now? You love each other. You've got this and if something does go astray, Leah won't care."

"I know." Briley flopped down on the bed and picked her phone up, switching to Facetime. "I just want everything to be perfect."

"Oh, Briley. Nothing's perfect. Get dressed and have a good time. I'll see you tomorrow."

"All right. I love you."

"I love you, too. Now go."

An hour later, Briley was dressed. She opted for a pair of charcoal gray trousers and cream sleeveless V-neck silk blouse. She'd told Leah to dress up, though she wasn't sure she was prepared for seeing her. She lifted her phone when a text message came through from Evan giving her a thumb's up.

It was time.

With a spring in her step, she grabbed the red rose off the kitchen counter and made her way to Leah's front door. "I can do this." Before she could lift a hand to knock, the door was opened. It took her a minute to remember to breathe when she got her first look at Leah. "Hi."

"Hi."

The deep blue knee length sleeveless sheath dress with a plunging neckline that Leah wore set her heart racing. Her hair was down and a locket lay around her neck.

"This is for you." Briley handed over the flower.

"Come in while I put this in water." Leah took the red rose and smelled it.

Evan waved at her from the couch. "Have fun, but not too much fun."

"We'll try."

Leah kissed Evan bye, grabbed her shawl, and followed Briley out the front door.

"You look amazing," Briley said, opening the truck door for her. "You're always beautiful to me, but." She shook her head. "Wow."

Leah cupped her cheek. "You look nice as well. I love that outfit." She ran her fingers along Briley's bare arm, causing goose bumps to pop up along the flesh.

"I...Yes." Briley felt the heat of a blush. "We should go. I made reservations."

"Okay."

Briley didn't know why she was so nervous. It was just Leah. Her Leah. The woman she was in love with. She gave herself a pep talk before climbing in the truck. As soon as she clipped her seatbelt, she received a text message from Kat.

You've already got the girl. Calm down.

She took a deep breath, then turned to Leah. Kat was right. "I'm happy you're with me." She lifted Leah's hand and kissed the knuckles.

"I feel the same way. There is no reason to be nervous, Briley. It's just us."

Twenty minutes later, Briley pulled into the parking lot of A Midnight Tale, one of a handful of five star restaurants in Garriety.

Leah grabbed her arm. "Do I need to ask how you got reservations here? I heard they needed to be made months in advance."

Briley smiled coyly. "I called in a favor."

"Do I want to know how many favors people owe you?"

"After tonight? None."

A slow smile graced Leah's lips. "You called in all your favors for our date? I hope it's worth it."

"You will always be worth it."

After they were seated, and drinks ordered,

Briley reached across the table and held Leah's hand. "I can do fancy."

"That you can. I enjoy our time together so much." Leah unfolded her napkin and placed it on her lap.

"I'm glad.," Briley said.

"I also enjoy our time as a family and am looking forward to our fishing trip tomorrow."

"It's going to be great. I have a gift for you in the truck."

"What do you have planned? I can see the wheels turning in your head," Leah said.

"Dinner is only the beginning. Next is dessert and a special treat. One I hope you will enjoy."

Leah laced their fingers together. "Now you have me intrigued. A special treat like last night?"

A blush raced up Briley's neck. "Not exactly, but that can certainly be put in the game plan." She winked.

"Dork." Leah pulled her hand back when their drinks were delivered.

"Are you ladies ready to order?" The waiter asked.

After a spot of back and forth, Briley decided on the grilled lamb with roasted asparagus and mashed sweet potatoes, and Leah opted for the filet mignon with garlic roasted potatoes and sautéed green beans.

"What's on your mind, Briley?"

Briley fidgeted with her glass of wine. "I thought about being with you. How it would be. What we'd talk about. Just everyday things."

"I've thought of you as well. I hope I've lived up to your expectations."

"No." She shook her head. "You've far exceeded them. The fantasy doesn't hold a candle to reality."

Leah grinned. "I had set a plan in motion to talk to you, but could not get myself to carry through with it. I'd see you running a few times a week and see you out and about, but never in a million years would I have expected this. It blows my mind sometimes. The fact that you want me."

"I don't think I'll ever stop wanting you. If this is a dream, I don't want to wake up." Briley took a deep breath. "There is something I've been wondering about. Things changed for us after the toy convention."

Leah got a knowing smile on her face. "It did."

"Why?"

"Do you remember Captain America?"

Briley scowled, but softened when Leah squeezed her hand. "How could I forget?"

"Don't be so quick to judge, Briley. She told me that she knew my interests were elsewhere and she told me life was too short not to take chances. That's one of the reasons she came up to me to begin with. I took her advice."

"She gave you the push you needed?" That was not what she had expected.

"She did, yes."

Briley picked up Leah's hand. "Well, then, I'm grateful for her push. Though, we would have made it here eventually."

"Eventually, yes."

The waiter setting their food down interrupted them. He filled their wine glasses and walked off. Briley really had promised herself no more heavy or emotional talks, but that had failed. Time to bring things back down. "How is your steak?"

"The best I've ever had."

"Wait until you try Kat's. She is a master at

grilling." They were both content to share casual conversation for the rest of dinner, and when the waiter brought the dessert menu, Briley waved him off.

"No dessert?" Leah asked.

"Not here. All part of the plan." Briley paid the bill and offered her arm to Leah, who took it.

When Leah was seated in the truck, Briley took a package out of the back seat, then set it down beside her. "I know you enjoy photography, but when you showed me your collection, I didn't see one of these. I know this is a newer model, but when I was younger, I always enjoyed using it. I know we normally take pictures with our phone, but I thought this would be fun. I think Griffin will enjoy it and it's all ready to go." She handed over the bag.

Leah pulled a Polaroid camera out. "Oh, darling, this is wonderful." She then turned to Briley. "Smile." She lifted the camera and snapped a picture. When the picture came out, she shook it to dry it, and laid it on the dashboard. Briley made a gimme motion for the camera, then took Leah's photo, and one of them together. "This is fantastic, Briley. I had one years ago, and have been meaning to get a new one, but never got around to it."

"I figured we could buy a few photo albums and put all the pictures in. You know," she rubbed her neck. "Of all of us."

Leah grasped Briley's neck and kissed her. "You're amazing. I don't know what I did to deserve someone like you in my life."

"You moved next door to me."

There was a look of awe on Leah's face. "I did, yes."

"It's only 8:19, and our next destination closes

at ten. Still plenty of time to make it." Fifteen minutes later, they pulled up in front of C and C, Garriety's largest chocolate and candy store.

"Is the chocolate as good as I think it is?" Leah asked.

"Even better." Briley led her into the store, but bypassed the candy section and guided her into the chocolate portion of the store. The sheer amount of chocolate available was overwhelming.

Leah smiled. "Do you have something in mind? I'm sure you did when you brought me here."

"I do. You just stand there and browse, while I get our chocolate." Briley walked up to the counter and smiled at the girl behind it. "Can I get a twenty-piece sampling?"

"Which ones?" the girl asked.

"You pick."

The girl's eyes lit up. "No allergies?"

"None." Briley walked to Leah. "I was going to get some for the kids. I don't know what they'd like but you can pick them out some."

Leah gave her a quick kiss on the lips. "All right."

With Leah's items in hand, Briley paid for their order and not twenty minutes later, they were on to their next destination. "I wasn't sure about this last place and I hope you like it."

"I'm sure I will. Tonight has been wonderful."

When Briley pulled into an alley, Leah frowned but didn't say anything. As the truck left the alley, and pulled into an empty parking lot, save for one car, Briley knew Leah had questions. She put the truck in park and turned it off.

"What are we doing at the astronomy center? I didn't think it was open yet." Leah took off her seatbelt and turned to Briley.

"It's not. I helped the manager get a house and I asked him if we could get a sneak peek."

Leah's eyes widened. "Are you serious?"

"Yes."

"What are we waiting for?"

"Let's go." Briley grabbed their bag from C and C and a backpack from the back seat. She laced her fingers with Leah's and slid a key card into the slot on the door. It clicked and Briley led Leah in. Before the door shut behind them, a man was walking up to them.

"Good evening, Briley, and you must be Leah."

"It's nice to meet you," Leah said.

"You as well. I'm Harold and I will give you a tour, then leave you to it, Briley."

"Sounds good."

The building was state of the art, costing nearly twenty million dollars to build, and was set to open next month. It was steel, and glass, with dozens of interactive activities. Briley would have loved to have seen the planetarium, but that wasn't on the agenda tonight. She knew Leah wanted to explore, but they had a destination in mind.

Harold stopped at a door that led onto a large observations deck equipped with over a dozen telescopes. "I'll leave you two to it. Briley, you have two hours."

"Thanks, Harold." She pulled Leah onto the deck and set her bags on a bench. "How am I doing so far?"

"This is wonderful." Leah beamed. "Can we look through them?"

"Yes. The five in the middle are computerized and set to track and stay fixed on a celestial object, but the other ten we can adjust and explore." Briley had never seen Leah so excited before and vowed to bring her and the kids here when it opened. Harold had already promised her tickets to the grand opening. Briley watched Leah look through the lens of the nearest computerized scope. How had she gotten so lucky?

An hour later, Briley laid a blanket on the floor by the wall, and helped Leah down before joining her. From their vantage point, they could see the star splattered night sky.

Leah snuggled into her side. "I didn't expect this, darling."

"So, my powers to woo are still intact?"

"Your wooing powers are definitely intact."

Briley wrapped her arms around her. "I wanted to do something special for us."

"You've succeeded."

"I know I've said it before, but I'll keep saying it. I'm not going anywhere. You're stuck with me. I've gorilla glued our hearts together." Briley made a heart with her fingers.

Leah's chuckle quickly turned into a full-blown laugh, which Briley shared. Briley stopped laughing when Leah cupped her cheeks.

"I love you." Leah's voice was hoarse with emotion.

Briley closed her eyes and concentrated on her breathing. It felt like her heart was going to beat out of her chest. Her eyes flew open when Leah placed a hand over her heart. Briley brushed the hand away, pulled Leah into her arms, and peppered kisses along her neck. Leah had often told her she loved her since the first time she said it, but something felt different about tonight.

"I don't think I've ever left you speechless before," Leah said.

Briley closed her eyes again. "Every time you walk into the room you leave me speechless."

"I love you, Briley.

"Say it one more time." Briley grinned into Leah's neck.

"I love you." No matter what the future held, one thing was for certain—the risk was definitely worth the reward.

Epilogue

Briley hummed, adjusted her cap, then proceeded to staple the last of the Christmas lights along the porch. This was the last item on their to-do list for decorating the house. She and Evan had been out all morning, and he held the ladder steady on the ground for her.

They'd been working on the house and yard for the better part of five weeks, and she was finally happy with the way things were turning out. Multi-colored lights ran in straight lines along every available surface of the front on the house and the porch.

Griffin had picked out an inflatable Santa, reindeers, and sled that adorned the roof. Then Evan had the bright idea to turn the roof into a landing strip for the sled and had an elf directing it with a light. Briley hadn't been sure about it, but had admitted when it was up that it looked good. Dozens of snowmen, reindeer, ornaments, and elves that were made from wood pallets and painted accordingly littered the yard. One weekend, they'd made it a project.

Solar candy canes lined the walkway into the house and the driveway. Briley and Evan had debated for a week on what color to wrap around the big oak tree in the corner of the front yard. When they still couldn't make up their mind, Leah wrote all their choices on paper, threw them into a hat, and had Griffin choose. You could see the red from two blocks away.

After carefully climbing down the ladder, Evan high-fived her.

"This is awesome," he said.

"I know." She rubbed her hands together, and they both turned to the house next door. Briley had to admit Leah had done a good job. Mr. Balkin's decorations were placed in several sites in the yard, illuminated with spotlights. White Christmas lights outlined the windows and door on the front of the house. Red and green lights circled around the pillars on the porch and a large wreath that they had all made one weekend stood proud on the front door. Everything was subtle, but packed a punch. It was well done.

"Mom did a good job."

"She's good at everything."

He rolled his eyes. "You're only saying that because you love her."

"Touché."

She smiled when Evan pointed behind them, and they both turned and walked to the sidewalk. What used to be Mr. Balkin's house was decorated to the nines. Kat had gotten tons of decorating input from Mrs. Hanlin and Briley hoped that wouldn't give her an edge in the competition.

Several themes were scattered throughout the front yard. On one side was Santa's land, complete with Santa, Ms. Claus, and Rudolph. On the other side of the house was elf valley. Various elves were making toys, while others were climbing up a ladder that leaned against the house, putting up lights. In the center of the yard was Frosty and family. Multi colored lights covered the house and the roof. If she wasn't so sure of her and Evan's abilities, she would have been worried.

Kat had settled in well and Briley loved having her

just across the street from her. Kat grinned and turned her back on them so she and Griffin could finish their project. Ever since Kat had bought a pet ferret, she had quickly become Griffin's favorite person.

"I don't know why you two continue to stare at Kat's house," Leah said from behind them. Briley jumped at her voice, then relaxed when Leah slipped an arm around each of their waists and pulled them close.

"It looks good," Evan said, trying for cheerful, but it fell flat.

"It does," Leah agreed. "But, so does ours."

Briley continued to watch Kat and Griffin, then shook herself out of her thoughts and turned to Evan. "But, we have a secret weapon." She fist bumped Evan.

Leah groaned. "What have you two done now?" She took a step away from them and crossed her arms. She would have cut more of an intimidating pose if she hadn't been bundled in her coat, scarf, and green hat that was designed to look like a Christmas tree, down to the star on top.

Evan had picked hats out for all of them the previous week on a shopping trip at the mall. Briley and Griffin had been on board from the start, but Leah had taken a little convincing. She eventually gave in when Evan had chosen an elf hat for himself and Briley got designated the reindeer one and Griffin the snowman one. He'd even bought a Santa hat for Kat and a miniature one for Jackson, the Yorkie he had picked out from the shelter for his birthday. What sealed the deal was the hat designed to look like a tree they had bought for Stripes, Kat's ferret.

For the last several months, Griffin had been obsessed with kittens, but had warmed up to Jackson and Stripes. What Griffin didn't know was that Briley had picked up a kitten from a neighbor a few houses down a couple of weeks ago, with Leah's permission, and was letting her interact with Jackson and Stripes daily at her house, to get them used to each other. It was one of Griffin's Christmas presents. It was a tough decision, but once she and Leah saw how careful Griffin was with Jackson and Stripes, they decided to go for it. And if all else failed, Briley had already fallen in love with the kitten, so she would claim her.

"It's all good, Mom." Evan kissed her on the cheek.

"Yes, it's all good, tiny." Briley grinned and kissed the other cheek.

Leah didn't look convinced. "What have you two done?"

Briley bounced on her feet. She couldn't help it. Christmas was her favorite holiday. "All the lights on the house are synchronized to Jingle Bells." They'd tried to synchronize all the lights on the property, but came up short. It was still a win in her mind anyway.

"It's so cool," Evan said, grinning.

Leah looked between them, then cut her eyes to the house. "Does it work? Because I don't remember you trying it."

"Of course it works."

"Duh, Mom."

"Look." Briley sighed. "Last week Evan and I arranged to meet in the middle of the night and we tried it." She waited for the reprimand to come but it never did.

Leah smiled at her. "I know."

"How?"

"I got up with Griffin and noticed the lights. You and Evan were standing in the front yard, huddled together, talking. I didn't want to disturb you two. It looked like an intense conversation."

"We're so winning." Briley smiled.

Leah pulled out her phone and took a few pictures of them both posing and making funny faces. "Let's head in. I have hot chocolate and cookies." Evan didn't need to be told twice and took off for the house. Leah motioned Kat to join them and she nodded.

Briley touched Leah's arm, causing her to stop, then slipped her arms around her waist and pulled her close against her before dropping a kiss on the tip of her nose. "I love you."

"I love you, too."

Briley would never tire of hearing that one phrase. "Hmmm. There is something I've been meaning to talk to you about." She sighed and bunched her hands in Leah's coat to gather her nerve.

"You know you can talk to me about anything." Leah pushed the hair out of Briley's eyes and pressed closer against her.

"Yes. This is different, though. Okay. These past months have been amazing and I…"

"Just spit it out."

"Will you and the kids move in with me?" Briley started to doubt her decision when the seconds passed without an answer from Leah. "I mean…"

Leah shut her up with a kiss. "Yes." She tangled her fingers around Briley's neck.

God, that was easier than she expected. "Yes. Good. But, we don't have to move into my house. I mean yours has the awesome kitchen and basement, and the kids are used to it. I just don't want to miss out on anything with all of you and even though I only live next door and spend most of my free time with you all, it's not enough anymore."

Shivers raced down Briley's spine when Leah kissed the spot right below her ear. "God, I love you so much. I didn't think this type of love was possible, but here we are."

"You bet, and I don't plan on going anywhere. I'm afraid you're stuck with me."

Leah teased. "Careful, Briley, that almost sounded like a proposal."

"It wasn't, but for the record, when I do propose, there won't be any doubt what I'm asking." Briley kissed the tip of Leah's nose.

"Well, at least you haven't lost your charm." She laughed and pulled Briley toward the front door.

"You bring it out in me." Once in the house, Briley had to sidestep Jackson, who was yapping around her feet, and accepted the mug Evan handed her. After a sip of the hot chocolate littered with marshmallows, Briley plopped down on a chair on the other side of Evan. "Let's get this party started."

Fifteen minutes later, Kat pushed through the back door. She set Griffin on the floor, who ran to Leah to unbundle her. Once she was finished, she set her in her booster seat at the table.

Kat cut quite the figure with her Santa hat askew on her head, cheeks rosy, and her hands planted on her hips. "You couldn't wait for us. I see how it is."

"Kat, you know how it is when this one gets an idea in her head." Evan let the words hang in the air as he pointed at Briley.

Briley pouted. "The cookies were lonely."

"Well, we can't have that." Kat plopped down next to her and accepted the cup of hot chocolate with marshmallows. "Nice."

"Briley insisted on the marshmallows." Leah rested her arm across Briley's shoulders and made a face.

"Well," Kat said. "Hot chocolate isn't hot chocolate without marshmallows."

Briley was pulled out of her thoughts when Leah took her hand, led her into the living room, and stopped under the mistletoe. It wasn't the first time she'd found herself under the mistletoe with Leah. After the third time it happened, she realized Leah was doing it on purpose. Leah had placed sprigs all over her house and Briley's.

Leah wrapped her arms around Briley's neck, and Briley held her close. "Did you ever think we would get here? I feel we've hit our stride. It's nice to know where we started to where we are now."

"Ye, of little faith. Of course I did." She nipped Leah's ear.

"You're such a goofball."

"But, I'm your goofball." Briley's eyes caught on a photograph over Leah's shoulder taken this past Halloween. It didn't take much to convince everyone to dress as The Incredibles. With them all working non-stop, they were able to make the costumes in record time. They were a hit with the town and won first place in the family costume competition. Evan won second place in the individual placing. It left a lump in her throat just thinking about it. They were a family.

"Wait right here." Leah stepped toward the tree and picked up a small box that lay in its branches. She handed it to Briley. "It seemed we were on the same page." She brushed her fingers along Briley's cheek. "You have been our rock these past few months. I love you, darling. We all talked and this is what we want.

Open it."

Briley slid the ribbon off the box and lifted the lid. Nestled inside was a shiny key.

"I know you already asked, but we were also planning on asking you to move in with us. You're right; my house would better suited for our needs. Will you move in with us, Briley?"

"Yes." Briley hugged her tight.

They were knocked out of their bubble when Evan hollered from the kitchen. "Mom, we can see you guys and these cookies aren't going to decorate themselves."

"They have spoken," Leah whispered in her ear, before nibbling on it.

"Now, now. Don't start something you can't finish." Leah giggled when Briley picked her up and carried her back to the kitchen. "Lady Griffin, Sir Evan, and Peasant Kat. Lady Leah as requested."

Briley placed Leah back on her feet, and Leah curtsied. "My hero."

"Peasant, really?" Kat threw an M&M at Briley, where it bounced off her forehead and back onto the table.

Leah planted her hands on her hips and arched her brow. "We don't throw things, Peasant."

Kat chuckled and held her hands up. "Yes, my Lady."

"So, Briley, when are you going to move in?" Evan asked.

"Nice, Briley." Kat shot her a wink.

"It is. It really is," Briley said. "As soon as possible, Evan."

Briley sat down beside Leah, who laced their fingers together on Briley's thigh even as she lifted a squirming Griffin onto her lap. Leah was the woman that held her body and soul and she wanted to spend the rest of her life with her. The kids had weaseled their way into her heart and she couldn't imagine life without them in it. Madison, Bryan, and their kids were set to arrive the next day.

Briley kissed Griffin on the head even as Kat and Evan were busy throwing M&Ms into each other's mouths, mindful of Jackson underneath the table, who no doubt was watching their every move. Briley relaxed when Leah kissed her on the cheek, then slid several cookies in front of her to decorate.

It was these moments she lived for and couldn't wait to see what the future held. Life didn't get any sweeter than this.

About the Author

Born near Chicago, but raised in Southern Illinois, where she still lives, Shannon spends her free time writing. When she isn't writing, she enjoys binge watching fantasy, science fiction, or true crime shows.

You can contact Shannon at -

Website: smhfiction.com
Email: smh1981@live.com
Facebook: facebook.com/smharrisauthor
Twitter: @smhfiction

Check out Shannon's other books

The Adearian Chronicles - Book One - The Oath – ISBN – 978-1-943353-17-0

Ex-mercenary, Lanis Welsh, is finally at a place in her life where she is content with what and who she is; High Priestess Anya's Protector and Lover. After an unexpected request, she has no choice but to leave Anya's protection in the hands of someone else and travel back to the one place that holds nothing but bad memories. When she is manipulated into signing an oath she has no desire to fulfill, she questions the very truths she has built her life on. As strangers become friends and enemies become allies, Lanis must face the demons from her past. It doesn't take her long to realize there is more going on than anyone could have ever foreseen and nothing and no one can be trusted.

Adearian Chronicles - Book 2 – Revelations – ISBN - 978-1-943353-33-0

What would you do if you were faced with finding and saving the one person who held your heart, but you only had two weeks to do it?

When the unexpected happens and Lanis's world is turned upside down, her and Elson have no choice but to align themselves with two people from a strange land. With new enemies at play, and a Goddess that seems to have forsaken them, Lanis relies on the only people she can; her friends. To fight the demons that plague her daily, she has to separate her love for Anya, from the task she must perform. On top of the unknowns, she is gifted with a small black book that changes the way she sees everything and everyone around her. As her world starts to crumble, Lanis must face her fears and the nightmares that invade her dreams. With the hours ticking away, she must come to terms with the fact that she might already be too late.

The DragonWitch Tales: An Unexpected Beginning
– ISBN – 978-1-943353-43-9

Death ignited her powers. Love binds them.

Paisley's normal, boring life is shattered one evening when a strange, but sexy woman appears out of thin air in her living room and claims Paisley as her wife. Things spiral out of control when Paisley is informed by her mother that she is a witch that comes from a long line of witches, that other realms exist, and that the strange woman really is her wife.

As her choices slip from her grasp, Paisley must learn to navigate her new life, a new world, and a new wife. As if that wasn't enough, Paisley must deal with a growing attraction for a new woman in her life. Throw in a dragon egg, an angry queen, a traitor, and Paisley realizes she's going to have to learn to watch every move she makes.

As the push and pull between two women and her powers reach a standoff, Paisley makes a choice that will change the course of her life and the future of the world she calls home even if that means destroying her own happiness in the process.

The Details in the Design – ISBN – 978-1-943353-79-8

Every stitch tells a story.

Avery Michaels has longed to work in the fashion industry since she was six years old. Now at thirty-two she's fed up with her job as a food critic and signs up with an employment agency that promises to find anyone their dream job.

She is thrilled when she gets an interview with the fashion house of her choice, Catherine Davenport Designs. There's only one problem. For the past six years, Avery has had a massive crush on Catherine, one of the hottest fashion designers of the past two decades.

In the midst of a new job, nosey friends, Catherine's meddling daughters, difficult co-workers, and a dachshund named Polly, Avery also has to contend with a new woman that enters Catherine's life.

From the start, Avery knows winning Catherine's heart will be no easy feat. When curve ball after curve ball is thrown her way, does she scrap her design or make it work?